W9-BXO-558 10/2012

Ironskin

Ironskin

TINA CONNOLLY

TOR®

A Tom Doherty Associates Book
New York

IRONSKIN

Copyright © 2012 by Christine Marie Connolly

A Tor Book
Published by Tom Doherty Associates, LLC
175 Fifth Avenue
New York, NY 10010

www.tor-forge.com

Tor® is a registered trademark of Tom Doherty Associates, LLC.

Library of Congress Cataloging-in-Publication Data

Connolly, Tina.
    Ironskin / Tina Connolly.—1st ed.
      p. cm.
    "A Tom Doherty Associates book."
    ISBN 978-0-7653-3059-8 (hardcover)
    ISBN 978-1-4299-9304-3 (e-book)
    I. Title
    PS3603.O5473176 2012
    813'.6—dc23

                                              2012019874

First Edition: October 2012

Printed in the United States of America

0 9 8 7 6 5 4 3 2 1

For my family

Ironskin

Chapter 1

A HOUSE CRACKED AND TORN

The moor was grey, battlefield grey. It had been five years since the last fey was seen, but out here Jane could almost imagine the Great War still raged on. Grey mist drifted through the blackened trees, recalling the smoke from the crematory kilns. That was a constant smell in the last months of the war.

Jane smoothed her old pea coat, shook the nerves and fatigue from her gloved fingers. She'd been up since dawn, rattling through the frostbitten February morning on smoky iron train and lurching motorcar, until now she stood alone on the moor, looking up at an ink black manor house that disappeared into the grey sky.

The manor had been darkly beautiful once, full of odd minarets, fanciful gargoyles, and carved birds and beasts.

A chill ran down her spine as she studied the design of the house. You didn't have to be an architecture student to recognize who had drawn up the plans for it. It was clear in the imprint of every tower and flying buttress, clear in the intricate blue glass windows, clear in the way the gargoyles seemed to ready their wings to swoop down on you.

The fey had designed this.

The frothy structures were still perfect on the south end of the building, on the carriage house. On the north the house had war damage. It had been bombed, and now only the skeleton remained, the scraggly black structure sharp and jagged, mocking its former grace and charm.

Just like me, Jane thought. Just like me.

The iron mask on her face was cold in the chill air. She wrapped her veil more tightly around her face, tucked the ends into the worn wool coat. Helen's best, but her sister would have better soon enough. Jane leapfrogged the bits of metal and broken stone to reach the front door, her T-strap leather shoes slipping on bits of mud, the chunky heels skidding on wet moss. She reached straight up to knock, quick, quick, before she could change her mind—and stopped.

The doorknocker was not a pineapple or a brass hoop, but a woman's face. Worse—a grotesque mockery of a woman, with pouched eyes, drooping nose, and gaping mouth. The knocker was her necklace, fitted close under her chin like a collar. An ugly symbol of welcome. Was this, too, part of the fey design?

Jane closed her eyes.

She had no more options. She'd worn out her welcome at her current teaching position—or, rather, her face had worn out her welcome for her. Her sister? Getting married and moving out. There had been more jobs for women, once, even women with her face. But then the war ended and the surviving men came slowly home. Wounded, weary men, grim and soul-scarred. One by one they convalesced and tried to reinsert themselves into a semblance of their former lives. One such would be teaching English at the Norwood Charity School for Girls instead of Jane.

Jane stuffed her hands into the coat's patch pockets (smart with large tortoiseshell buttons; her sister certainly had taste), touched the clipping she knew by heart.

> Governess needed, country house, delicate situation. Preference given to applicant with intimate knowledge of the child's difficulties. Girl born during the Great War.

Delicate and *difficulties* had drawn Jane's attention, but it was the phrase *Girl born during the Great War* that had let Jane piece the situation together. A couple letters later, she'd been sure she was right.

And that's why she was here, wasn't she? It wasn't just because she had no other options.

It was because she could help this girl.

Jane glared at the hideous doorknocker, grabbed it, and banged it on the door. She'd made it this far, and she wasn't going to be scared off by ornamental hardware.

The door opened on a very short, very old person standing there in a butler's livery. The suit suggested a man, but the long grey braid and dainty chin—no, Jane was sure it was a woman. The butler's face was seamed, her back, rounded. But for all that, she had the air of a scrappy bodyguard, and Jane wouldn't have been surprised if that lump in her suit coat was a blackjack or iron pipe, hidden just out of sight.

The butler's bright eyes flicked to Jane's veil, glimmered with interested that Jane could not parse. She tapped her fingers on her bristly chin, grinned with sharp teeth. "An' ye be human, enter," the butler said formally, and so Jane crossed the iron threshold and entered the manor.

It was darker inside than out. The round foyer had six exits.

The front door and the wide stairs opposite made up two. The other four were archways hung with heavy velvet curtains in dark colors: garnet and sapphire on the left, forest green and mahogany on the right. Worn tapestries hung on the stone walls between the curtains, dampening the thin blue of a fey-lit chandelier. Fey technology had mostly disappeared from the city as the lights and bluepacks winked out one by one and could not be replaced. It was back to candles and horses—though some who were both wealthy and brave were trying the new gaslights and steam-cars. Some who were merely brave were attempting to retrofit the bluepack motorcars with large devices that burned oil and let off a terrible smell—like the car that had brought her from the station. The housekeeper must have husbanded the chandelier lights carefully to make it last so long, when all fey trade had vanished.

"I'll take your coat. That way for the artist," said the little butler, and she gestured at the first doorway on the left, the garnet-red curtains.

"No, I've come for the governess position," said Jane, but the butler was already retreating through the sapphire curtains with Jane's coat and pasteboard suitcase, grey braid swinging. In that padded room her words died the second they fell from her lips.

Her steps made no noise as she walked over to draw back the curtain. It was not a hallway, but a small chamber, papered in the same deep garnet and lit with one flickering candle.

On the walls were rows of masks.

Jane stared. The masks were as grotesque as the doorknocker. Each was uniquely hideous, and yet there was a certain similarity in the way the glistening skin fell in bags and folds. Clearly they were all made by the same artist, but what sort of man would create these monstrosities—and who would buy them? They would fit a person, but surely no one would wear them, even for a whimsy like that masked cocktail party Helen had attended. In the flickering oil light they looked hyper-real, alive. Like something fey from the old days, before trade had given way to war. She lifted her veil to see more clearly, reached up to touch one sagging cheek.

"Do you like my collection?"

Jane jumped back, wrapping her veil close.

A man stood in the curtained entrance. The garnet folds swung around him as he stepped inside, stared down at her. He was very close and very tall in that narrow room, and his eyes were in shadow.

"Do people actually buy these?" she said, and was aghast at having blurted out something so rude.

But he didn't look offended. "You'd be surprised," he said, still studying her. He was not handsome, not as Helen would describe it—not soft and small-nosed, no ruddy cheeks and chin. He was all angles, the bones of his cheek and jaw plainly visible, and his hair leaped skyward as if it would not stay flat.

Jane tugged on the corner of the veil. She knew how much the gauze did and didn't cover. The folds of the white veil obscured the details of her iron half-mask, but they didn't hide that it existed. She caught them all looking, men, women, children. They stared into her veil, fascinated, appalled, trying not to get caught.

But he was staring into her eyes.

Jane marshaled her thoughts. "I'm here from the city," she said. "I need a job." She had not planned to state it so baldly, but he and his leering masks threw her from her stride, and now the words were confused. They stumbled from her tongue, and she felt awkward and stupidly *young,* though she had been making her own living for nearly five years.

She especially felt foolish when he nodded and said, "I know. I bargained with old Peter to pick you up. Only reliable chap in town, when it comes to venturing out to Silver Birch."

"Oh," she said. Her driver. Of course. "Yes, thank you."

"I would've sent the motorcar, but we're down to the last full-size bluepack, and after that . . ." He shrugged.

"No horses?"

"They don't take to this house very well. The forest makes them skittish." He crossed his arms, his sleeve brushing her bare elbow. She had put on her best dress—a patterned navy one with short ruffled sleeves, though she had regretted it frequently in the cold and again now. *Almost* spring was the worst—the last cold and wet of winter when you were dying for bare arms and sunshine. "Tell me about yourself."

"I've been working as a teacher," she said, "and before that I was a governess. My strength is literature and composition, but I've taught all subjects. I speak three languages and I know how to help your—"

"I know," he said. "I saw your curriculum vitae before. I wrote you about it. I want to know about *you.*"

Her ruined cheek burned, hot under the iron. It was both at the implication that she'd said something foolish, and at the idea that he wanted to know her. The embarrassment was quickly consumed by anger, always close at hand since that day during the war. "What more do you need to know? You received my letters of recommendation."

He scratched his chin, studying her closely. "In five years

you've had four positions. Each one praised your knowledge, punctuality, and morals to the skies. Yet each one let you go."

She was white-hot inside her veil. Anger at the families who dismissed her, anger at the returning soldiers who took her positions, anger at him for probing her injuries. Barely trusting herself to speak, she said, "Yes."

"Let me see," he said, and before she could stop him he lifted her white veil and pulled it away from her face, revealed her to the small red room.

The iron mask covered her ruined cheek. It fit around one eye, crept over her temple where flecks of the fey shrapnel had hit. The hammered iron was held in place by leather straps that buckled around her head. And right now, with the rage that consumed her at his actions, it was probably leaking bits of orange light around the edges, as if Jane herself were on fire.

"How could you—!"

"I needed to know." He was looking at her as if something entirely unexpected had landed on his doorstep. "What's your curse and why can't I sense it?"

"It's rage, since you asked so politely. And you can't sense it because I'm ironskin." "*Wearing* ironskin," she had said the first few months, but soon enough she'd dropped the verb, imitating the other scarred children at the foundry. "The iron mask stops the fey curse. The rage can't leak through." Jane tore the veil from his hands and flung it over her face, but it was far too late. He stopped her from tucking the cloth down her collar.

"Leave it," he said. "You won't be veiled here." He gestured for her to precede him out of the room. His hand dropped as if it were going to guide the small of her back, but then it did not. It would be too forward of him, but perversely, she was hurt.

In five years she could list on one hand the people who had intentionally touched her.

Jane emerged into the round blue-lit foyer, half-thinking he was going to ask her to leave and not return. Despite her desperation—perhaps it would be for the best. To be stranded here in this house that reeked of fey, with this man who ripped down her barriers, who loomed over her with un-readable eyes . . . perhaps it would be easier if he dismissed her now.

But he pointed her up the wide stairs. "Come meet Dorie," he said.

The wide stairs led, logically enough, to the second floor, though Jane knew that "logical" was not a given with fey architecture. Not human logic, anyway. She followed his lead, unpinning her hat with its veil from her carefully crimped hair. Her straight dark hair did not hold crimps well, and there was little enough of it to see between the leather straps for the mask and the hat—still, Jane had tried to look her best today.

At the top of the landing was a suite of playroom and bed-room, and there was a small girl sitting on the playroom floor, dancing her doll in a ray of sunshine.

Jane was so distracted by the sudden appearance of sun-shine in the grey house, on the grey moor, that it took her several blinks to notice something that made her stomach lurch.

Dorie was not touching the doll.

Jane willed her feet to stay where they were, though every inch of her screamed to run.

How could this little girl be doing something only the fey could do? Was this child no human, but a fey in disguise, ready to attack at any second? Panic shrieked inside her, she clutched her hat as if to tear it to shreds—but again she willed herself: Stay.

Mr. Rochart reached down and confiscated the doll. "In this house we use our hands," he said. The doll's porcelain hands wrestled with his grip; the porcelain legs kicked his chest. "Dorie!" he said, and the doll flopped over his arm, unmoving.

"Mother," said Dorie.

He leaned to Jane's ear. "Calling it Mother is a fancy I can't shake from her," he said.

"They do look alike." Jane would not back away from this girl, though the sharp sense of something fey made her queasy, made her wounded cheek blaze. She had expected a girl with a simple curse, damaged like herself, like the others she had known at the foundry—a girl with red streaks on her arm who leaked despair, a boy with a scarred back who filled everyone who came near with a lust for violence. That child she could've helped, in the same way that the foundry had helped her: through acceptance and ironskin.

She did not understand this girl.

"She is not . . . like me," Jane said. "She is not cursed?"

"She's cursed, sure enough," said Mr. Rochart. "But she is not like you. I had heard that there were people like you, hit by fey shrapnel in the Great War, scarred with a curse that everyone around them feels. But she has no scar. And her curse is not like yours. Merely . . . ," and he gestured at the doll that had been dancing in the air.

Jane was all at sea. It was all wrong that this tiny mite

should wave her hands and have power dance behind them, should be able to make Jane recall the talents of the frightening, relentless fey.

Not to mention the creepiness of calling this doll with its waving porcelain hands "Mother." True, the strange Mother doll did look like Dorie. They had similarly perfect features: button noses, rosebud mouths, rouged cheeks. The doll had painted crimped yellow hair—Dorie had blond ringlets.

But at least there was life behind Dorie's blue eyes. And not behind the doll's glass ones. Both things were a blessing.

"I see," Jane said. She stood her ground and kept her trembling fingers in her coat pockets.

Dorie studied Jane. "Your face is funny," she announced, displaying tiny white teeth.

"I have to wear iron on my cheek to keep other people from getting infected," said Jane, though she knew this explanation would go over the girl's head. She was sure she had been told that Dorie was five, but even minus the curse, Dorie was unlike any five-year-old she'd met.

Already bored, Dorie turned away. She clacked her tongue rhythmically, sketched the air in time to it. Dots and swirls of blue light flickered behind her fingers.

The last time Jane saw that blue light was on a battlefield with her brother. She breathed, she swayed—she refused to run.

Mr. Rochart's hand came up as if he would steady her, but then he stepped back, his hands dropping. Twice was not etiquette, twice meant he did not want to touch her, and she was ice-cold inside. "We have tried a dozen governesses over the last year," he said. "None lasted a week. They all claimed it was not us—"

But Jane knew these words and they softened something inside of her. "It was them," she finished. "They were summoned home unexpectedly. Something urgent came up—a sickly mother, a dying aunt."

"You wouldn't believe the number of dying aunts in this country," he said. And even—he smiled, and Jane saw laughter light behind his shadowed eyes. Then they closed off again, watching the blue lights flicker.

Jane took a breath. Took the smooth-faced doll from his arms and handed it to Dorie. The floating lights vanished as Dorie grabbed the doll and held it close. "Pretty Mother," she said, burrowing her face into its cloth body.

"She likes pretty things," Mr. Rochart said. "Her mother was the same way." Silently he crossed to the window, looking out into the black-branched forest that crept up the grounds of Silver Birch Hall as if it would swallow the house. In the sunlight she saw that his slacks, though fine once, were worn along the crease and at his knees.

"She is gone, then?" Jane said softly. Unbidden she neared him, him and that wide window onto the choking forest. To live here would mean to live in its dark and tangled grip.

Mr. Rochart nodded. "The last month of the war." The words landed like carefully placed stones, a heavy message grown no lighter with repetition. "She was killed and taken over by a fey. She was pregnant with Dorie."

Jane sucked air across her teeth. The mother killed, the daughter still unborn—no wonder this child was different from any she'd ever seen. Her heart went out to the two of them.

Mr. Rochart turned to Jane, looking down, down. In the filtered light through the window she could finally see his eyes. They were amber, clear and ancient, a whole history trapped inside of them just as real amber trapped insects. He reached to take her hand; she knew he wouldn't—but then he did. "Will you help us?"

She had not been touched like that, not simply like that, since the first year of the war. Unbidden, she recalled the last boy to touch her: a baker's apprentice she'd loved, with blond hair and a smile of gentle mischief. She was fourteen, and he'd invited her to her first dance, taken her waist, whisked her around the piano and out into the garden, where her stockings had splattered with spring mud. Someone's mother had stumbled on them laughing together and sternly ordered them back inside. . . .

A touch and an unwanted memory should not influence her decision, but in truth her decision was already made. It was made from the moment she saw Dorie, from the moment she saw the clipping, perhaps even from the moment almost exactly five years ago when she knelt by her brother's body on the battlefield, blood dripping from her chin. If this man would take her on, she would bend all her will to the task. She would help this girl. She would help them.

"I will stay," she said. "I will start now. This morning."

Relief flooded his eyes—almost too much. He pressed her hand and was gone from the room before Jane could decide what it meant.

Chapter 2

FEY LIGHT

The enormous estate had all of three servants: the butler Poule (who was also in charge of the grounds and the pre-war motorcar), the cook, and one maid. When Jane, aghast, said: "One?" the maid merely nodded.

"How can you clean this whole house by yourself?" said Jane.

"Can't."

"Just the laundry alone—"

"Poule built scrub tank. Nice bits hired out."

The young maid's name was Martha, and perhaps she was treasured more for her monosyllabic qualities than her desire for cleanliness. She was tall for a girl, rangy, with ginger hair closely braided to her scalp in defiance of any current fashion. Her dark dress and apron had clearly seen better days, though they were clean and neatly patched. She showed Jane an abbreviated tour of the house. All the open rooms were in the south wing, the undamaged wing. The sapphire curtains opened to a hallway that branched off to drawing room, dining room, sitting rooms. The kitchens were beneath them in the cellar. Martha did not take her through the curtains that led to the north wing, but she explained in words of one syllable that forest green eventually led to Mr. Rochart's studio, and mahogany only to Poule's quarters and damage.

Jane's rooms were on the back of the second floor, down the hall and around the corner from Dorie's room. It was a family room that had been given over to the governess, so it was bigger than Jane had expected, and hung with a threadbare tapestry depicting a maiden taming a dragon. (A fanciful design, Jane thought critically, as the maiden was blonde, pink, and rather buoyant, but dragons had only existed—if ever—in the Faraway East.) A nearby spiral staircase appeared to go all the way up and down the house, but Jane reminded herself to check that to know for sure.

During the tour, Jane pestered Martha with a flurry of questions about the house and its schedules, but the only time the maid offered more than a grunted yes or no was when Jane asked about Dorie.

"All yours now. We told him no more. Had to get *you* to keep *us.*"

"Is she so naughty?" said Jane.

"Not a bad child. It's what she does when she's good," said Martha, and shuddered.

"Can you feel when she's doing, um . . . not-quite-human things?"

Martha nodded. "I'm not one to start at naught. Nor Cook. That's why we're here when the rest fled. Though some days the blue lights and air dolls make your hair rise." She gestured at the iron covering Jane's face. "Could be you'll fare well. Since you're a cripple too."

Jane stiffened at the one word Martha had given two syllables to say, and perhaps the laconic, unimaginative maid saw that, because she fell silent again. More questions brought no more answers, and the only other piece of information Jane could extract was that Dorie's supper—and thus Jane's, for today—was at six.

When the maid was gone, Jane unpacked her small pasteboard suitcase. It was not everything she owned, but near enough. Her trunk with her winter woolens and a few books and pictures was still at the boarding house in the rooms she'd shared with her sister—though by the time she returned to the city to retrieve it, it would probably be at Helen's new home.

As short a time as the other governesses were there, they had left traces of their passing, perhaps due to their hurried departures. A calendar from last year hung on the wall, stopped at November. A scrap of orange wool, a pen nib, a cinema stub firmly wedged between the mirror and frame— that one must be an abandoned souvenir; the films had stopped running in the first year of the war. Hairpins everywhere.

Yet someone had put a snowdrop, surely the first of them, in a tiny cream pitcher on her dresser. Jane looked at its curved white petals as she thought: Well. Someone expected me to stay.

She hung up her best dress and changed into a shapeless dropped-waist dress of dark wool, a pre-war hand-me-down a decade out of date and never in fashion to begin with. Changed her good stockings for a woolen pair she'd knit that winter while listening to the Norwood School girls recite poetry they didn't understand or care to. The ribbed stockings were far too thick to be fashionable, but they were warm, a necessity in this house where the fires seemed few and far between. She put her few things in the drawers, checked her hair. The crimping had completely fallen out, of course. The white lock of hair was loose, torn free by *him*. She grabbed one of her predecessors' hairpins and shoved it ruthlessly in place within the dark brown hair, the pin digging into her scalp. She nudged the leather straps that held her mask higher on her head, where they would start the long process of slowly dropping again.

Jane was used to adjusting the alignment of the mask without really looking at herself. It was not her disfigured side that made her throat clutch and her anger rise; it was her good side. The reminder of how she should look. If she turned her profile to the mirror she could imagine her face whole again, as she hadn't seen it since sixteen, when her life was normal and full of possibility. But that luxury was too costly. The times she gave into those imaginings, she wept, after, and was unsettled and resentful for days.

So Jane glanced just enough to see that every bit of the scarring was hidden by the cold iron. Rage, she had told Mr. Rochart. Rage was her curse, and it coiled on her cheek, suffused her soul. But at least the iron stopped it from leaking to other people. She had not known that she was cursed, at first. There were so few survivors, and each of them stranded at different understaffed city hospitals, far from their country homes. Besides, when everyone was angry, afraid, miserable—who knew that the effects were emanating from these scarred people who refused to heal? So she hadn't known, until an ironskin came through the hospitals, searching for people like her, and sent her to the foundry.

But she knew how she looked. She'd known that since the moment it happened.

Jane turned from the mirror and set off to find Dorie.

Jane found Dorie sitting on the kitchen floor. Oddly, there seemed to be more sunlight down here than in some of the upstairs rooms. In the edges of the ceiling there were skylights that let light in somehow—perhaps with mirrors? Jane seemed to recall that as a feature of fey building. Regardless, the thin sunlight was an improvement over blue-tinged chandeliers and sconces.

The cook was stirring a soup pot and flicking through an old magazine, clearly read many times. She was thick and sturdy, with reddened face and arms, and grey-blond hair that escaped in curling wisps from her faded cap. Her name was Creirwy, which is perhaps why she went by Cook.

Dorie was on the floor, tracing the square tiles with the palm of her hand. When Cook wasn't watching, Dorie painted the tiles with patterns of light. When Cook caught the blue flash out of the corner of her eye, she said warningly, "Dorie . . . ," and the lights disappeared.

Cook looked up and caught Jane's eye. "Oh, and you must be the new one," she said. She left her soup long enough to clap Jane a friendly and floury pat on the shoulder. "I'm Cook."

"I'm Jane. Jane Eliot."

"Jay," said Dorie, jumping up. Her white frock was smudged with jam.

"Miss Trouble is having that good of a day," said Cook. "It'll last a bit, if you're clever with her. She got some lunch in her belly just now. I'll be sending Martha with your tea in the late afters, but are you needing a bite now? Sure, and you haven't had lunch, have you? Sit down, lass, and eat right now."

Jane's stomach was vast with hunger. The sunlight fell on a half-empty jar of sliced peaches on the sill, on a dented tray of buns cooling on the stone counter. Yeasty steam scented the air. She had been too nervous to eat when she left the city at dawn—though a half-awake Helen had tried to make her eat a toasted stale crumpet—and she wasn't sure she could do much better now. Besides, she was clattery with anticipation to try working with Dorie straight off, to see what it was like, to see what her new life would be. "No thank you," she said, resolutely turning away. "I'd rather get started with Dorie."

She reached down for Dorie's hand but Dorie eluded her, backing away and crossing her arms behind her back.

"Sure and she doesn't like to be touched," Cook said over her shoulder. "I'll be sending buns up with you. Wouldn't do anybody good to have you fainting." She packed several buns in a little basket with a chunk of sausage and a wedge of white cheese.

Jane withdrew her hand and looked soberly at Dorie. Chalk up the first thing she wasn't going to push on Day One. "Will you lead the way, then?" she said.

Dorie smiled sideways up at her in the manner of children everywhere when they'd gotten away with something. Perversely, it comforted Jane to see a behavior she could label. Dorie scooted sideways through the door and set off down the hall, Jane after.

Cook followed the two of them out into the hall, chattering about how the sourdough hadn't been rising as it should, the early spring lettuce wasn't coming quick enough, and entertainment wasn't the same since the tech for the blue-

and-white films died and you never saw the matinee idols anymore. Local talent on a hastily built stage just wasn't the same as a lusty star-crossed clinch from Fidelio and Frida, now was it? Not that Jane would know, as that was nearly ten years ago now, and Jane probably hadn't given tuppence for a good romance as a child. Despite Cook's complaints, her casual manner was a welcome relief from the pervasive gloom of the rest of the house. She dropped two pieces of wax-wrapped taffy from her apron pocket into the basket and handed it to Jane.

"Thank you," said Jane, and she turned for the stairs.

But Cook grabbed her arm. "You won't be taking those stairs," she said. "Those will be going to the master's studio."

Jane looked in surprise at the stairs—and then, at the identical staircase at the other end of the room. "Oh," she said. "All right." She could not tell if Cook was cross or just curt. And what would there be to be cross about?

Dorie scampered down the hall and led Jane up the correct stairs, away from Cook.

Cook watched them until they were out of sight.

Dorie knew the proper way back to her rooms, and she liked stomping. Another positive trait in a child—Jane wondered how long she would treasure every disobedience as proof of humanity. Not that gleefully stomping up the stairs was particularly disobedient, but it was a normal behavior that parents expected governesses to put a stop to.

Jane just followed.

She thought back to her first day as a governess in the city. She was not quite seventeen; her mother had died a few months before, and with her, her small living. A neighbor had taken

Helen in to let her complete school (in exchange for their cow, which amused Jane on the days she could find something to laugh about) and Jane found herself being pushed from the safety of the foundry. The Great War was over and the soldiers were slowly coming home, attempting to reclaim their former lives. War-scarred Jane was finally, begrudgingly, given a place with a long-ago friend of the family's. They had three children, nine, seven, and four, and the first day Jane spent doing nothing but playing ring around the rosy and sardines with them until they were used to her strange face and would let her touch them and tickle them and tuck them in at night.

Jane didn't think any amount of playing sardines would help with Dorie.

She sat down on the neatly swept floor by the white bed and watched her charge, hoping that by familiar association *she* would get used to Dorie. Sardines would have been helpful for the governess this time, she thought ruefully.

Dorie stood in the center of the room, looking intently up at the corner of the silver-papered ceiling. Her arms were slightly away from her sides. She clacked her tongue thoughtfully.

The hairs on the back of Jane's neck pricked up. "Dorie?" she said calmly. "Are you looking at something?"

Dorie turned and smiled. "Mother was there," she said.

"Mother?" said Jane. "Your doll?"

By way of answer Dorie looked around for the doll. It was hanging off the bed, arms limply flopping down the sides. The instant her gaze fell on the doll it rose in the air and began swimming around the room.

Though the last thing in the world she wanted to do was touch that doll, Jane made herself calmly reach out and grab it as it flew by. "In this house we use our hands," she said, quoting the girl's father.

The doll tugged in Jane's grasp, but Jane held firm. She searched the room, looking for distractions. What would Dorie find familiar, comforting to do with the new governess? Was there anything she enjoyed besides flying the Mother doll through the air?

There were puzzles and activities stored neatly on the shelves—so neatly that Jane doubted they ever saw use at all. A small alphabet book lay on top of a chalkboard, and it made Jane suddenly curious as to whether anybody had ever attempted to teach Dorie anything. Did she know any of her letters?

Despite Dorie's one-word answers and tongue clacks, Jane sensed that the girl was not stupid. Just . . . different.

Whether any other governess had stayed long enough to find out how much Dorie *could* learn was another question entirely.

The main obstacle to Dorie's learning was revealed almost immediately, and it was obvious as soon as Jane saw it. When Jane handed Dorie the alphabet book, she didn't reach out for it. Jane was looking at the bookshelf, so she thought she felt Dorie grab it. But when she turned, no one was touching the book. The book was being wafted through the air to Dorie's lap.

"No, Dorie," said Jane, and she picked up the book. "We use our hands." She held out the book and watched Dorie reluctantly take it, her hands clumsy like a toddler's. "Open it to the first page."

The book opened, but not to the first page. Dorie tried to grasp the pages, but she could only grab several or none. She threw it down. "You don't like to use your hands, do you?" said Jane under her breath. She brought the book back. "It's okay. A little bit at a time. Page one is the letter A."

Dorie clacked. She tried again to grab the page and turn, but her fingers were not used to fine movements. The page accidentally ripped. She bounced and clacked, her curls swinging. She threw the book down in frustration and Jane felt an answering crossness inside. She had chosen an activity that was far too challenging, and now she had Dorie riled up.

Jane replaced the book on the shelf and sat cross-legged by Dorie. "How about a game?" she said. "Do you want to play pattycake with me?" No, that would involve hands. She groped for something less confrontational. "Ring around the rosy?"

Dorie's face stayed blank.

"Maybe you don't know it. Okay, I'm going to sing it for fun, and if you do know it you can sing along." Jane sang, but there was silence from her charge, though Dorie's feet twitched as if she felt like dancing.

Frustration pricked behind Jane's mask but she tamped it firmly down. No one had said this would be easy. She was here to make a difference in Dorie's life. She was here to help her be normal.

No matter how long it took.

"Let's play something else for a while," Jane said.

Dorie's face creased into a mutinous scowl that Jane much preferred to blank porcelain.

Jane amended, "Something fun." She carefully did not mention that the activity was going to involve Dorie holding things. She brought a stuffed bear and stuffed monkey from the shelves and let Dorie point to one to choose it—a minor success. "Now, Mr. Bear and Mr. Monkey are friends." The monkey was dressed in a scarlet felt coat and hat. Jane walked him over to the bear, which lay in Dorie's lap. "Hi, Mr. Bear!" She said it in a squeaky voice, and Dorie laughed.

"Now you," said Jane.

Dorie raised her arms. The bear levitated.

Monkey gently pushed him back down. "Flying makes my tummy upset," Monkey said. "Let's stay on the floor."

Bear shook his head and rose again.

"What's your favorite color?" said Monkey.

Bear shook his head.

"Can you talk to me?"

Bear shook his head.

Jane gently plucked the bear from the air and set it back in Dorie's hands. The bear zoomed back into the air. Back into Dorie's hands. Back into the air. Hands. Air. Hands—and then Dorie squealed and the bear went flying across the room.

Jane sighed. The child was as stubborn as the governess. She was determined that she wouldn't be the one to break . . . but how was she going to get through to Dorie?

Jane spent the rest of that first morning trying different activities, searching for one that might serve as a lifeline to reach Dorie. Stubbornly Jane went back to the shelves and pulled out puzzles, games, chalk, toys.

One after another they went through Dorie's roomful of activities. They attempted drawing, but Dorie would not hold the chalk. When tea came, she floated the bun to her mouth. And when it was finally time to get dressed for dinner, Dorie's jam-stained frock flew off and the new one on without either girl touching them at all.

An exhausted Jane trailed Dorie down to the dining room.

The dining room was lit with another blue-lit chandelier as well as candles—and yet the light fled, sucked into the corners of the dark-papered room. The house was a mish-mash of styles from different generations, Jane thought. Her rooms had been furnished a very long time ago, judging by the white-washed walls with the worn tapestries. Dorie's were modern—wall and ceiling papered with an intricate silver pattern, the trim and furniture crisp and white. The dining room was in between—heavy dark furniture, oppressive scrolled paper on the walls. Jane ignored the fey-blue flicker of the chandelier glancing off the dark paper and hoisted Dorie into her high seat.

"Little Miss Trouble, were we now?" said Cook. She leaned on the back of Dorie's chair and gestured with a wooden spoon.

Jane stood up for Dorie—she wasn't sure why. "She's not a bad child," she said. "She just gets frustrated because her way is so much easier and better than mine. She doesn't get it."

Dorie wafted her milk glass over, sloshing milk on the table in the process.

Cook snorted and wiped the table with her apron. "It's kind you are to think so. A regular terror, I say."

A tall figure entered the room and Cook straightened up immediately, jamming her wooden spoon into her apron pocket and feigning innocence. "Evening, sir," she said, nodding. Mr. Rochart looked down at her until she turned and fled, muttering something about the potatoes.

Dorie jumped down from the chair, buried herself in her father's knees. "Did you manage all right this afternoon?" There was worry in his dark eyes as he gently stroked his daughter's hair.

"I'm not giving up yet," said Jane. She stopped Dorie's chair from falling over, steadied the table.

"No, of course you wouldn't," said Mr. Rochart. He was still in the worn wool slacks he had on earlier, though now they were covered in a faint white dusting of powder. A similar smudge streaked one shirt cuff. He ruffled Dorie's curls and lifted her up. "You're too stubborn for that, aren't you? You don't back down."

Jane felt pleased by his accurate assessment—and that made her feel cross and prickly. She was not going to roll over like a puppy dog just because he seemed to be paying attention to her, *Jane,* and not her, *the ironskin.* She said, "How do you know I don't?"

Mr. Rochart's black eyebrows drew together at her tone, shadowing his eyes once more. "A less principled girl might've sought refuge in her sister's new home," he said, laying out his chain of thought for her. "And no one would've faulted her."

"Except the new husband, who might not want an extra mouth to feed," retorted Jane.

"So stubbornly this wisp of a girl seeks gainful employment," continued Mr. Rochart, "and she will not be turned from doing it to the best of her measure. Not be frightened off by all the demons in hell. . . ." He looked down at Jane, and she took a step backward from the peculiar warmth in his eyes. "You are indeed determined to help us, are you not?"

"Of course, sir," she managed, chin up. "Have I given you reason to doubt it already?"

He still studied her face, and she was surprised to find that it did not feel like he was judging her deformity, but was simply curious what made her tick. "When what you hope for appears on your doorstep, there is every reason to doubt its reality, Jane."

She did not know what to say to that, but then from the front of the house the twisted doorknocker sounded, just as Cook bustled in with the potatoes.

"What, at dinner?" Cook said, but a glance from Mr. Rochart forestalled any other protest.

"Have them eat," he said, setting Dorie down. He strode off toward the front of the house.

Jane took Dorie's arm, guiding her back to the dinner chair, but Dorie wriggled free and was suddenly trotting after her father. Jane grabbed for her frock but missed, the cotton skirt slipping through her fingers.

Jane took off through the maze of rooms and halls after the fleeing girl, caught up with Dorie just behind the sapphire curtains that opened onto the foyer.

Dorie was peeping through. "Pretty lady," she said, and clacked.

Jane stopped, looking at the foyer through the narrow gap Dorie had made. The short butler was saying, "An' ye be human, enter," and the woman swept over the threshold. Mr. Rochart bent to bestow a kiss on the visitor's hand. "Miss Ingel," he said. "The honor is mine." She had kind eyes; she smiled and corrected him: "Blanche."

An odd pair, Jane thought, for the woman, though more smartly dressed than Mr. Rochart, looked unformed next to him. Perhaps his hair stood up, perhaps his cuffs were mended, but still he wore his clothes and they did not wear him. Whereas the woman's figure was good enough, and her coat and frock were smart, but she looked ill at ease, lost inside her fur and aquamarines, almost nervous. Her brilliant bobbed red hair was frozen into stiff pin curls that did not suit her face, which was plain, with pouched eyes and a large smashed nose like a prizefighter. Her eyes lingered on the sapphire curtains, then slid away, as Mr. Rochart ushered her into the red room of masks.

Mr. Rochart turned as he entered the garnet curtains. He glanced at the darkness behind the sapphire curtains, and even buried in shadow, Jane was suddenly positive his eyes fell on hers. Embarrassed at being caught spying, she drew back immediately, grabbing Dorie by the back collar of her dress and propelling her down the hall toward dinner.

Nerves made her wobbly on the worn soles of her old workaday boots. Dorie twisted free, scampering back toward the dining room, and Jane slid on the smooth floor of the hallway, which was poorly lit. Indeed, though there were rows of sconces, there was only one blue fey light left, at the far end of the hall. Dorie had already disappeared around the corner, so Jane set off firmly toward that, chin raised. She did not want to get lost on her way to the first good meal she'd eaten all day.

She was nearing the wall sconce when it suddenly winked out, and Jane found herself in the grey-black of a windowless hall at twilight. There was a dart of wind past her hair, as if dry leaves had flung past and departed, and a crackle that sizzled in the air like after-lightning. And then nothing, nothing to show that the fey technology had been there, except a bare copper sconce on the wall, barely visible as her eyes adjusted. She had seen the aftermath of fey lights or blue-packs winking out before, of course, but it was rare to catch one the moment when it fizzled and died. Always abruptly; no transition between something working and not—not like a candle that sunk into itself, giving you warning of its coming death.

And now here she was, in a black hallway, and no dinner in sight. Her jaw set, her teeth ground anger out as she willed herself calm. This was not the end of the world, just the end of a very long and trying day.

A small touch on her skirt made her gasp, almost shriek. In the dim light she saw a tiny figure with blond curls stretch out a hand.

At the other end of the hallway.

No smile crossed that doll-like face, but Jane's skirt tugged again by that invisible hand, and Dorie turned and set off around the corner.

Patience, Jane counseled herself. Patience.

She followed the invisible tug on her skirt all the way back to a hot dinner.

Chapter 3

SEQUINS AND BLUEPACKS

The first month went very slowly. So did the approach of spring, which refused to fully commit itself to the moor. Wind and rain ground on outside of the nursery window, and Jane and Dorie's days continued in a relentless impasse. It occurred to Jane that she and Dorie were circling each other like two wounded creatures wanting to drink from the same stream, each wary of the other's intentions, each unwilling to either strike or run away. The stream was the house they had to share, or perhaps it was the positive regard of the man who ran it. Dorie adored her oft-absent father, and Jane . . . Jane wanted to do a good job in her new position, that was all, end of story.

Dorie was not interested in anything but being left alone to amuse herself with flying dolls and light pictures, as she had been for all the five years of her existence. She did not start the day stubborn, and if Jane did not try to make her change, all was well. But she resented any attempt on Jane's part to make her do even simple activities with her hands. As Jane had said that first day to Cook, Dorie's way of doing what she wanted was so much easier that she had no reason to try Jane's.

There were, however, two neutral territories.

Dorie would cheerfully walk or run around outside on the moor, anytime the rain lifted—though Jane had to keep a strict eye on her whereabouts to make sure she didn't run into the forest. And she liked dancing. The gramophone's bluepack had long since died, but someone had rigged it with a hand crank. So Jane sat and turned the handle, and Dorie danced. And if she danced a little too gracefully for a backward five-year-old . . . well, Jane could ignore that.

But dancing ability seemed little compensation for everything Dorie lacked. Of course, what she might be extra clever in was the fey talent.

But that would not serve her well. She would be shunned the first time she left the house. If people could not stand looking at Jane and the other victims, what would they do to a girl who moved dolls with her mind? At the least she would be an outcast, at the most. . . . Jane had heard of a few fey captured, their flickering blue forms studied in secret as the scientists tested for ways to fight back. A gruesome thought when it was the enemy you were talking about. If the subject were a tiny five-year-old girl . . . Jane shook her head.

Each night, Jane ran through the days in her head, assessing where she'd gone wrong, considering where she'd gone right. Dorie liked new things, and so when Jane found new activities, there was a short window of time where Dorie would try the new game before getting frustrated. Small progress, though hardly sufficient to introduce Dorie to the world.

Jane wondered if there was something she could withhold from Dorie, but what would that be? Her meals? The child was used to having everything she wanted, just the way she wanted. And in the case of meals, that meant eating with her fey tricks—wafting food through the air to her mouth—and not with fingers or fork. Jane told Cook to start sending a set of silverware up with Dorie's meals from now on, but so far Jane had only placed the silverware beside Dorie's plate, and not insisted. She had not quite had the fortitude to go into that inevitable battle.

After one not-too-terrible morning of watching Dorie dance in time to the three-quarter beat of a waltz, Jane started to wonder if Dorie had any natural math ability. Sometimes children afflicted in one area were extra clever in another, Jane knew—there had been a girl at the Norwood School who could hardly speak or look you in the eye, but she could add sums with startling proficiency.

Jane brought up a jar of dried beans and tried counting. Dorie liked counting. She could count to a hundred, and Jane's estimation of her human skills went up. But when Jane asked her about adding she shook her head. Bolstered by the good morning, Jane decided to find out what it would be like to try to teach Dorie something.

"This may be new, but I know you can do it," said Jane. "It's just like counting." She had found two crystal buttons in her dresser and she brought them out now.

"Pretty," said Dorie, and Jane perked up at this show of interest.

"Yes," she agreed. She put the two buttons in Dorie's palm. Dorie's fingers did not close around them, but lay as stiff and unmoving as if her hands were porcelain. "Do you know how many buttons are here?"

"Two."

"And how many here?" Jane put two green buttons in Dorie's other palm.

"Two."

Jane pushed Dorie's hands together. "Now count how many."

Dorie clacked and shook her head. She turned her arms till the buttons slid off her palms and clattered to the wooden floor.

"Let's have another go." Jane separated the buttons into two piles on the floor. "How many buttons here?"

"Two."

"And how many in this pile?"

"Two."

"So if you have two buttons and you add two more . . ."

Dorie threw the buttons across the floor in a flash of blue light.

Jane sighed and picked them up. The one that went under the white chest of drawers came back covered in dust. The other one rolled to the windowsill, and Jane saw a flash of movement through the window, a shadow disappearing into shadows, as she stooped to retrieve it. She straightened up and looked more closely.

Dorie's window faced west into the forest. The forest was dark today; it was always dark. Grey pine, blood-dark cedar, and black briar tangled through its undergrowth. Thin strips of the silver birches the estate must have been named for glinted in the darkness, but even they looked oppressed, their branches swallowed in poisonous mistletoe. The forest stretched across the entire back of the estate and curved down its sides as if it were encroaching on the house, year by year. A creeping arm of forest came so close to the damaged north wing that Jane was not even sure if you could walk between them. The forest had a foothold it would not relinquish.

So surely she hadn't seen a tall form slip between those thorny locusts; surely no one would choose to be swallowed up by the dark.

Jane turned away from the window, painted buttons in hand. Dorie's chin was lifted toward the window, her perfect face expressionless and smooth. "Father," she said calmly.

Jane looked back, but the shadow was gone—and she was pretty sure that Dorie couldn't have seen the shadow on the ground from where she stood.

"Let's go back to counting," she said, but the attempt at math had gotten Dorie's back up.

"Father," Dorie said mutinously. "Father, father, father."

"Perhaps he'll be at dinner," said Jane, though truthfully he hadn't been down in days. She looked out the window at where she thought she had seen the figure. *Was* that Mr. Rochart? Of course, the man was allowed to walk around his own estate. But to deliberately go into the woods, the dark woods where the fey had lived, hidden in the twists and turns of the dark branches, inside the knotholes, between the thorns of the locusts . . . No, the fey had not been seen for five years, since the war ended. But they had not been openly vanquished. Merely they had disappeared one day, leaving a breathless taut waiting for the next attack that never came.

"Counting," Jane said firmly, turning back to Dorie.

But Dorie was gone.

There was one stone-cold moment when Jane thought the girl had literally vanished. Then she heard small feet pounding on the staircase and her heart came stuttering back to life.

Jane took off from the room, shoes skidding as she hurried after Dorie. Most unladylike, she thought to herself as she hiked her skirts up to better maneuver the slippery stairs. Small wonder so many governesses had given up. It wasn't the fey after all—it was the lack of dignity.

Jane chased the small creature out the back door. Her first shout of "Dorie" had gone completely unheeded, so she saved her breath and remaining shreds of dignity to run silently after the child, who was running pell-mell toward the black forest. The old saying sprung sharply to mind: *Don't go into the woods past the last ray of sunlight.* Her iron mask threatened to slide around her head as she ran, so she held it with one hand and grabbed her skirts with the other. Jane pounced on Dorie about ten feet from the edge of the clearing. Her foot slid as she caught Dorie's shoulders—Jane stumbled to one knee, nearly knocking Dorie off her feet.

So much for dignity. Jane held Dorie there, panting. "You are not to go into the forest," said Jane firmly. "It is not safe. Your father would be worried." She looked past Dorie into the dark woods, but saw nothing but trees, trees and the flat black shapes between them. Sunlight did not reach very far in these woods.

Dorie turned under her arms and twisted to look at Jane. With Jane on her knees, the two were nearly at eye level. "Father?" Dorie said wistfully, and Jane felt a small tender twist at her tone.

Jane squeezed Dorie's shoulders. Through the layers of skirts her knees turned damp in the grass. "Your father is very busy," she said gently. "He can't always be around to play."

Dorie's shoulders slumped. She pulled away from Jane and went slowly back toward the house, kicking stiff legs through the clumps of wet grass. Jane heard a sharp clicking sound—Dorie clacking her tongue in frustration, in time to her steps.

Crossness rose as Jane stood and followed—but it was *for* Dorie this time. Where *was* her father, and why couldn't he come down more often for Dorie?

The hair rose on the back of her neck as a low voice said behind her, "I thought she was going to run straight into the forest."

Her dress suddenly seemed too warm for the foggy day, all hot and constricted around her wrists and throat. "She might have," Jane said, and tried to sound calm and firm, a wise and skilled governess with no grass stains on her skirt. "But I caught her."

The faintest smile hovered around the corner of his mouth—she identified it and it was gone. "I saw the tackle. You see you are our soldier; I hired you for your trim fighting form."

"Father!" said Dorie, and she ran to him, even as Jane tried to puzzle out whether she should be flattered or made cross by the comparison.

Mr. Rochart dropped a kiss on Dorie's head and steered the small girl back to the house. "Do not go in the forest, love," he reminded her firmly. Dorie rubbed her head on his leg and did not answer. "Now march quietly back to your rooms with Miss Eliot." Dorie went as bidden, twisting back every few feet to check that her father was following.

"You are settling in?" he said. "Your rooms are sufficient; the fire is lit, the floors swept; all ets are ceteraed?"

"They are," affirmed Jane, suddenly at a loss. She offered, "The dinners are very good. Creirwy is an excellent cook." Her fingers twisted in her skirt. Weren't there things she had wanted to say? Truths to ask, riddles to unriddle? And all she could do was mouth bland nothings about the food.

She fell silent, and so was he, as they trailed Dorie up the stairs. He walked them to Dorie's rooms as if escorting them back to a cell they should not have left, Jane thought.

He stayed in the hall, clearly not intending to come in. Dorie looked up at him with big eyes. Jane was sure she read behind that blank face the desire for her father to stay. If only some of that hero worship could be transferred to Jane! Then perhaps Dorie would try reading and adding and using her hands. . . .

Using her hands.

Lunch had been delivered while they were outside. Stewed beans and bowls of applesauce sat on two trays by Dorie's room. Seized with a sudden impulse, Jane said, "We were going to try using a spoon today. Perhaps you'd like to watch."

"Of course," Mr. Rochart murmured. He did not come over the threshold, seemed poised to flee. But he stood, watching, and Dorie looked up at him expectantly.

"We're going to try applesauce," Jane said, and she set one of the blue-rimmed stoneware bowls in front of Dorie. She used the spoon to demonstrate eating a bite herself, then she held it out to the girl. "Now you try," she said.

Dorie looked sideways up at her father, as if deciding whether to humor Jane. Mr. Rochart just stood, waiting patiently, so Jane carefully took Dorie's arm and showed her how to lever her spoon into the applesauce and up to her mouth.

Jane let her hand fall away. "Now you try," she repeated.

The presence of her father seemed to be the deciding factor in trying the new game. Dorie turned a look of intent concentration on her applesauce and carefully raised the spoon. As it neared her mouth she forgot to hold her wrist level, and the applesauce fell in a plop on her skirt. Immediately she turned her blank face to Mr. Rochart.

"Good try," said her father. He reached down and wiped the blob from her dress. But to Jane he murmured, "I have seen her play the trained monkey before, when she wants something. But the minute your back is turned . . ."

"Baby steps," said Jane firmly. She turned Dorie's hand level again. The spoon still had applesauce clinging to it. "Try again."

Dorie brought the spoon back, and after banging it into her chin, she slid it in. She sucked the applesauce off the end of it.

"Very good," said Jane. "Much better. Let's try it again."

They got in two more bites, and then Dorie looked up at her father for praise.

He was no longer standing in the door. He had melted away. No doubt trying to avoid a parting scene, Jane thought in exasperation.

Which meant Jane was going to have to deal with the aftermath he shied away from.

Dorie's face stayed blank, perfectly blank. Her hand opened and the spoon fell. Drops of applesauce spattered the clean floorboards.

"Oh no you don't," Jane muttered under her breath. She grabbed the spoon and put it back into Dorie's hand. "Let's continue to eat our applesauce," she said. She attempted to close her charge's fingers around the spoon handle, which was probably her first mistake.

Dorie glared, struggling to pull her palm out of Jane's grip.

She squirmed free and threw the spoon down. "Father!" she said.

"He's gone!" said Jane, temper rising. "Let's show him what a good job we can do."

The bowl of applesauce rose off the floor and floated up to Dorie's chin.

"No!" said Jane, and she pulled the bowl away. "No applesauce unless it's with a spoon." She wiped dust off the spoon and put it back into Dorie's unwilling hand. Keeping her hand closed on Dorie's, Jane maneuvered Dorie's stiff arm toward the bowl. Carefully Jane scooped up one spoonful of applesauce with Dorie's spoon and put it in Dorie's mouth. "Good," said Jane, letting go. "Now you try again."

Dorie stared obstinately at the spoon in her hand. Then she threw it down, mentally yanked all the silverware off the tray, and set it whirling above Jane's head in furious clanks.

"No!" Jane shouted. She pulled Dorie's tray away, shoved it out into the hallway, and shut the door. She sat down beneath the whirling silverware and plucked it out of the air, one by one, until she had a fistful of spoons and forks. She kept her hand tight on the silverware and stared down at the little girl. Yanked the bowl of applesauce back in front of Dorie. "Try again."

Dorie lifted the bowl of applesauce and dumped it on Jane's head.

There was absolute silence in the room as Dorie stared blankly and stubbornly straight through Jane, and an angry Jane counted to thirty, willing her temper to calm.

I am not on fire, she told the hot orange rage that licked the mask around her cheek. *I am cool water, putting out the fire. This little girl will not beat me.*

Apple mush dripped around her ears.

At long length Jane rose slowly and went to her room. She changed her dress, ran a washcloth over her face and hair, drank a glass of water. Stared out the window for a while, considering her options.

When she returned, Dorie was standing at the window, looking into the forest.

"Dorie," Jane said, then stopped.

The applesauce was neatly wiped off the floor and piled back in the stoneware bowl. All the silverware was tidily stacked next to it.

Dorie turned from the white-trimmed window. Jane could not tell if the blank expression was guilt or pretend innocence. She decided not to push it.

"Let's listen to your gramophone," she said.

A week later, Jane sat on the stairs for a while after her charge had gone to bed, leaning against the railing and thinking. In the twilight the foyer chandelier burned half-blue. One of its two mini-bluepacks had fizzled that morning, so half the foyer was dim, while the other half was decorated with blue sparks from the hanging crystal prisms. Jane absent-mindedly rubbed the bridge of her nose where the iron weighed down on it, watching the sparks dancing across the walls like tiny lights. Helen would like the way the chandelier sparkled. So would Dorie.

Dancing and walks. It was little enough to build trust out of, and Jane was reluctant to turn their only positive times together into rewards to be dangled overhead. She wondered if Mr. Rochart would have any ideas. She wanted to ask him— but he was always gone, and when he was there, like the day with Dorie and the applesauce, he melted away as soon as he'd appeared. Day after day he shut himself in the attic studio, or was mentioned casually as being "away," though the motorcar remained in the carriage house. She knew all too well how much Dorie missed him. He had been at dinner twice during the month, and Dorie was much better the next day.

Down below in the foyer, Martha emerged from the forest green curtains, dragging a ladder backward that scraped on the stone floor. She wrestled it into place on the rug beneath the chandelier, tucked the hem of her skirt in her waistband to keep it free of her legs, and went up.

Jane did not speak, not wanting to startle Martha on the ladder, or embarrass her about her hiked-up skirt. But she wondered what the maid was doing—bluepacks didn't have an empty container, a shell to remove. When they were gone they were gone. And with the rationing nowadays of the final stores left from before the war, when the bluepacks were gone they were generally gone for good. Hardly anyone had spares left to replace them. Mr. Rochart himself had said they were on the last of the big ones—the ones that would run a motorcar.

But Martha pulled a small bit of wiggling blue from her apron pocket and tucked it into the power source on the chandelier's right side. Jane watched the motions that used to be familiar to everyone—pushing the blue stuff into the copper container (never iron, of course, or it wouldn't work) with one finger, clapping the lid shut to keep the squirming substance in. It wasn't that bluepacks tried to get free, exactly, but they did thrum and move in your hands.

Jane had dropped one, once, when she was young and

changing the porch light. The old bluepack had fizzled that morning, bursting out of the copper cylinder that screwed into the light bulb, leaving the lid rattling on its hinge. Jane balanced on a kitchen stool that really wasn't meant for balancing. She leaned wrong and had to grab the base of the light, opened her fist, and there went the bluepack. It hovered *pretty much* where she had let it go, as if it knew she owned it. But it was that *pretty much* that was the trick, since it made feeble darts up and back, as if attached by elastic to the spot in the air. Jane knocked the stool over twice more before she finally caught the bluepack and put it into place.

The foyer was fully lit again. White-blue light glittered crazily from the jostled prisms as Martha descended the ladder and clapped it shut. She shook out her skirts, and as she did so Jane saw her apron quite clearly.

Her apron pocket was full of mini-bluepacks.

Martha hoisted the ladder up and headed back through the curtains, the ladder's feet catching on the velvet.

Jane suddenly stood. Quietly she went down the stairs, following the silent maid. She did not know exactly why, except that the question: *How many bluepacks does Mr. Rochart still have?* was uppermost in her mind. Why, he could sell them on the black market if he'd a mind to—certainly the various attempts at replacements were nowhere up to speed.

Jane slipped through the forest green curtains and saw that the hallway, which had gone completely black that first night she was here, now had every sconce lit with white-blue light.

Martha strode down the hallway, ladder under her arm now, and Jane followed her down the stairs and around the cellar as she replaced one, two, five more bluepacks. Jane was about to give up out of both boredom and feeling ridiculous when

Martha stacked the ladder against a wet stone wall, left the house by a back door, and struck out down a paved walk that led to the carriage house.

Jane waited a cautious interval before following her. She felt rather silly at this point—why was she following Martha back to some closet where they kept supplies? But on the other hand, Martha had replaced a good twenty bluepacks this evening—still had some in her pocket—and Jane had not seen anything like that in ten years.

It was the deep blue of twilight. They were almost to the spring equinox, and though the days were chill, at least they had been getting longer more and more quickly. She longed for summer, true summer on the moor, when there would be perhaps a full month of sunny days, days that lasted well past dinner, when you could run around outside with bare arms. Between the war and her time in the city, she had not had a real country summer in years. Her best memories were all from childhood, when both her parents were alive. Memories of finishing her chores and being allowed to play tag with Charlie and Helen and the other children late into the night, well past when they should have been in bed. But summer only lasted a month, and they all went a bit mad for it.

She wondered what summer would be like here, at Silver Birch. Almost, she could not imagine that she would still be here when the days lengthened and the sun warmed the grass. It did not seem a place for summers, or perhaps it was just that she was still uncertain that she was doing any good at all. They would dismiss her well before summer, and Jane would be on her own again.

She shook her head, clearing her gloomy thoughts. The walk to the carriage house was not used as much now as it had been, as it took you straight between the ruined wing and the forest. Jane watched as Martha glanced side to side, then hurried through, her elbows at sharp angles as if they would ward off trouble in the night.

Jane hurried after. Grass grew thick between the uneven stones. The air was crisp on her arms and the wet grass left cold imprints around the tops of her boots. She had seen Mr. Rochart at the edge of the woods, hadn't she? That day from Dorie's window? The iron mask was chill through the padding—she touched it with one finger and shivered.

Where had Mr. Rochart gone slipping through the trees? There—no, there, perhaps. Past that thorned locust, although that wasn't a good reference as the forest was thick with them. Locusts and birch, and the silver birch were dense with clusters of mistletoe, which Jane knew would kill the trees if left to spread. Still, who was going to wade into the woods, these woods, in order to peel a parasite from the trees? No one with sense.

Martha was vanished now, out of sight around the ruined wing of the house. Jane moved more slowly, cautiously following the flagstone path as it curved around the black and shattered walls. There were broken stones here that had fallen and never been moved. A blown-out window with sharp glass teeth, ragged curtains silent behind it. Mr. Rochart's studio must be up above this somewhere, a workroom perched on crumbled stone, black gaps, decay.

Far ahead, at the end of the curving path, the door to the carriage house cracked open. The twilight was quite dim now, and Jane stood silently next to the house, hoping she would go unnoticed if she did not move. A figure emerged.

But it was not Martha.

Even in the twilight, Jane could tell it was a man, an older man with a stoop and a cane. He held something small—fiddled with it and tucked it into his back pocket—it looked like a wallet. Then, with a nervous glance over his shoulder at the forest, he moved off down the long driveway that led back to the road. Jane wondered if he was headed all the way back into town, for that was a long road for a man with a cane. He must be some visitor—perhaps Martha's father, and the girl had just been meeting him to hand over her wages. Still, Jane could not imagine why such a rendezvous would happen at this time of night. She kept her eyes peeled, looking for Martha, but she did not see the thin figure emerge.

Night was coming up faster now, blue-black fuzzing the outlines of the sturdy carriage house, the black and crippled wing of the estate. She should go.

A crack behind her and she whirled, but saw nothing. Another noise—a crackle, a *bzzzt*—a fey noise, she was imagining things—! Jane cursed herself for a fool. No sane person went even this close to the woods at night, especially not to satisfy some silly curiosity about the state of her employer's supply closet.

Jane turned back. She left the curving path and struck out straight across the lawn, skirting flowerbeds on a direct line to the house. There was nothing behind her, nothing.

Nothing.

Nothing. Another crackle—she turned around—and *he* was suddenly standing where she had been a moment before, as if he had been following her, unseen.

"What are you doing out at night?" he demanded, and he took her elbow, crushed her against his side, moved her forcibly across the lawn and into one of the back doors to the house. Inside the entryway he freed her from his grasp but not his gaze.

Jane drew back, crumpled into her shell, a thousand things whirling through her mind so not one of them was able to get free on her tongue. He was here, when she had wanted to see him. He had too many bluepacks. He was right to be worried; and of course she knew better than to wander near the forest, like some sort of witless city girl.

He locked the door behind them and stood, his amber eyes intense and black. Then he sighed and said with a self-mocking lilt to his tone, "I am sorry. I am a beast; I roar." His hand went to her shoulder, and the gentle touch, the apology, disarmed her. She would have to watch herself—it was not right to be undone every time someone casually touched her. "Yet I cannot afford to lose you, and you of all people should know not to tempt fate."

But that made her angry, and the anger tangled up with the embarrassment, leaving her further tongue-tied. From her tongue spilled the thought: "Perhaps if you were around for me to ask questions about Dorie, I wouldn't have to come looking for you."

"You were looking for me?" He had still not released her shoulder.

"For Dorie," she repeated, firmly. It was true. She had been, earlier. Further, he should be around for Dorie; she shouldn't have to hunt him down.

He glanced upward, as if he could see back to his studio. "I have someone waiting just now," he said. "I only left her because I saw you on the lawn."

Someone.

"A client," he amended, as if he could hear her thoughts. "I would put her aside if I could, for you."

"For Dorie," she said.

"Yes."

She suddenly thought that he meant it, that she had a momentary power that meant he would stand there until she told him yes, it was okay to go, yes, she could do without him just now, just at this moment. She looked at him and still he stood, his amber eyes studying her thoughts and waiting.

"Go," she said.

He nodded. "We will speak later."

And then he was gone, and she was not sure that she believed his promise, though he probably meant it as much as he could. She could not puzzle him out. He seemed to put up barriers—old walls, formal language. A man who seized every opportunity to melt away to his world of work—his masks, his clients.

But then—he had come down from his studio for her? Was that because he cared about Jane—or cared about what she might see? Did he know, all through that conversation just now, that she had been shadowing the maid? For that matter, what door had he come out of? She pulled aside a curtain from a back window, looked back toward the walk that led to the carriage house. But it was dark now, too dark to see.

Jane walked slowly through the fully lit halls, back to the foyer, brushing the dust from her skirt—sitting on Dorie's floor did little for her dresses, old as they were. She had not even received any help from him for Dorie. All she needed was a way to reach her—

And then she saw a glint of blue-lit gold, just near the garnet curtains. She crossed the foyer and picked it up. A coin-sized sequin, no doubt fallen from one of the pretty ladies' dresses.

Jane pulled the crystal buttons that she had tried the other day out of her pocket and considered them as she wandered down the hall and into the kitchen.

Shiny buttons. Sparkly sequins.

Rewards.

"Cook?" she said. "Do you have any aluminum foil?"

Chapter 4

THE BEAST-MAN'S PROMISE

Jane spent the next several days scouring the house for forgotten treasures: scraps of ribbon from a governess, bits of foil from Cook that she cut into stars, small gold sequins fallen from a party dress in a long-unused guest room.

She did not see Martha until by chance in the parlor—the maid cleaning the window, Jane examining a beaded lampshade and reluctantly deciding that there was no way she could declare a certain swinging bead both about to fall off and unfixable. Jane watched Martha cleaning in energetic circles, her unpinned ginger braid swinging in tempo, and could not think of a way to admit she'd been spying.

So for now she did not seek out any new mysteries, but only shiny things, until she had a full double handful, ready to go. That day after Dorie's nap she brought all the sparkly bits to the nursery in a little bag and showed them to Dorie, whose blue eyes lit up.

Yes, thought Jane. This might work.

"One at a time," Jane said to Dorie. "I'll give you one pretty sparkle for every one of my games we play. Shall we start with catch?"

Jane tucked the bag of treasures in her skirt pocket and got up to get the ball.

She tossed it to Dorie, who did not put up her hands to catch it. The ball fell at Dorie's feet, and she looked past it, at Jane's skirt.

There was a tug on Jane's pocket.

Jane whirled, grabbed for the bag, caught the bottom edge of it as Dorie whisked it from the pocket and up into the air. The bag untied itself and a froth of silver stars, gold sequins, and blue ribbons spilled out. They circled over Jane's head like a planetarium display, and Jane, furious in a way she knew even in the moment that no savvy governess should be, lunged after the sparkling swirls.

The orbiting stars rose higher, out of Jane's hands. She shouted, grabbing for them, and Dorie looked solemnly on, her arms raised and her face as blank as a porcelain doll.

The sparkly bits that Jane had so painstakingly collected rose to the ceiling. Then they swirled into one starry line, shot to the top of the wardrobe, and deposited themselves well out of Jane's reach on top of the tall white cabinet. Well out of Jane's reach, but she had no doubt that Dorie could now take the tinsel down at her leisure and play with it anytime Jane was gone.

She skidded to a halt and stood panting, staring down at the girl.

If, in that moment, Dorie had looked mischievously up at her and laughed, Jane might have calmed down. But Dorie merely turned from her, walked to the window, and stood, watching the forest with no expression at all.

Jane left the nursery, slamming the door behind her.

* * *

Day after day and the frustration didn't lessen. The more Jane coaxed, thought up new games, took Dorie's Mother doll away, the blanker and more stubborn—and more infuriating—Dorie got.

By the end of the month Jane was wondering whether she had the temperament to stay after all, no matter how much she wanted to help the girl. She had heart for the task, she had determination—those weren't the problems.

It was the self-doubt that was getting to her. The anger lumped along behind her like a black dog nipping at her heels. It raged inward, telling her it was her fault that Dorie was intractable. You should leave, it told her. You expected a lonely girl like you; you expected you could swoop in and solve her problems with a bit of iron and a hug. Never mind that yours weren't solved so readily. Never mind that when you finally found Niklas and the foundry, you wouldn't speak to anyone for weeks—just sat hidden under a worktable and watched the other scarred children try to master their ironskin, their curse.

Jane hated her inability to make a difference in Dorie's life, and she hated how exhausted the girl made her. Where was her patience for this poor waif, battle-scarred just as she had been? Where was Jane's loving kindness?

Gone since the war, Jane thought. Gone with her brother.

Jane and Dorie were sprawled on the stone floor of the kitchen, heedless of dignity, when the weekly mail came. Jane had momentarily given up the battle and was watching Dorie waft cut-up chunks of the last mealy storage apples into her mouth.

"Sure and you'll never get that one to use her hands," said Cook.

"Maybe she just wants to use her feet like a monkey," said Jane. "I should take off her shoes."

"Being tired makes you sarcastic," said Cook. "Now you'll be seeing what we went through." She held the white bowl against her broad hip, beating air into the cake batter.

"All you had to do was let her draw light pictures on the floor while you worked," said Jane. "I'm responsible for her mortal soul."

"She'll be having a soul, now? Ha," said Cook.

There was no real rancor in these exchanges. Jane rather liked Cook's lazy cynicism. It meant there was one place in the house she didn't have to guard her tongue and bite back the sarcasm that spilled over it. That was a rarity—even Helen had not suffered Jane's black dog moods very well.

But even if she could be caustic with Cook, they had little else in common. And Jane couldn't stay in the kitchen all the time, anyway. She got to her feet. "Finish your apple, Dorie, and then we're going back upstairs."

Dorie looked mutinous and Jane sighed inwardly, careful not to let it show on her face. You couldn't let children know when they were shredding your last bit of patience.

The old butler, Poule, appeared in the kitchen doorway. She nodded at Cook and reached up to hand her a circular. She was nearly as short as a dwarf, Jane thought—not that the dwarves were seen much anymore either. And for Jane—

"A letter?"

Bright eyes gleamed, but the butler didn't answer the obvious. As Poule reached up to hand Jane the letter, Jane saw a stray flash of light from her sleeve, as if light glanced off metal. Jane's eyes narrowed. Just what kind of roles were Mr. Rochart's servants really playing? The woman turned and left, her worn black shoes stirring up a small puff of flour that Dorie had spilled.

Jane slit the envelope with a silver paring knife and tugged out a thick fold of heavily written-on paper. "It's from Helen!" she said. "I was almost getting worried. I've written her twice."

"And she not once?" said Cook. "*Tsk.*"

Jane laughed and dismissed the implied rebuke. "Helen probably has twenty letters started to me by now—seventeen of them mislaid. Goodness knows what the flat looks like anymore." She unfolded the page, pleased that Helen had managed to get a letter actually out the door to her. "Dearest Jane . . ." began the letter, and then, typically Helen, it launched into a flowery description of the latest ball she and her fiancé had attended, replete with tidbits of gossip about people Jane had never met. The flow of minutiae was occasionally interspersed with a command for Jane to return to the city immediately and have as delightful a time as Helen was having.

Jane flipped over the page, and an engraved card fell out and fluttered to the floor. Jane picked it up—and stopped.

"It's a wedding invitation," she said.

"As should be," said Cook. "You said she was betrothed."

"Yes, but I thought she was waiting till the summer," said Jane. "When the family left on their summer travels." A familiar worry tugged at her inside—that Helen was busy making rash decisions without Jane there to advise. Not that Helen always listened. Jane was not entirely certain about the character of Helen's fiancé, but when she had dared mention any concerns, Helen had stormed about, insisting that she adored him, that any faults were easily mendable, and what did Jane know about marriage anyway.

"Soonest's best," said Cook. "Otherwise the man might be

finding a new lass, or the woman getting in a spot of trouble."
She beat the batter hard, her wooden spoon hitting the side
of the bowl with muffled thumps.

"Helen would not," Jane said positively. "She is not, I'm
sure of it. Likely she's lonely without me, and dying for something new to happen. Neither of us were born with much
patience." Jane flipped the engraved card around in her fingers, the attendant letter almost forgotten. "The wedding is
soon—just after her eighteenth. Do you think he'll grant me
leave?"

"Only way of finding out is asking," said Cook.

Jane looked up at the older woman, startled. "Am I allowed
to go up there? To his studio?"

Cook tapped the cake tin full of batter against the counter,
leveling it with sharp thwacks. "He'll not be having any ap-
pointments today, so I expect you'd be safe. Mind you, you're
not to be saying I said so. And knock first."

"All right," said Jane. She stood up, brushing her dark
skirts clear of flour and crumbs. "I'll go." She glanced down
at Dorie, now lying on her back and pointing her toes at the
ceiling for no discernible reason.

"Sure and I'll watch her," said Cook. "This is her I'll-be-
an-angel-if-no-one-is-crossing-me stage. I know it well."

Jane nodded, folded the unread letter in her pocket, and
took a breath. "I'll go," she said again. "It's just a studio."

Just a man.

She repeated that to herself as she climbed the stairs outside
the kitchen. Where they opened on the first floor she stopped
and peeked out, calculating that this should be the damaged
wing she had studied from the back lawn. The hall was nearly

pitch black, and she couldn't see if there was damage or not. At the far right a thin slit of light implied a break in the forest-green curtains she had seen in the foyer.

Jane continued climbing.

She wondered as she went past the floors if she was supposed to know immediately where Mr. Rochart worked. Would it be obvious? Or was it off one of the black landings, branching off one of the dark and destroyed rooms?

But at the fourth floor the stairs stopped and it *was* obvious. The landing was lit with the most light she'd seen yet in the house. This was the top floor, and the roof was sloped overhead, the great beams visible. It looked like it should be the garret, she thought. It shouldn't be where the master worked—it should be servants' quarters, dark and cloistered cubicles of space, twisting corridors.

But perhaps those walls had been removed, knocked out. Perhaps this area had been transformed.

On one side of the landing was a large empty area, bright and filled with light. Its polished wood floors were brighter than anything in the house.

On the other side was a long white wall with one door. The door was ajar, and Jane could just see a form moving around inside.

She walked over and knocked. "Mr. Rochart?"

"Come in."

She pushed open the door and entered. She had seen shadows moving, heard him—but now, where was he? The room was empty.

Jane turned slowly, looking around the broad rectangular space. The long side opposite was a wall of windows that should face the backyard and the woods, if she hadn't gotten completely turned around. On one end of the room was a second door, and on the other was shelving filled with supplies—some of which Jane recognized as pens and charcoal and pastels, some of which were unknown to her. A heavy worktable sat in the middle of the room, covered with tools and more stacks of materials. The walls in the wide room were white, and all the remaining available surfaces were lined with more of those same skin-colored masks that encircled the red waiting room off the foyer. It was strange that anything with hollow eyes could seem so much to leer.

A noise from behind, and she startled. "Sir?"

Quiet. Then Mr. Rochart emerged from that other door in the north wall, pulling it closed behind him. "Miss Eliot," he said, formally polite. Perhaps he was remembering that he had not come to speak with her as he had promised. "Did Poule send you up here?"

"She brought me a letter," said Jane, temporizing in case she would get the cook in trouble for pointing her the way. "I hope I'm not intruding."

"Of course not. I see you are studying the masks."

"They're hideous," Jane said bluntly. Too blunt, but it was the second time that he had caught her looking at them, and she was annoyed by their intentional ugliness. As if he knew that people would stop and stare at deformity, as if he were taking what she had to deal with every day and warping it for his own amusement. "I gather they're supposed to be." The masks caught and held the eye with their perversity—rows and rows of protruding teeth, cruel scowls, cauliflower ears.

"They're the worst in people," Mr. Rochart said. "Extracted and displayed. A reminder."

She could not decide how old her new employer was. When

his eyes were shadowed from her, hidden, then he seemed relatively young—late twenties perhaps. But sometimes she saw those deep amber eyes, and then he seemed a hundred years old. It was a strange feeling. "I don't understand why you need a reminder of how evil people can be," she said. "It's something I try to forget."

He moved closer, the formality fizzling off and away, as if by coming to the studio Jane had given him the necessary permission to indulge in speaking with her, watching her. His lean frame was so near to her own. "Sometimes we have to remind ourselves what we are capable of." There was a well of sorrow in those amber eyes, and Jane didn't know what to say. Her heart beat fast, without her permission. "I wonder what we all would be like, without the Great War. You would not be here to rescue me, Jane, so what life would you lead . . . ?"

Jane drew away, turned her iron cheek into the shadows. Anger and strange hungers bubbled inside her, so to hide them she looked at the wall and said, "I see you've made none with war scars." There were poxed cheeks, there were knife scars. But there were no masks blotched red, ridged and bubbling as if death crept beneath them. No victims of the fey.

Maybe even he couldn't stand that much ugliness.

"I show the worst in people," he repeated. "Not the best. Not bravery." He was near again. He touched a bare spot on her jaw, and his fingers were warm and flecked with clay dust. "You were trying to protect someone; I'm sure of it."

Jane set her lips and pulled back, turning away from that touch, that level gaze. Warm looks he couldn't mean; invasive words that flicked her wounds.

No options.

The workbench in the center of the room was covered in tools, paints, glue. A damp towel covered a mound on the workbench; a lump of clay sat in a white-grey bucket of water. White and pink dust was everywhere. "Are you working on something new?"

"As always." He drew aside the damp towel to reveal the start of a mask. At this stage it did not look ugly. He was still shaping its basic contours: cheekbones and chin, and the eyes were merely two depressions of his thumb.

"A mask you cannot look through," said Jane. She imagined wearing a mask like that, imagined her own iron creeping over her eyes, her nose, her lips. The thought was suffocating, and not just from the imagined lack of air. "Your eyes sealed shut."

"Perhaps there are more masks like that than we think," he said. He covered it with the cloth, his fingers gentle around its form. He studied the cloth-covered mask as he said: "I am sorry I have not been back to help you. My work—"

"You are busy," Jane said. She was helping him out, granting him excuses. Anything to avoid revelations of truth, which would be—what? He did not know how to help Dorie, he did not want to see Jane. . . .

"Tell me now," he said. "How have you and Dorie been getting on? Have you made progress?"

"Not so much," Jane admitted. She weighed all the frustrations and decided not to admit defeat just yet. "She is speaking a little more to me now."

"She trusts you, then," said Mr. Rochart.

"I don't know about that," said Jane, "since I keep trying to get her to do things she doesn't want to do. Perhaps I am familiar now, is all. I know she understands everything I say—she could speak in full sentences, if she wanted to." She remembered that shadow slipping into the forest. "She talks of you sometimes. Says she sees you from the window."

The lines of his mouth fell; a weariness crept over his cheeks. A tiny shake of his head. With an effort he roused himself and said, "But tell me, Jane, what matter of import weighs on your mind? A letter, you say?"

"From my sister," Jane said, recalling herself to her mission. "She is to be married quite soon—within the week, in fact. She wishes me to be there, and indeed, I wish it myself." Jane found herself slipping into the archaic language he so often used.

The weariness returned. "You would give up on us so soon," he said.

"No!" said Jane. She remembered her frustrations with Dorie and felt sharp guilt. "No," she repeated. "This is not an invented dying aunt, I swear it." She held out the engraved notice to show him. "I had thought it would be a couple months from now."

He did not look at the invitation, but instead leaned in closer. "Decades ago, before the Great War, there was still trade with the fey. Contact, even if it was rare and limited to your friend's cousin, your neighbor's father. Those bluepacks were everywhere, ran all the trains and streetlights, trolleys and gramophones, and yet you never knew anyone personally who had met the fey—it was always a friend of a friend, or a faceless business who shipped the lights and bluepacks to the local stores. Stories about the fey spread, of course. Some compelling, some disturbing; and if you saw a fey at a distance, wearing a human shape—well, you never quite knew if all the stories of curses and stolen children were true or slander. The tales of the fey were fireside tales to entrance your friends and family, and not gruesome fodder for the newspaper."

Jane nodded, uncertain what this had to do with her leave of absence.

"There was one tale of a lass who was tricked into staying with a ruined man," he continued. "A human man, who had been cursed by the fey. A damaged man, nearly a beast. When this girl goes home for a visit, he bids her promise to stay only a week, for without her he will surely fade and die, return to the clutches of the fey that once claimed him. . . ."

She could not fathom this despairing mood, but she liked it little. It poured from him like a poison, clutching at her throat, overpowering even her rage. From a distance she heard herself saying, "The circumstances are very alike, then. For I clearly see your beastly fangs and sharpened claws."

Mr. Rochart straightened. Laughter broke through the somber expression. "Go to your wedding," he said. "I will not even hold you to the beast-man's promise, make you swear to return to me."

"No?" said Jane.

"No. I will fetch you home myself."

Chapter 5

FEY BEAUTY

Six days later, Jane sat on a pink tufted stool in Helen's new sitting room, watching her sister flit back and forth. Fair Helen, lovely Helen, pink and white, unscarred Helen was dressed in nightclothes that looked like pre-war underclothes: a white chemise and bloomers, both heavily worked with eyelets and satin ribbons. Strange to think how sharply fashions had changed in one decade after seemingly centuries of head-to-toe layers. Dresses were sleeker and clingier by the day; glimpses of legs were displayed in the thinnest stockings you could afford (and oh, weren't stockings dear these days as the factories all labored to make coal and steam technology work as efficiently as the bluepacks once had). Soon, Jane reflected, they would all wear nothing at all, and yet her head would still be swathed in mask and hat and veil.

Helen's copper-blond hair streamed free, her big brown eyes batted lashes at Jane. "The pearl combs or the tortoiseshell, Jane? Why won't you make me choose?"

"I thought you had chosen," said Jane. She was seated next to the fireplace. The fire felt lovely, warm—too warm on her iron cheek. She turned her face away from the blaze. "The tortoiseshell, then," she said. "To offset your hair."

Helen held one up, then dropped it on the rosewood vanity with a sigh. "No, the pearls, of course. It has to be pearls for a wedding. Come twist them in, will you?"

Jane obeyed. She always obeyed Helen on the little things. It was easier that way. And yet no matter how many small battles she let Helen win, Helen fought just as hard on the big ones. And there met Jane's temper, and called Jane stubborn, no matter how stubborn Helen was herself.

"It's a lovely mirror," said Helen. "Not all wavy and silvered like ours was in the flat."

Jane twisted the copper-blond curls over her finger, carefully not looking at the mirror.

Helen shifted, disrupting Jane's hands. "And my rooms are lovely, don't you think so? Did you see the fixtures for the gaslight? I selected them. All on my own."

"Hold still."

"Ouch," said Helen, and her fingers flew in the way of Jane's and back down. "I said, aren't you fond of my rooms?"

"I'm not sure why you're here in these rooms before the wedding," said Jane. "Since you asked."

"Don't be prim," said Helen. "Nobody here thinks anything of it."

"I passed two cousins and a maidservant this morning that thought something of it."

"Is that why you've been so cold to me all week?" said Helen. "You barely wished me a good birthday on Tuesday, and I am now eighteen and quite ridiculously adult."

"I have not been cold to you," said Jane, nettled. "You've been busy with teas and ordering the servants to twist bows and make cakes. I've had errands to run. There are things I can only get in the city and not—" But she stopped short of criticizing her new home.

"Not out in the sticks," said Helen. "I understand our real trouble this week, don't you worry. My simply divine new life will not come between us. You absolutely must give up that dreadful job and come live with us. Alistair is quite wealthy enough to feed another mouth, and I refuse to strand my sister in the remains of the war zone."

"A touching invitation, if melodramatic."

"Bother your sarcasm. You know what I mean. No one would think anything of it if you left that position." Helen untied and retied the ribbon between her breasts. "Your Mr. Rochart is well known."

"Is that so?" said Jane. She tamped down a surge of interest in the subject and calmly tucked a manufactured curl into the pearl comb.

"There is a mysterious air around him, that's what I know," said Helen. "Is it true he killed his first wife? Like the fey story of Bluebeard, you know, a forbidden locked room, and when the new wife enters it she finds all the dead wives hanging on the wall, and then"—she drew a finger across her throat with gruesome relish—"*snick,* she's next." Her eyes grew wide at her own imaginings. "Ooh, what if you're in danger? Maybe you shouldn't even go back to turn in your resignation. Stay here with me. They can ship your trunk."

"His wife died in the Great War," Jane cut in. "Fey bomb, I believe."

"You believe. But you don't know."

"I've seen more of him than you, and I don't believe he's a Bluebeard for one instant," said Jane. "If he were, he would've advertised for someone beautif"—a gesture with her hand cutting off the word—"someone not me. Besides, I've been there for a month. Surely he would've chopped me into bits by now."

"Maybe he likes it to be a surprise when it happens," said Helen thoughtfully. She cast around for more gossip. "Well, everyone knows his daughter has some sort of deficiency, so he keeps her locked up in the garret and no one ever sees her."

"Untrue," said Jane. "She can go nearly everywhere in the house."

Helen pounced. "Nearly?"

"Well, not the studio, but that's off limits to everybody. And not the western wing, but you see it's damaged. . . ." Jane trailed off, annoyed by Helen's raised eyebrows. "Well, tell me the rest of the lies."

"Well, he had an affair with the Prime Minister's wife, and that's perfectly true and not lies at all, despite the fact that his cheeks are thin and he never pomades his hair. She met him at a dance last spring, and then she went down all the time to see him, and finally stayed down there for a month. And when she came back she was so refreshed and glowing, she looked ten years younger. The Prime Minister didn't even have a clue, but everyone else was laughing and making cuckold horns behind his back. How's that for facts?"

Jane was cold inside at the thought. "Facts?" she managed. "You haven't produced one. There, now your hair's done. Let's put you in the dress."

A knock on the door was followed by a maid backing in with a tea tray.

Helen jumped up. "It's not time for my dress," she said.

"First there's morning tea, and then there's you to get dressed and brushed and curled, because like it or not, I intend for you to be stunning. Two sisters, each more ravishing than the next! Men dropping dead at their feet!" She staggered dramatically to Jane, sank to her knees, and laid her head in Jane's lap. "Now come eat something."

The tea was delectable—little cream-filled cakes, slices of crisp hothouse cucumbers, chocolates and sugared almonds piled in silver bowls. Helen replenished Jane's plate faster than Jane could empty it. She cradled a warm cup of black tea and tried not to think of Mr. Rochart's past affairs. Of course men had them. Eyeing her sister's frothy nightclothes—of course *people* had them.

Helen caught Jane's eye. "Are you still thinking about me living here? I was perfectly well chaperoned, I promise you. Everyone knows I have no family. Where was I supposed to live?"

"By yourself, in our flat," said Jane. "I would've sent you money." Most governesses lived with their families, of course. But Jane's school had refused to let an ironskin board there with the pupils. Helen's family had agreed to let her share a flat with her sister so Jane wouldn't have to live alone. But they had insisted it be a *nearby* flat, and in that part of town it had taken both girls' scanty salaries to barely cover the rent. Though Jane could be cross, she suspected that deep down Helen was grateful not to have to live with her charges. Helen was never the mothering type.

"In our *empty* flat I wouldn't be chaperoned," said Helen. "Positively much more scandalous, I assure you. Not to mention dull as dirt. No Jane to fuss over me and keep me from spending all my earnings on shoe buckles and fizzy wine. Why does it bother you?"

"It doesn't," said Jane. If she probed deeply, it was probably because she felt guilty at leaving Helen to make her own decisions, manage her own life. Which was ridiculous. She'd only left Helen because Helen was leaving her. Well, that and the no-job thing. She'd been fired from the Norwood School over winter holidays, and hadn't that just made them pleasant. "Forget I said anything."

Helen carefully took apart a cream cake and licked the insides out. "Can you remember when we used to have this sort of thing at home?"

"Just," said Jane. "Never every day though." Father had died in the Indis of brain fever when Jane was eleven. Though the estate went to Charlie, there had been no family money left, except what Father had earned by his wits. After the dust and the debts had been settled, they were left with Mother's tiny annuity. Still, even those times had had joy in them. Jane had seen the terrible conditions at the Norwood School, and that had just been as a teacher. If both her parents had died when Jane was eleven, she and Helen might have ended up as charity pupils at a school just like that, cold and hungry and at the mercy of typhus or polio. She could scarcely imagine how that Jane would have turned out—equally scarred, perhaps, equally angry.

But when Jane was thirteen, the war started, and the poor-but-happy time grew fainter, thinner as the terror dragged on and on. Until one day on a battlefield her brother was gone and it was all over, all of it.

After the war, after *no Charlie,* the estate went to the cousins, and Jane could not even keep Mother in her own home while she wasted away. All she could manage was huddling in Niklas's foundry, lost and confused and trying to recover from a wound that would never heal.

But down that road lay guilt and rage. Jane blinked back the orange fire that warmed her mask, doused it with thoughts of lakes and streams and pure cooling rain. She refused to be angry today.

"No, not cream cakes every day," Helen was saying, "unless Father sailed home with a windfall. But better than never. Better than grubbing in the gardens, and depending on neighbors' charity, better than watching Mother take in tatwork and ruin her eyes by hoarded candlelight. Tatwork! Do you hear how old-fashioned that sounds? No one wears lace now. Mother wouldn't know what to make of it, if she were here." Her voice faltered on the final word.

Jane touched Helen's arm. "I know you miss her."

"And I'm sure you missed her in the city, after you left us," said Helen, brightly, sharply, and Jane's hand fell away. "But we're not digging up unpleasant pasts today. Not for my wedding." She dropped the decreamed cake sections to her saucer and smiled at Jane as if willing things to be all right. "Go on, eat, before I clean off this entire tray." Helen's fingers hovered over another slice. "But everyone says Silver Birch is enormous, one of those grand old fey-built estates. They probably have cream cakes out the ears. I suppose if he doesn't chop you into bits, you can sneak me into some brilliant party there and we'll make off with a bottle of sherry and an entire cake and go looking for all those slaughtered ex-wives."

"I don't think he has parties," said Jane. "They live simply."

In truth she suspected that money was tight, but she didn't like the idea of gossiping about her employer. To assuage Helen she picked up a small triangle of rose-scented cake and tried to turn the subject away from Helen's gruesome imaginings. "Won't there be lots of food today? Were there problems with rations?"

"Bosh," said Helen, separating another cake slice. "The Great War is *over,* Jane, no matter what your country friends think. Rations simply don't apply to someone like Alistair. Why do you think I picked him? Not just for his charm. People with money can *save* you, Jane—if they want to. But you take the bad with the good—you see how practical I have become, on my own—and today that means excess. He has the staff making mountains of cakes, chilling waterfalls of champagne. And really, it will be glorious, won't it? But I can't do this while people are watching." She demonstrated what she couldn't do by sucking pink cream filling from the sponge. "Anyway, that's ages away. I still have an entire ceremony to get through without fainting, and so do you. Did you bring something nice to wear?"

"My best," said Jane, referring to the navy frock with short sleeves. "You've seen it."

Helen made a face. "You'll wear something of mine." She raised a cream-smeared finger, forestalling Jane's protests. "You will. We're the same size in everything but shoes. If you had a blond wig then from behind we'd look the same. Not even Alistair could tell us apart, I'm sure of it. You could take my place today, and wouldn't that be a laugh? I wonder what he'd say when he found out."

Jane's protest subsided under this flight of fancy. Even

knowing Helen's sartorial tastes, the dress was a small battle, and the next point was a bigger one. "All right," she said. "As long as I can wear my veil."

The wedding was beautiful, the reception long. There were plenty of the little cream-filled cakes, but Jane didn't see Helen eat anything at all. She moved through the party in her slim white frock like a ghost, her honey-hued hair in coiled curls contained by the pearl combs. "Fey beauty," croaked an old auntie next to Jane, and then she was rewarded by hostile stares from the ladies around her. That was a saying from long ago. Not today.

Jane herself felt quite odd and otherworldly. Helen had insisted on fixing her veil so it was short and gauzy, not the long swathes of fabric Jane normally used. If Jane had had her normal veil she would have adjusted the layers to cover the front of her borrowed dress. Helen's dressmakers had been busy providing her with a whole new wardrobe, and this was one of those dresses.

"But I can't stand it," Helen had said. "I don't care how chic the color is, it washes me out. I wore it to Mrs. Wilmot's tea party last week and her daughter Annabella just bumped right into me, in front of everyone. And then drawled, 'Oh, I'm sorry I didn't see you; you blended into the wallpaper.' When their wallpaper is clearly pewter and not dark silver. Of course she's just jealous because she wanted Alistair, not that that makes it any easier. Alistair assured me I was more beautiful than anyone except the Prime Minister's wife. But I'm never wearing this again."

The dress was a silvery grey silk, shot through with silver and jet threads that shimmered in the light. It very nearly matched her iron mask, though Jane could not decide if this was a good thing or not. The dress was in the very newest style—slinky and close-fitting, gathered at one hip and falling in a swish to the tops of Jane's T-strap shoes. The décolletage was low—not as indecent as some of Helen's dresses, but quite low enough for Jane. Helen had had to lend her a tight and low-cut slip that would work underneath.

The dress might have not worked well with Helen's coloring, but it worked splendidly with Jane's. Helen curled Jane's dark brown hair with the tongs, then made her leave it down around her shoulders, tucking only the white fey-blighted lock up into the combs and veil. The dark silver transformed her pale, peaked look into something luminous, into a creature who was marble-skinned and elegant. It was the most beautiful dress Jane had ever worn, and she was very nearly in love with it, even if she felt an utter fraud.

As she came downstairs and found a seat outside under the erected tents, she noticed people looking at her. Relatives, servants—people who had seen her around the house all week suddenly stared at her as if for the first time. There was a brief moment where men looked at her as if she were a *girl*.

And then one by one they looked closer at her veiled face and remembered, or saw, the ironskin beneath. They discerned who she was, and they dismissed her.

But not all of them figured it out immediately. And not all of the men stopped looking at the silver lines of her dress.

Jane felt quite light-headed as she watched the wedding, struck by the idea that this might be how it was supposed to be. How even now she might wake up from her terrible dreams of the war and be happily sitting here whole and unveiled, watching her younger sister marry. Mother would be next to her, Charlie on the other side, the tall strong man she had never gotten to meet. Even in her imagination, the clock would not turn back far enough to put her father on the bench with them.

But it would turn back to that dreadful morning in the last month of the war. It would turn back to that dawn, and somehow she and Charlie were the lucky ones who made it home, who made it out of that war alive, until now they sit here on the bench as the minister recites Helen's vows, and Charlie nudges her and whisper-recites the tale of Helen writing a love letter to their old clergyman in her ear, and they try not to giggle. For now Helen is saying the final words, and then it is all over, and Alistair is kissing the bride, and Mother clutches her hand, because she has promised Helen she will not cry.

They are done, they are smiling. And Jane turns to watch Alistair and Helen go solemnly down the aisle, and she should be looking over Charlie's shoulder, her chin should be touching his arm.

But there was no Charlie, and her light-headedness popped, and then she was standing on her feet clapping with all the other men and women she didn't know, who didn't know her, who looked at her and looked away, again and again and again.

Jane sat down with a rush as the crowd swarmed after Helen and Alistair, cheering their names and congratulating them for this wonderful, glorious day.

There was dancing, but Jane deliberately found another room to sit in, where it wouldn't look like she was wanting to dance and not able to find a partner. She ended up sitting next to the old woman who had called Helen fey earlier, and two other old women who loosened their shoes and watched the girls on display flit back and forth from the crammed ballroom to the room where the cakes and tidbits were laid out. A smaller dance with some of the youngsters was going on in this room, and an old man with a fiddle played for the kids and competed with the string quartet's sound emanating from the larger dance floor.

The sea of slinky gowns sliding back and forth between the rooms was arresting. Décolletage was low, T-strapped heels were high. Desperation was on more than one dewy cheek, plainly mixed with the waxy lipstick, the false eyelashes, the tight waves of curls. Single men were few—a lost generation.

But one beauty slinking past in an apricot gown needed no such ornamentation.

"Ah, the Prime Minister's wife," said one of the shoe-loosened women.

"The lecheress," said the other, fluttering her handkerchief, and they cackled.

The woman's face, elegant and porcelain-smooth, gave no sign that she had heard.

"She's beautiful," whispered Jane under her breath. Her face was peaches and cream, symmetrical, classic. Her apricot frock with its beaded net overlay clung softly to her lines, an elegant column. So this was the woman Mr. Rochart might have loved. An idle summer fling? Or passion, loved and lost, a tragedy bound by the rules of society?

"Fey beauty," croaked the woman who had said it before. "It's not smart to be that beautiful." The other old women were in dresses thirty years out of date: full dark skirts and corsets, kidskin boots, and rows of tight buttons everywhere.

But this one was modern. She wore a silk dress in sea-foam green with net flowers at the shoulder and waist. It draped oddly on her hunched and sagging form, and the leather heels slipped from her thin feet. She had a tiny pair of jeweled pince-nez that she studied the Prime Minister's wife through. "Not smart at all."

"Why not?" said Jane.

The women bent in, free of the restrictions the younger generations placed on their words. "They used to say the fey were drawn to the exceptionally beautiful," said Pince-Nez.

"Or exceptionally talented," said Shoes.

"May you be blessed with ordinary children," contributed Handkerchief. "May you be born plain."

"Why? What did they do with extraordinary children?" said Jane. She knew one of those, though surely the women meant a different kind of extraordinary.

"Steal them. Take them back to the forest," said Pince-Nez.

"Eat them," said Handkerchief.

"Bah," said Shoes.

Pince-Nez agreed with Shoes. "They take them for enter-tainment."

"And because they covet mortality," said Shoes in sono-rous tones.

"My granny knew someone who got eaten," Handkerchief said obstinately.

Jane did not believe that the fey had ever eaten people. And "covet mortality"—well, the bodiless fey had certainly taken over corpses during the war. They killed with fey bombs that prepared dead bodies for the fey—then reanimated them, used them to fight hand to hand. That was why the crematory kilns had been going nonstop during the Great War, to save their loved ones from that wretched fate. But that was a war tactic, a horror designed to strike fear into humanity. A very effective horror, but not the desired end in itself.

But entertainment... "What do you mean by that?" she said to Pince-Nez.

Pince-Nez stretched her feet comfortably into the path of a woman towing two marriageable daughters away from the food. "Anything that lives forever gets bored," she said.

"Like you, you old bag," said Shoes amiably.

"Even if I reach my hundredth I will never be bored," said Pince-Nez, rapping on the iron of her chair for luck. Her ropes of necklaces clacked against each other. "But the fey were."

A woman walking by shushed Pince-Nez, out of habit.

"So they stole humans to feed on," Pince-Nez said.

"I told you they ate them," said Handkerchief.

"Not that kind of feeding," said Pince-Nez. "They used to steal children, and everyone knew that. They fed on their beauty, their artistry. Sucked up everything that made them good. Then they let them go ... each one a dried-up, shriveled old thing."

"Like you," said Shoes.

"Least I was a beauty to begin with," returned Pince-Nez. "Fey beauty, they said I had. It's a wonder I didn't get stolen."

"That's enough out of you, Auntie," said a male voice.

Jane looked up to see Helen's new husband shaking his head at them. Handkerchief and Shoes cackled at the intrusion, while Pince-Nez hummed softly.

"But each stolen child is given a gift," said Pince-Nez

dreamily. Her face softened, and for a moment Jane saw a glimpse of the beauty she might have been. "A gift to take back to the human world, years and years later. . . ."

"Where's yours, you bat?" said Shoes. "In your knickers?" Handkerchief roared with laughter.

"Bah—enough!" said Alistair. "Come, Jane, you mustn't become one of these harpies already. Take a turn with me." He took her hand and pulled her up and into the children's dance.

There was a moment of shock as she realized this was the second man to deliberately touch her this month. Though Mr. Rochart had not needed the attraction of a clingy silver dress to touch her shoulder (twice), press her hand.

Jane did not find Alistair Huntingdon handsome. She was not sure that Helen truly did, either, despite him having the features that Helen had often designated as male beauty. His hair was curled, his nose straight, his teeth white and present, but Jane did not find the arrangement of it all pleasing. More to the point, his ruddy face lacked character—both in the moral sense and in the individual sense. But perhaps she was biased from having only seen the face of one man for the last month, a man with a million oddities inscribed on the map of his face, a man who had lived. The comparison— the fact that she was thinking about this comparison—made her pause.

Alistair was looking at the silver curves of her dress, not at the iron behind her veil. Jane could not decide if that was a blessing or not. But then he smiled politely and raised his gaze to somewhere around her ear. Nodded at the old fiddler, who started one of the popular waltzes—"The Merry Mistress," Jane thought. Though the family she worked for would never have approved, Helen had snuck off to the ten-penny ballroom (girls no charge) more than once, dragging Jane along as chaperone. Jane did enjoy the music. She would sit on a white-painted metal chair, sip a sugared coffee, watch her sister flit and flirt.

Now Alistair's free hand took her waist and he led her smoothly into the steps of a waltz. "Helen was very glad you came," he said. "She would hardly talk of anything else. You must come back at holidays."

"That is very kind of you," said Jane. She had waltzed be-fore the war; she was pleased to find the movements still in her feet. She did not like the touch of Alistair's hand on her waist—it seemed too warm, too insistent—but she smiled at her sister's husband and tried not to think about it.

"We don't want you to give up on life," he said. "No sitting around with the old biddies anymore."

"I was enjoying watching the children dance," said Jane.

"You are easily amused," he said, laughing.

Alistair seemed harmless enough. His foibles were evident from her short study of him—he was indolent, too fond of a life of pleasure and drink. From the way he'd avoided the war he must be a coward, though it wasn't likely that his inability to fight would affect his marriage. Helen herself had admit-ted these faults—stated in the same breath that she was sure he would mend them, once he was settled—but counted her-self lucky for more reasons than just his wealth and relative charm. So many men of their age had been lost in the Great War. Alistair might be a decade older, his birth might be no better than the Eliot girls' own. And yet, for the penniless governess to land him was a coup.

But was it worth it?

"... and the roses alone cost—oh, but you would be shocked. And then that man couldn't tell the difference between 'open' and 'overblown.' It's the difference between a woman who wields her assets wisely and a common ... well. Not a polite word, but he understood the analogy once I made myself clear."

Jane focused her wandering mind on Alistair's boasts. "But surely Helen would've been satisfied with something simpler. She is not greedy."

Alistair laughed. "I told your sister that your affliction had made you innocent. You have no idea of what is required to maintain one's position." He leaned in closer to the good side of her face, his breath hot on her ear. "They are ravening wolves, my dear. Each harpy ready to tear me and my bride down. This is the world we must live in. Your sister and I must be ... perfect."

"And you fear you are not?"

"I see you smirk, but your cynicism is truly naïveté, Jane! The common folk weary of the endless sacrifice yet to be made *after* the war. They must be shown, and indeed, they thrive on our doings. We are the morale of a lost generation, and as such, my cravat must be sharp and new, my plain yellow hair curled and set. My home must be stocked with the latest technology even as it is invented—did you mark the gaslight? And yet there are so few men left, everything is easier for me, you understand."

"Of course," Jane murmured. Her temper was flaring at his assessment of her as *naïve*.

"Your sister is a natural beauty, but she lives in an age where beauty plus art can equal perfection. No matter the state of the rice imports or whatever boring thing is claiming her husband's attention, you see how the Prime Minister's wife draws the eye. Helen must learn her art."

"The art of taking a lover?" she said pointedly, but he laughed this off, unaffected by her rudeness. He was insufferable, and she let go of his hands, pulled back from the dance. "Thank you, Mr. Huntingdon, but I tire easily," she said.

Alistair's fingers lingered at her silver waist. "You will never land a husband that way, you know. Keep your veil over your face, dance even when you are fatigued. It is the only way to win the war between men and women."

"The only way, is it?"

He leaned closer and she could smell the spirits on his breath. His cheeks were flushed. "Perhaps you are not as naïve as you seem. Perhaps you know that your charms could win a man in the dark, before he sees the imperfections under your mask. Come to the ballroom and I will whisper in your ear what man may be thus caught. I know all their secrets, you know. I will find one for you. Tell you his weaknesses, tell you in what curtained room you may find him tonight. . . ."

Jane squirmed free from his touch. "I do not require such assistance, sir." Her cheeks flushed as her temper struggled to burst free. "Perhaps you had better return to your guests."

He straightened, smiled, seemingly not offended. "Remember I am ever at your service." A short nod and he was gone.

Jane backed against the wall, her breaths short and furious, rage lighting her cheek, bursting flame against the iron mask. "The Merry Mistress" finished with a flourish, and the old fiddler eyed her with concern. For a breath only, then he swung into a foxtrot. The children danced, the women cackled, and Jane felt as though the air had been squeezed from her chest.

Pince-Nez's face swung in front of her, the old woman dreaming of a time when to be snatched by the fey might still be romantic—a shattered illusion, a vanished past. . . .

Helen drifted in on the arm of a young man, her face lit with laughter. Halfway through she saw Jane's mutinous expression and excused herself with a smile and flutter.

She whisked Jane into the corner. "What is it?"

"I have employment," Jane said through fierce breaths, holding back angry tears that flickered orange at the corners of her eyes. "I am independent."

"Shh, I know," said Helen. She rubbed Jane's arm in a calming gesture she often used when Jane became overwrought. "You're my brave sister. Breathe."

But Jane was too incensed to stop. "I am not grasping blindly for a husband, no matter what yours may think of our family."

"Come, Jane, that's too unfair. What did Alistair say to you?"

Jane did not think that Mr. Huntingdon's infuriating words were meant to be a pass at her—they were merely his own horrid assessment of the world they lived in. A brief shut of the eyelids—thoughts of cooling water, putting out the fire. Feel Helen's calming touch, let it soothe the rage.

Jane studied her sister's face, her heart rate slowing, the orange fog clearing. "Tell me, Helen." A breath, another. "Do you love him?"

Helen's pink-and-white face closed off and she let go of Jane. She laughed, copper curls tossing backward; took a swallow of her champagne. "Enough to grace his bed tonight."

Jane knew the look: stubborn Helen, determined to see a madcap course to the end of it.

Helen's eyes danced back to her young man. She pulled away from Jane and into his waiting, willing flirtation, her champagne sparkling green-yellow in the gaslight. The room was an extension of Helen, chartreuse-glowing champagne, the glitter of citrine, topaz, aquamarine, waxy pearls, and the shiny tops of curled hair. Glittering and silent, a shiny mask of gaiety hiding all.

Jane would get no truths from her.

Chapter 6

THE FOUNDRY

The next morning was very long. Mr. Rochart had wired Alistair that she would be picked up after lunch, and Jane longed for that time to arrive. She did not belong in that house, and every bored remark and cutting observation of the others over their strong tea or hair-of-the-dog cocktails confirmed that.

But if she did not belong there, did she belong at Silver Birch Hall? At least she was needed there. Perhaps she would never be comfortable anywhere; perhaps she had not that gift. Jane sat on a loveseat and tried to amuse herself by sketching the languid figures as she listened to Helen and Alistair and the remaining houseguests trade snide news from the wedding. Every one of them had a hangover, and they complained about that, and their gossip that morning was particularly caustic and cruel. The ropes of jewels and bright silk day dresses seemed too gay for the tired and cranky bodies underneath. Jane stirred milk into the bitter dregs of her tea and lukewarm sip to quell the sick feeling from the o much sugar, too much nerves, too much

"Why, that's Helen to the life," drawled one of them, and Jane found a rope of pearls dangling into her sightline as Gwendolyn or Gretchen or Gertrude Somebody-or-other peered at her sketch. The woman had red bow-painted lips that did not match the lines of her mouth.

"Jane is quite talented," agreed her sister.

"Are you going to color it in?" said Gertrude.

"I'm not very good with a brush," Jane admitted.

"You should've studied art at a good school," said Gertrude. "Then you would know how to use color, for a picture without color is like . . . what is it like, somebody?"

"Like a girl without a figure," said Alistair. "Technically correct, but not worth looking at." Gertrude laughed appreciatively.

The casual words flicked like a whip. Didn't they think she would love to have studied with real artists? It was too easy to see that other life, the one without the war. Oh, she was not fooling herself, she would never have been a real artist, but with a better education she would have been skilled enough to teach. She might have been a special instructor at a private school, and she would not have been asked so casually why she chose to be so unskilled. A lack of money had killed off one avenue, a lack of normalcy the next, and she had been pruned into this strange and twisting branch that should never have grown at all.

Jane sat fuming until Gertrude and her candid observations withdrew to the card table, to flirt with Alistair and down her morning champagne.

Even dreadful mornings eventually end, and at long last a footman entered with the observation that there was a driver at the door for Miss Eliot.

If in the back of her mind she had thought that "I will fetch you home myself" meant Mr. Rochart would literally be the one at the door, she was disappointed. Not that she had dared think that.

Still, it was thoughtful of him to arrange her journey for her. He had selected a later train than the cheaper dawn one she had taken to get here, and he had wired for an agency to send a car. The footman hefted her trunk into the hansom while Jane said goodbye to her sister on the front lawn.

Jane looked at Helen in her pink crêpe de chine frock and collar of garnets and considered, briefly, how many paths a life might take. Her sister's cheeks were pale from the excesses of the day before, and exhaustion hovered in her eyes. "I wish you well," Jane said.

She meant it, but Helen trembled at perceived coldness, and for a moment the barriers of last night broke. She flung her arms around Jane, clouded her with the sharp smell of gardenia perfume. Her rings dug into Jane's shoulder blades. "Don't think badly of me," she said passionately into Jane's shoulder. "I mean to be good to him, you know. He's better than you think. And I'm just so tired of being out of options."

Jane patted the copper-blond hair. "It wasn't so very bad, was it? The two of us?"

Helen pulled back, and Jane's skin seemed cold where Helen's body heat had been. "You'll never understand, you know," she said. "You're too brave. You have a history of it, and I have a history of not living up to you. You have memories of being brave to sustain you when you are tempted."

The look in Helen's eyes made Jane falter. As if there was an old hurt in them that had never healed. As if, deep inside,

Helen blamed Jane for going into the battle that morning when Helen could not. But that couldn't be right.

"I have a history of cowardice and foolish decisions," said Helen. She untangled the garnets of her elaborate collar and patted the chains back into place. "That's all I have, Jane. I have to plan for the future knowing what I have inside me— plan around my own folly. I'm being very sensible and independent like you, you see? It's just that when I do, it comes out—oh, it's a muddle." She gave up on the tangled collar. "You won't understand."

"I might . . . ," said Jane, groping for lost ground. How could you avoid old wounds when you didn't know they existed? Yes, Jane had been there with Charlie, but Helen had been there while Mother wasted away, and Jane had still been huddled at the foundry, lost in rage and self-pity. Should Jane blame Helen for that instead of herself? As Helen said, it was a muddle. No, she didn't blame Helen for running off to marry Alistair; she just didn't always understand her, and at this minute that gulf seemed very wide indeed.

"No, you won't." Helen patted Jane's cheek, sending out more gardenia from her perfumed wrists. "Ooh, your mask is so cold. But I suppose it's the only thing that stops you from being angry with me all the time. If you hadn't found that foundry, I'd have had to live with a fey in truth. Now kiss me, Jane, and promise you'll come again to see me. Or stay forever and always. But at least come."

"I promise," said Jane, and now her tangled thoughts were derailed by Helen's mention of living with fey. Of course! She should visit the foundry and ask Niklas for advice.

A man's hand fell on Helen's shoulder—a curly-haired

man smiled down at them with all his perfect teeth. "Don't forget to return and see us," said Alistair. "We'll find you a man yet."

"She'll return," said Helen, forestalling any rebuttal by Jane.

"Excellent," said Alistair. "Now Helen, my sister wants to know if you'll join her for a round of hearts."

Helen kissed Jane's cheek. "Write to me," she said, squeezing Jane's hands, and then she was gone, whirling away in a froth of copper curls and fluttering pink skirts.

Down in the heart of the city the air was thick, a tangle of river smells and factories. Dead fish and new machinery wove a thick miasma that lay along the river like a wool shawl drenched in a storm. Jane closed the door on her reluctant driver and walked down where the streets were too narrow and filled with carts and waste to drive an actual car.

And yet despite the smells, the dirt, this area called to Jane, plucked at her with strings of warm memory. She had spent half a year here after the war, half a year broken and raging. The worn heels of her old boots slid on the wet cobblestones. It was always wet here, and always slimy, too, as if whatever they were spewing from the factories was welling up through the ground, through stone-scaled roads, coating the paths and walls and sky. It had not been so long since the air had been clean down here, she knew. Since the heart of the city didn't automatically mean pollution. But need for the blue-packs had begun to outstrip supply a generation before the war. Factories sprang up like cattails along the banks, and the dirty coal that poured into them—chokepack, it was sometimes derisively called—slowly began to poison the home of the poor.

There were rough men down here in the grey sooty air, and ladies in loose red dresses, but if they looked at her, if they saw her face, they merely nodded. Something uncoiled within her at this, at the memory of this. The ironskin were familiar here, and no one startled at the sight of her. And the ironskin belonged to Niklas, and that was a community of sorts, and one you didn't mess with.

Then, too, perhaps they merely saw in her someone who'd had enough trouble for one lifetime. Maybe they felt guilty; maybe they chose easier targets. A host of maybes that Jane didn't know, so she just walked to the foundry, head held high and veil flung back so everyone could see her iron.

There was a high fence around the place—an iron fence, of course, and Jane gave the bell clapper a mighty tug and set it to ringing with sharp clanks. Through the bars the foundry loomed, its sooty walls as familiar as the day she left. The yard around it was a patchwork of dirt and brick, heaped with salvaged iron, slag—everything Niklas or the kids could drag home for cheap or free. A thin knobbly boy with an ironskin leg hobbled unevenly to the gate, tugged down the heavy iron bar, and let Jane slip inside.

"Thank you," she said, and looked down at his thin frame while he studied her with curious eyes.

The ironwork was crude here. Niklas didn't believe in fancy flourishes, even if he had time for them. Except for Jane's mask, which had had to be hammered to fit her shape if it was to do any good at all, his work was cast iron from roughly carved molds, designed to fit as many as possible and therefore fitting no one perfectly. The boy's leg was covered from ankle to knee with two pieces of iron, fitting around his calf like a clamshell, and lashed in place on either side with leather ties. The bottom tucked into a boot that someone had tried to adjust to keep the weight of the iron from digging into the top of his foot. The ironskin was too big for him, meant for him to grow into, and the excess space was taken up with rag padding between the iron and the shin.

She wondered what his curse was. Ironskins always wondered what each other had, and yet she would not rudely ask, as Mr. Rochart had. But the boy volunteered, as forthright as his curious stares at her face. "I got hunger," he said. "No matter how much I eat it's gone and I'm still hungry. Afore Niklas set me up it made me little sisters all hungry too an' drove me mum off her head. So I told you mine and that's polite, so now what you got?"

"Rage," said Jane. Hungry rage, that could take a crumb of irritation and turn it into a banquet. Like the sharp orange fire she'd felt at Gertrude that morning, when Gertrude's only real crime was thoughtless stupidity. Perhaps someday it would incinerate her entirely; Jane would go up in a sheath of orange flame. She did not say any of this to the boy.

"Rage," he repeated. "That's fierce, ain't it?" He pondered, weighing the merits. "I guess I'd rather be hungry and have my leg all tore up. I'm used to it, see."

"And you have ironskin from Niklas to help," said Jane, gently prompting.

"Right. Niklas." He shrugged a thin shoulder at her, motioning her toward the foundry. "C'mon, I'll take you to him." The boy limped quickly over the uneven bricks, using a crutch to take the weight off the heavy iron leg. At the threshold he turned and gave the impudent greeting favored among the lower classes during the Great War, and since. "Stay out," he said.

Jane crossed the iron threshold, proving she was no fey. He grinned and jerked his thin body away from her, into the workshop.

There had been more kids here, once. More misfits like Jane, scarred and lost, scarred and orphaned, scarred and rejected. But the number had dropped with time, since the last fey had vanished five years ago. This boy must've held out for those whole five years—his family must've held out, too—till an ironskin saw him and sent him here.

Five years ago. Niklas's work might be less, but the scarred still wandered in, Jane knew. She wondered if his task had only gotten harder with the passing years—the number of people might be diminished, but their emotional pain was surely greater, as they'd lived with their anger or fear or pain for five years, and not known its cause.

She walked through the crowded workshop, remembering. She had only stayed here six months, after the hospital and before that first governess job. She had been too devastated by the loss of her brother, her mother's illness, and by the inexplicable and terrifying rage that filled her, to think of this as home, or even a refuge, or anything except the place where she *was* one moment, and then the next moment. Perhaps that was the skill she had learned here, to make one minute follow the next, like making one foot follow the other, leading yourself out of hell by only thinking about one foot touching the ground and the other foot rising. Step by step, moment by moment, back into the land of the living.

The boy paused ahead of her. "It's an ironskin," he called out, and around that turn in the workshop she saw Niklas. He was just as she remembered: tall and broad, his cropped black beard striped with grey, and the curious dwarven-manufacture work glasses he wore fitted around his eyes like the crystal facets of spiders. He wore close-fitting hoops of iron in his ears, iron bands on his wrists. An iron circle hung from a string around his neck. String for safety reasons—if the hoop got caught on something, it would snap long before his neck would. She did not know if the iron charms worked, as clearly none of them were touching his veins, but she knew that he had always worn them since the war, would always wear them, and that gave her comfort.

He glanced up at her, then back down at his work. He was making a mold of a leg, gouging the wood with a sharp chisel, and apparently it was more interesting than saying hello.

The boy shrugged at her, as if to say, "That's Niklas, what can you do?" then scampered off as quickly as his leg would let him.

"It's Jane," she said. "Jane Eliot."

"I'd recognize that face if it were forty years instead of four," he said.

The wide back doors were opened for the light, and the river smell mingled with the hot iron and burnt wood. *There,* she had huddled on her first day, as if she were six and not sixteen. *There,* she had met a boy with despair running across his breastbone and understood what it was like to be on the other side. *There,* she had stood when Niklas brought the cooled mask from his desk, and showed her how to wrap the padding in place, slide it over her cheek, adjust the leather straps.

Niklas's heavy hands turned the mold back and forth as his chisel slipped along the contours. "What did you come back for?"

She remembered the driver waiting at the gate and said,

"I don't have much time. But I know someone who needs your help."

"Where's the scarring?" said Niklas.

She stalled before the part he wouldn't believe. "Niklas," she said. "You've seen a lot of curses."

"That I have."

"Do you know of one that doesn't hurt the people around the person? Like mine makes people angry, and the boy who let me in—his makes people feel starving. Do you know of one that doesn't cause pain?"

"Where's the scarring?" Niklas repeated.

Jane shook her head, admitted it. "There is none. None visible."

He looked up from his work. "What makes you think there's a curse at all?" he said, reasonably enough.

Jane clasped her hands together, to stop them from shaking as she described it. It was ridiculous how strongly the girl still affected her, even though she'd worked with Dorie every day for several weeks now. "She can do . . . fey things," she said. "She makes pictures out of light. And she can move objects around."

Niklas clasped the iron at his throat, as if to ward off her mere words. His voice rumbled, deep, angry, and he leaned toward Jane as if he would shake her. "Then this woman *is* a fey," he said. "A fey in disguise. Where did you meet her? She must be destroyed."

Jane started. "Oh, no!" she said. "No, no, no. This is a little girl. Her mother was the one cursed, while the girl was unborn. It's affected her strangely, that's all. And I have to figure out a way to stop it. I thought maybe you would have heard of somebody else like this."

She had forgotten the effect of his work glasses up close. She felt pinioned in their faceted gaze. "There's nobody like this," he said. "A fey could take over a dead child's body as easily as an adult's. You need to reveal her for what she is and destroy her."

Jane pushed the billowing panic back down at his words. He couldn't possibly be right. It was all wrong to come see him. He was too fixated on what he thought he knew to be true, and now Dorie could be in danger. She made her voice very calm. "Listen carefully," she said. "The girl is five years old and has lived with her family and the servants that whole time. You know perfectly well that fey-ridden bodies last no longer than a year, tops. Thus the old story about King Bertram's lover, who started to stink, but the King couldn't be convinced of that. This girl is human, but because of the circumstances around her birth, the curse is different. I still need a way to help her. Just as you helped me when I needed it."

The fanatic tension in his posture slowly died. He gestured at his furnace, at the bars of pig iron, the empty casting molds. "How can I send you back with ironskin if she doesn't have a scar to cover?"

Jane exhaled, tension unwinding. "That's my problem," she said. "One of them. I'd hoped you would have an idea."

"Short of welding her into a solid iron box?" His face twisted in a way that said it was only half a joke. When Jane did not move, he said, "Well, since you won't be put off. I do have something. Something new."

He turned from his workbench to rummage around a thick wooden table piled high with slates covered in nota-tions, papers, scraps of metal, stubs of lead, links of chain, and coils of rope—Jane wondered if that desk had changed at all since she'd been there four years ago. No, nearly five, now.

"Ah. Here," he said. He picked up a small, greasy looking jar containing a brown-and-black substance.

"What is that?"

"Tar," he said. "Tar with flecks of iron. I've tried it out and it works almost as well as the ironskin itself. It's horrible stuff and gets on everything, but you might find you can use it to find her weakness. The fey point of entry."

"Maybe I could," agreed Jane, awed by the possibility. She turned the jar around in her hands. Even the outside was tacky to the touch, smeared with bits of iron-flecked tar Niklas hadn't managed to scoop into the jar. "I remember you had a theory that the location of the curse might influence the type of curse—that similar curses cluster on similar parts of the body. I know you haven't encountered one like hers . . . but do you have a suggestion of where to put the tar?"

Niklas closed his fingers around iron, his expression closed off. "Say again what she does," he said.

He listened attentively as Jane told him everything she could remember. "You say she often waves her hands when she's making things happen. Or looks in that direction, which sounds like her eyes or her mind. I'd try one of those three."

Jane shuddered. "Tar in her eyes?"

Niklas shrugged. "If she is fey, maybe it'll kill her off for you."

"If the witch drowns, she wasn't a witch," Jane said wryly. She slipped the jar into the pocket of her dress. Took the few bills she'd brought inside and stuffed them into the iron cauldron Niklas used as a bank.

He watched her out of the corner of his eye, while saying gruffly, "I guess you have a job now and that's only right."

"And I didn't when I came, and you helped me anyway," she said. "You don't know how much that meant to me."

Niklas shrugged, picked up a hammer, started pounding on an iron bar that didn't look like it needed pounding.

She knew that the gruffness, the dismissal, was only his manner. A side effect, perhaps, of the howling depression he'd once confessed to her was his curse. The outline of his shirt caught on the iron underneath, the tough cotton snagging on the metal ridges, the hang of the leather jacket deformed by the iron chest that squeezed him like a vise, as if a tighter cinching could drive out the poison. She remembered the shape of that rigid corset from when she'd tried to hug him goodbye. Old Ironsides, one of the boys had called him, trying to make an affectionate nickname for the man they worshiped.

But Niklas didn't take to affectionate nicknames. And the name was never mentioned in his presence again.

The boy appeared in the doorway. "Hey miss, there's a man says you're gonna miss your train." He shouted around Niklas's banging, slipping his words in with the familiarity of practice. "He says if you don't come quick there may not be a car when you get there, as some hoodlums looked int'rested in dismantlin' it." A grin showed what he thought of the driver's worries.

Niklas did not stop pounding the iron bar with his hammer, though Jane turned again, said, "Thank you, Niklas. Thank you."

There was maybe a half-nod in return.

"All right," she said to the boy, pressing a coin into his

hand. "You take care of him, right?" The boy nodded, his sharp chin bobbing, his knobbly fingers shutting tight around the coin.

Jane clutched the jar in her pocket. She hurried through the door of the workshop and out the gate, hurried into the impatient orbit of the worried driver, leaving the foundry of the ironskin behind.

Jane's thoughts flew back and forth as the train clattered into the country station. First Helen and her new, utterly foreign society. The cruel rumors about Mr. Rochart and Dorie. Then—the paste might work, the paste might work. She could try it on Dorie the very next morning—starting with her hands.

As long as Dorie could touch iron without injury.

Iron was the only thing that stopped the fey. The rules had been hard to pin down—still were inconclusive—because the fey didn't take well to capture, after all. Besides, the war had gotten so tied up with superstition, as soldiers draped themselves in lucky iron charms—it was hard to tell what did and didn't work.

But one thing seemed pretty firm.

If a fey took over a dead body, that fey could be killed. An iron spike—a feyjabber—directly into an artery destroyed that fey forever.

Iron weakened fey, barred fey, wounded fey—it was why the iron mask on her cheek kept the fey curse from crossing the barrier and spilling out into the air, infecting others. If Dorie's talent was similarly a foreign part of her, a fey parasite on a human host, so to speak—then it should work. But was Dorie more human . . . or more fey?

The train jerked to a stop and Jane disembarked, thinking of the exercises she would have Dorie try. With the tar in her bag, suddenly all the frustrations with Dorie seemed possible to overcome. New ideas, new methods, spilled through her mind, firing her with new energy. She was startled to see a tall shadow spill over her, to hear a voice near her ear.

"Ah, my little soldier is returned to fight by my side," said Mr. Rochart. "Miss Eliot."

"Sir," she said, and she composed her suddenly trembling fingers by dint of shoving them in the wool coat's patch pockets. Her heart seemed to leap at seeing him, but she reminded herself that that was merely her excitement over Dorie's paste. The man was aggravating, with his hideous masks, his disappearing act, his Prime Ministers' wives.

Even if his conversation was more intelligent and entertaining than anything she'd heard the whole week in the city.

He loomed over her, a tall figure in a coat just as worn as hers, she suddenly saw, powdered with more of that white dust that followed him in a fog. A button was loose—didn't he have anyone to mend it? She was cross at herself for wanting to put it right. She was not allowed to be this relieved at returning home. Home? No. Returning to her job.

"You forget us for an entire week," he said in a low, mocking voice. "I myself brave the moor and damn the last bluepack to fetch you at the station, and I merely rate a respectful 'Sir?' Oh, Jane, Jane."

"In that you have the advantage of me," she said demurely.

He laughed—a sharp bark at odds with his foreboding appearance. "So I do. Well, Jane, my given name is Edward and you must call me it from now on. I am tired of this 'Rochart' nonsense." His black brows lifted, knit. "I believe you should have a trunk, little one."

"Indeed I do," said Jane. "But you mustn't carry it yourself; you will throw your back out."

He looked at her sharply, as if trying to decide if she had really called him old. Jane smiled politely, feeling that in some obscure way she was staying level with him; that two could play the game of aggravation, and that by being sticky she was staying more truly *Jane*. It was a brief thought, with little time to untangle it, for he was speaking again, moving, his eyes searching her face.

"As soon as we are in the black beast," he said, gesturing to the motorcar, "you shall take off that veil. I dislike it when I cannot see your eyes. I am certain they are laughing at me now."

The sparring was a stimulant to her train-deadened wits, and Jane's spirit rose. The contrast between his sense of humor and Alistair's could not have been sharper. He did carry her trunk, and he hefted it into the old car, ushered her in, and closed the door.

"There's no top," he said, though that much was obvious. "We are both ancient—there, I will say it so you do not have to." The car was indeed so ancient Jane wondered it didn't need cranking. It clearly had been old even before the end of trade almost a decade ago. "We'll drive slowly so you don't get mussed."

"Not for my sake," said Jane. There was an undercurrent of warmth to the spring air tonight; it caressed her fingers clinging to the metal ridge of the door, promised summer ahead. The car lurched forward and the wind blew her veil back, and she let it.

"What's on your mind?" he said, and she felt him looking sideways at her.

A million things, but one the most pressing to tell him. "I have an idea for Dorie," Jane said. "I don't know if it will work, so I don't want you to get your hopes up. But I need to ask you something before I try it."

"Of course."

"Can Dorie safely touch iron?" Jane thought the answer must be yes, or he would've warned her about it the moment she entered the house. She tapped on the rim of her iron mask anyway, for luck.

He nodded. "Certainly. She may have difficulties, but she is still human."

"Good," said Jane. "I'd like permission to try an experiment with iron and Dorie, then."

"I will support anything you do that is trying to get her to be more human," he said. "You've found that slow going, haven't you?"

His kind words made her admit in a rush: "Truthfully, yes. How do you get that child to *mind*?" And then she reddened at how exasperated she sounded with his offspring.

"Very poorly," he replied. He sighed. "I love her greatly, but I confess every fey-touched thing she does pains me, makes me remember—" He bit off that thought and with an effort raised his spirits again. "But though I am wretchedly busy, shut away in my studio, you mustn't be afraid to come to me. Seek me out, *make* me listen. Anytime you have trouble with her."

"I have trouble," Jane said dryly. "But I have a feeling the iron might help."

"You have my full support in anything you do to rid her of

those fey traits," he repeated. "It's why you are here. You have my trust." He was driving, so he did not look meaningfully at her when he said it, but all the same Jane felt her breath catch in her throat. It closed off any words she might have said about her experiment, or about Dorie's behavior.

When no more information was forthcoming, he said: "Well, keep your secret for now, but report to me within the week."

"I will," said Jane.

"Did you enjoy your sister's wedding? I let you off the leash for it, so I propose the answer should be yes. Though on second thought, I don't wish you to have enjoyed it so much that you will leave us for another wedding in a week."

"That is my only sister, sir."

"Carefully avoiding a real answer. I suppose there were a good many fine ladies and gentlemen there?"

Before Jane could stop her tongue, it leaped forth with "Do you know the Prime Minister and his wife?"

"Your sister travels in fine circles," said Mr. Rochart. "Yes, I do. She was a client of mine last summer."

"A client," said Jane. Surely he couldn't mention her so casually unless "client" was the entire truth.

"She sat to have a mask painted," he said in answer to her implicit question.

"It must have been a beautiful mask," said Jane. She could not imagine that woman wanting a hideous one, to wear or to hang on the wall.

"It was," said Mr. Rochart. "Do you know they have five children? She told me at length about all of them. I was tempted to make the mask with a permanently open mouth."

Jane looked up at him, startled—then laughed.

"So you can laugh," he said. "I was worried that our gloomy house would wear you down. That the black moor would swallow you whole. Or perhaps your week in the city has refreshed you, and you shall be hungering to return soon for more of its lavish pleasures."

"Not a chance, sir," said Jane.

"I am selfishly pleased," said Mr. Rochart, and then they were both silent. Silent—but the air seemed charged. Small tendrils of happiness curled off the spring air, coiled around Jane's skin.

The sun was setting now. For a rarity the clouds were thinned enough that the sunset could be seen, and its pink and orange rays lit the underside of the white-grey sky. The moor was transformed, each blade of grass clarified, each clump of heather gilded with pink. Here and there daffodils ran along in drifts, bending in the evening breeze.

It was an odd happiness, and Jane couldn't tell where it came from, only that it danced through the golden light, the air, thrummed in the quality of the silence between the two of them. She could not break that silence for anything, and when he did, it was half pleasure, half pain as she leaned into his voice, cupping each word to see what would be revealed there.

"When I was young I painted the moor," he said. "When I was your age. No—younger, even." Her heart shattered and swelled at the same time, his words both worse and better than they could be, even if she could not have said for the life of her what worse and better would have been in that moment.

The house was in sight now, the ancient car nearing its drive. The black walls soared overhead, and now she had to speak, and her words would undoubtedly fail him—supposing that he even cared what her words were. But she knew nothing about art—no, worse than nothing, for as Gertrude had pointedly reminded her she had had no money for tutors, for training, and so she was treading on a subject she would love not to be ignorant in, and yet, could not help but be. She remembered a series of grainstacks she had seen at a museum once, the same grainstack in shifting lights, seasons. "Did you paint it frequently?" she said.

"Yes," he said, and stopped the car at the front door. "But my travails are a story for another time. Come Jane, you are home again, so take up your coat and come see what Cook has prepared for us. Why, what about this black fortress has brought a smile to your face?"

Home, thought Jane, stepping from the car. Home.

Chapter 7

HANDS OF IRON

Jane woke the next morning with renewed purpose. She was almost joyful as she jumped from bed. The white walls of her room seemed fresh rather than sterile; the dark-paneled halls were warm and inviting. She munched the toast and tea that Martha left outside her door while she dressed and settled the iron mask and fresh padding on her face.

If this worked, she would have a way in. A way to reach Dorie, a way to convince the girl to learn things before she was hopelessly behind. Stubborn Dorie might be, but if her fey skills were taken from her, she would have few options. Jane ran scenarios of Dorie's stubbornness in her head while she coiled and pinned her hair, looping locks of it over the leather straps of her mask. The one white lock outlined her skull, twisted a pattern in her coiled bun.

An hour past dawn, and Dorie would surely be up and eating breakfast.

Time to tackle the lion. The lion cub? No, no lion—just a mule.

Jane hurried down to the kitchen. Martha was fitting the teapot onto a loaded tray, talking over her shoulder at Cook.

"If he'd keep those late hours for good. But no, now it's up at dawn. It's bell-rings. It's Martha where's my tea. He won't eat the fish."

"You just take the kippers along anyway," said Cook. "Sure and you'd think we were in the poorhouse already from the way he starves himself. Tell him if he doesn't eat those they'll be going to the dogs and hang the expense."

Martha shook her head at Jane as she bustled past her with the tray. "You. Put him in a good mood," she said. "Don't know as I like it."

Jane grinned. Morning light lit the kitchen stone, softened the folds of her dress. She wondered if Martha were right, if she could possibly take credit for something so lofty and far-removed as the moods of Mr. Rochart. "He's not an early riser?" she said.

"Stays up near to cockcrow, sleeps till lunch," said Cook. "Unless he gets excited about something, then Katy bar the door." She eyed Jane, but Jane turned to Dorie, who was waving her hand and wafting raisins from a blue-striped stoneware bowl into her mouth, one by one.

Last time for that.

Jane scooped up the bowl. "Come on, Dorie," she said. She half expected a mental tug on the bowl, but Dorie was not an intractable child at heart. She was willing enough to see what they were going to do next. It was only when "next" involved "hands" that everything went to hell in a handbasket.

"Maybe I'll take these, too," said Jane, nodding at the raisins.

"Suit yourself," said Cook.

They made their way up the stairs to Dorie's playroom, Jane studying the girl as they went. As she had told Niklas,

Dorie seemed to use her hands to direct her fey curse. Though she did not use her fingers in any dexterous sense, she often waved her stiff hands in the direction of what she was mentally moving, or to direct the light pictures she made.

It did not necessarily mean that that's where the fey curse resided—especially since there were no visible signs of the curse—but it gave Jane hope. After all, if Dorie had to be entirely covered with paste from head to toe, that wasn't a workable solution any more than Niklas's trenchant suggestion of eyes or mind.

Once inside the white-and-silver playroom, Jane took the precious jar of iron-flecked tar paste out. Dorie looked interested, until her eye fell on her Mother doll. She wafted the doll through the air and started it turning somersaults.

Jane smeared paste on the back of her hand and studied it, considering. Iron was a barrier to fey—the iron on her face kept the poison sealed in just as the iron in the threshold kept the fey out. Or a feyjabber in a fey-ridden corpse killed it for good.

Jane realized her hand was shaking. Nonsense! Dorie went in and out all the time over iron. Mr. Rochart—Edward—had said it had no effect on her.

The experiment might fail, but it would not harm Dorie. Jane was really very sure of it, but it didn't seem to calm her nerves.

"Dorie," she said. "We're going to try a little experiment. Does my hand feel cold to you? Touch it very carefully."

Dorie looked suspicious at this directive, but curiosity trumped it. She touched the tar with her flat palm. "Funny," she said. Jane regarded her closely, but she did not shriek or shudder, and when Jane picked up Dorie's hand and studied her fingers, they were free of blisters and scars.

The iron on Jane's own face didn't hurt her at all. It merely stopped the fey poison from leaking its power past the barrier. If iron had the same effect on Dorie's abilities, no one might have noticed. There were few enough people like Dorie, or like Jane—and so no real exploration into how they could live normal human lives, besides what they themselves figured out and shared with each other, what Niklas shared with those lost souls in the city. Besides, everything iron during the war had been melted down to make strips for windows and doors, for shields and feyjabbers. There was little enough of it for Dorie to come in contact with when she was sitting in the middle of her room playing with Mother.

Jane patted the brown tar all over Dorie's hands, smoothing it around her fingers and up her arms, checking several times—"Does that burn? Does it feel cold?" But Dorie said no, interested in this messy new game.

Jane was dying to see if the tar worked. But if she asked Dorie to try her light pictures and she failed, Dorie would immediately connect that with the tar. Better to carry out her plan of distraction. She quickly cranked up the gramophone with Dorie's favorite piece—a cheerful ditty from the Southern Continent with a bunch of made-up words like *jumbuck*. "Show me the dance you do," she said to Dorie over the music. "I want to learn it."

This remarkable novelty swung Dorie's attention away from her sticky arms. She demonstrated her made-up dance for Jane, and even seemed faintly interested in Jane's inability to do it properly on the first try. But Jane could tell the wheels in her head were turning.

Jane took them straight from the jolly jumbuck song into a Gaellish one about cockles and mussels, and then into another of Dorie's favorites. About then, she saw Dorie's steps fading, her attention growing focused on her arms. So she brought out her pièce de résistance: a new dance record her sister had been tired of. That caught Dorie's attention.

"But first, some blocks," said Jane. Her stomach tensed with the coming conflict. She got down the blocks and started forming pyramids. "Now your hands will make the blocks sticky. Isn't that silly? It's a new game."

Dorie touched a block with her palm and saw that, indeed, the tar made the block sometimes stick to her hand without her moving her fingers at all. Her expression grew interested. For the moment she had completely forgotten their usual point of conflict, captivated by this game that was halfway between using her hands and not.

This was an unexpected bonus, and Jane made the most of it, encouraging, joking, distracting. For the rest of the morning, Dorie tried building with blocks with Jane. Jane alternated between triumph and tension—Dorie working with her hands was brilliant, but nothing had been proven one way or another.

And then Dorie's block house fell. And then the next one. Her attention shifted, and Jane clearly saw the moment when Dorie's inner eye focused, as she attempted to rebuild the blocks in her preferred way.

Breath held, world stopped.

Nothing happened.

Tension poured out, turned into cautious triumph as Dorie's face blanked out, her focus caught by what was not happening. This time Jane saw the tiniest of blue lights scatter over the blocks and die away.

And still nothing happened.

Dorie's mouth opened in a wordless, taut cry, and she kicked the blocks across the room in frustration.

"Dorie, bring those back, please," said Jane.

Dorie stomped her feet and clacked. She kicked the remaining blocks, stack by stack, banging them across the room.

"Bring them back this instant," repeated Jane. She levered the kicking girl to her feet. "Blocks. Now."

Dorie kicked and squirmed, freeing herself, and Jane's temper rose to match Dorie's. She caught one of Dorie's sticky angry arms and forced it down to pick up one block and bring it back. Another. "No more disobedience," said Jane. "No more throwing blocks."

Dorie's mouth opened in a silent howl.

One by one Jane marched her to pick up every single block. Dorie was a sticky dead weight in her arms, her arms and legs stiff and her jaw set. When the last block was picked up Dorie collapsed on the floor, as if Jane had destroyed her.

Martha's knock on the door was a relief. "Bean soup," the maid said. "Cod in white sauce."

Jane's heart sank. She looked at the sauced fish and porcelain bowl of stew on the tray.

Dorie stared up mutinously. Jane knew that look. The look of trying to waft the tray through the air.

But the tray would not go.

Dorie looked down at her tar-covered arms and wailed, a thin miserable sound. She raised her arms—rubbed them furiously together, trying to scrape the paste away. But her motions were clumsy and the tar sticky. Her scrapings only smudged the paste around.

She lay down and starting yelling in earnest, drumming her feet on the side of the dresser.

"What's wrong with her?" said Martha in disbelief. And then, "You put tar on my floor?"

"It's an experiment," Jane said briefly. "This food won't work."

"Won't?"

"I need something she can eat with her hands," Jane said. "Tell Cook I need plain cut-up vegetables, plain cut-up bread. Apologize from me for the extra work."

Martha was still peering at screaming Dorie.

"I'll tell you all about it after I tell Mr. Rochart tonight," said Jane. "Lunch—please?"

Martha backed out with the tray, and Dorie's howls and kicks redoubled. After a while, Jane heard Martha return and leave the new tray outside, but she did not open the door. Jane waited until the girl wore herself out, till the furious kicks became languid thumps of the heel, and the howls were just a rhythmic grunt in the back of her throat.

Perversely, Jane was almost glad to see the tantrum—it made Dorie seem more human, to see her throw a full-blown, audible tantrum that looked exactly like any other frustrated child might have thrown, rather than her usual trick of calmly walking to the window and ignoring Jane. No, this tantrum was real, even down to the petulant part of being too tired to continue, but too stubborn to totally give up. Jane watched the kicks die away. Then she brought the tray in and set it down in front of Dorie.

Dorie sat up, sniffling.

"I know this is hard," said Jane to the tear-streaked face. "But I promise you it's important. Your father wants you to use your hands. Will you try again for me?"

She wiped the tips of Dorie's finger and thumb, pushed the tray toward Dorie and held her breath, hoping the promise of food would lure the girl into one more effort. Sniffling, Dorie ate most of the bread and all of the carrots.

That was the last thing she did as Jane asked.

The minute lunch was finished, Dorie plopped down in an afternoon sunbeam and lay on her stomach, her hands flat to her sides. Her eyes were open, her lips pressed shut, and she refused to budge. Finally Jane went and retrieved a book from the library, sat down with her back to the window, and calmly read. Or at least pretended to calmly read—the book she had grabbed turned out to be about the politics of the Ilhronian city-states in the 1600s, a subject she would've found dull at the best of times.

Twice Jane set down the book, got up, and built herself a castle from the blocks, hoping the game would lure Dorie back to life. But Dorie refused to budge.

Eventually Dorie fell asleep. Jane brought in warm water and towels and wiped the tar off the limp arms. She settled Dorie down for her nap. Dorie did not stir, and Jane gazed down at her, wondering how she could look so innocent in her sleep. Dorie's fingers twitched on the coverlet.

Jane stepped from Dorie's room, softly closing the door behind her. Martha was dusting in the foyer below, one ear cocked to the room above. Her eyes widened as a bedraggled Jane came down the stairs, covered in bits of tar from stem to stern, a book tucked under one arm and dirty towels in her hand.

"You lost the war," Martha said.

"It's a draw," Jane said grimly. "Are there old clothes stored somewhere?"

Martha furrowed her brow in question.

"I need gloves for Dorie," said Jane. "Long gloves, a lady's gloves."

"Won't fit."

"I know," said Jane, grabbing for the last thread of her patience. "I don't need them to look nice. Just an old pair."

"Chests in the north roof," said Martha. "You won't go there 'less he says so."

"Of course not," said Jane. The rules and restrictions oppressed her, overwhelmed her for that moment with her insignificance. But she had expected nothing less.

She plopped down on the stairs for a moment, felt the tired muscle ache in every corner of her frame. She wasn't sure how long the tar would last. Not long, clearly—and every day Dorie had it on was another day of more work for the maid and laundress. Jane would stand up to their wrath if she had to, but she was sorry to provide them with more work if there was a way around it. And how would she get more tar, anyway, without going to the city herself? The thought of Mr. Rochart going to Niklas's foundry on one of his city trips made her grin.

But the question of where the ironskin needed to go was solved, and it certainly was all about the hands. Maybe it even made sense. Dorie's curse was not rage or hunger or misery, but it was a variant of fey talent—fey technology, perhaps; who knew how bluepacks were made, after all—and so perhaps it made sense that it was directed by her hands.

Chainmail would work, she thought. Chainmail like the

dwarves wore, but crafted into gloves. But no, immediately—how would chainmail allow delicate use of the fingers? Jane flexed and unflexed her fingers, pondering. Had Niklas ever tried chainmail for scarred hands? Perhaps there was a reason it didn't work, or perhaps the chainmail was simply so bulky that those people lived with the curse rather than live in iron gloves.

No, keep thinking. Something with the tar she had, but that wouldn't get on anything. Two pairs of gloves, perhaps, cut to fit Dorie, and the tar sandwiched in between. Leather—no, oilskin for the gloves. There'd be some evenings of stitching ahead, she foresaw.

But first there was an artist to tackle.

Jane retreated to her room to freshen up before reporting to Mr. Rochart. Her apron and dark day dress were grimy with bits of the iron-flecked tar. She would have to attempt to remove those tonight, and then hope that the hired laundress Martha had mentioned could do a better job on them. There was a reason that her small collection of dresses and skirts were all dark.

But now she had a couple things Helen had insisted she take. ("You *must* dress up occasionally, Jane. I don't care two pence if you 'get applesauce on them.' That's what life is *for*.") The dark silver gown hung in her closet like a promise. It insisted that someday she would get to wear that gown again, though she couldn't think why or when. Next to it hung a pressed sapphire blue linen, an old summer dress of Helen's that she had always admired. It was simple and neat, with a boatneck and three-quarter sleeves, enlivened by embroidered white dots that Helen had done one week in a fit of boredom with the old dress. But it was new to Jane. And it was quite appropriate for a dinner dress at the end of a day chasing Dorie.

Or for bearding an artist in his den.

She unbuckled her mask and laid it on the bed. She scrubbed her face and arms scrupulously clean before stepping out of her dirty dress and into the sapphire blue one. She changed out the padding in her mask for fresh—and then rather than twist her hair up, she suddenly decided to leave it down. The brown and white locks did not hide, but they softened the side of her cheek, obscured the lines of the iron.

Her mood lifted as she cleaned up and changed. Helping Dorie was not going to be easy, no. But she had proved that the tar would work. She had a way to get through to the girl, to break her of her disturbing fey habits.

The rest was just going to be hard work for the two of them—but Jane knew what hard work was like. She could do this.

Jane brushed down her skirt, looked down at her boots. They suddenly looked unbearably workaday, and she tugged them off, replaced them with Helen's castoff dance slippers, white and embroidered with silver thread. They were a touch too long, and she was overdressed, certainly—but it seemed to suit her expanding, lifting mood. The twilight sky with stars and clouds, that's what she was, and the thought was light and joyful.

Jane checked on Dorie—still sleeping, exhausted—descended to the foyer, and slipped through the forest green curtains. The landing she had stood on a week ago should be in sight—yes, there it was. She flew up the stairs to Mr. Rochart's studio and slipped trhough his open door, knocking on it as she entered.

He was just closing the far door behind him, entering the main studio. "Jane," he said, surprise in his voice. "You—" He stopped. "You look different in colors."

"Black is a color," said Jane. "So is grey."

Mr. Rochart snorted. "You're laughing at me, and I'm the artist. You might show your elders some respect."

"Indeed I had forgotten you must be almost thirty," said Jane, and then added, laughing, "I will call you Grandfather Rochart henceforth."

"Grandfather Edward," he replied. He crossed to her and then the worry was back in his amber eyes. He touched her arm. "You look too cheerful to be up here with bad news—but tell me. How did your day go with Dorie?"

"It wasn't entirely perfect," Jane admitted, "but I think I have a way to reach her." Briefly she explained the iron paste, and concluded, "It seems to stop her from using her fey abilities." And that one tremendous success could offset even such a day as she had.

"Just like the iron on your cheek," he said. He shook his head in wonder. "So simple, and yet it never occurred to me."

"Don't blame yourself," she said, and daringly she touched his shoulder. She was unprepared for the tremor that ran through him, as if he was as unused to touch as she, as if a mere friendly gesture was enough to undo him. His hand rose even as she withdrew hers, and she didn't know what to do with any of her limbs anymore. So she smoothed down the skirt of her sister's dress, feeling the embroidered dots slide underneath her palms. That fluttering happiness went sharply through her chest. "She did not want to use her hands, of course," Jane said, trying to sound casual. "She was quite frustrated."

"I imagine." He was not polished like the gentlemen at Helen's wedding, but that did not matter to Jane. He was arresting, with those strange deep-set eyes that stayed in shadow, those amber eyes whose meaning she could rarely catch. "I will have a talk with her after dinner."

"That would be helpful," said Jane. "I believe the tar is a tool we can use to catch her up to where she should be. But she will still have to do the work." She remembered the rest of her purpose and added, "And I need to get into the north attic. Martha said there might be some gloves I could use for Dorie. So she doesn't get tar on everything. I also need some linen, and linseed oil to waterproof it."

A shadow of pain drew across his face. "Yes, I believe Grace had some gloves. She always liked parties more than I did. Tell Martha I said you might look in her trunks. Have Poule find you everything else."

Jane nodded. "Thank you." To distract him from the memory of his deceased wife she said, "I didn't like Helen and Alistair's party very much either."

"Nasty things," said Mr. Rochart. "Parties, that is, not your sister and her husband."

He smiled at her and she laughed, her heart warming. She realized that she was still poised on the threshold of the studio, and she let her laughter carry her boldly past him, into the studio where the natural light poured over the golden floors, the rough working table, the mounds of white clay. Her blue skirts floated around her, the fine linen weave brushing against her legs, the legs of the table.

Her momentum carried her all the way to the window and there she stood, the afternoon sun bathing the lines of her dress as she looked away from him. Alistair's pointed comment about her figure flickered into her mind, and then she banished it. She was not trying to seduce Edward, not trying some ploy to entrap him in the night. No, it was more the thought that with her face turned away perhaps he would see her as she should've been, a girl in a blue dress with embroidered dots like stars. A glimmer of her metal reflection danced in the window, but she looked past it, out into the black woods.

"I used to paint back there," Edward said. "In the woods." The intimacy of his words lapped her ears, like he was spilling secrets meant for her alone.

"Wasn't that dangerous?" Even before the Great War there had always been the stories. *Don't go into the woods past the last ray of sunlight.* There was always someone's cousin's friend who knew a girl who chased a blue will o' the wisp past the edge of sun and never was seen again.

"I didn't get on well with my father," he said. "I avoided him. I spent every possible hour outside, painting." She could feel him moving closer, though he made no noise. It was implicit in the way the air moved, in the way soft eddies of warmth and scent curled past the wisps of her hair, changed the folds of her dress. "When I grew tired of painting the moor, I turned to the forest. It occurred to me that there were very few forest paintings around. An untapped niche."

"Ah, a mercenary," she said. With her head turned away she was a different Jane, a Jane who still had a brother and a mother, a Jane who had taken this job as a calling to help Dorie, and not also because she was desperate. This Jane could flirt, she could tease, she could even call him "Edward." As long as she didn't turn and look at him, the moment would hold.

"In my head I would be the bravest artist of them all—and the wealthiest besides," he said, and there was laughter in his voice. "You don't have to give up your artistic merit for riches if everyone knows you were tremendously brave to get that painting."

"I thought people with ancestral estates and good family names were supposed to despise the acquisition of money," said Jane.

"Ah, but I didn't get on with my father, remember? I was going to show him—show them all."

"Wicked child," said Jane. "Won't go to parties, defies his parents, goes into the woods . . . it's impossible to see where Dorie gets it from."

"And you?" he said. His voice was rough; it caught at her, intense and burred. "Where do you get your stubbornness from? Your independent streak? Your strange, fierce spirit? Where?"

There was a sound from behind the far door and she turned, startled, and her eyes met his. He did not turn to look for the source of the noise, but no matter. The instant he saw her face in its mask, the other Jane popped like a burst bubble and she was plain damaged Jane Eliot again.

"Are Martha's quarters on this floor?" she said.

"No." He leaned forward, urgency in his voice—deep, tense—passion in his simple words. "Tell me who you are."

She started to speak, though not knowing what she'd say— but then the door opened and a lovely woman sailed out.

Her face was perfectly symmetrical, carefully chiseled,

framed by a mane of red hair, by a chain of aquamarines at her white throat. She glanced in the mirror at her perfect reflection, then beamed at Edward. "In the pink of health, I knew it. You are divine, dear, but I must run." She saw Jane and her fine eyes widened. "Is this a new one?" She crossed to them and leaned in confidentially to Jane. "You'll just love him. We all do." She kissed Edward on the cheek, whispered something in his ear. A flash of worry flickered on her pretty face, her shoulders tensed, as she told him something Jane couldn't hear. Then she was sailing toward the door, all smiles again. "See you in a few weeks for that coming out you've promised me. Don't worry about me, I can see myself out."

Edward shook his head at Jane. "Just a moment." He hurried after the beautiful woman and ushered her to the stairwell door, his head close to hers. Jane saw his finger touch the woman's rose petal cheek before she managed to look away.

"I'm sorry about that," he said as he returned. "Miss Ingel is a client. I didn't want you to think—"

"There's something familiar about her," Jane interrupted. A familiar anger coiled around her heart, suffused her head.

"Really? I wouldn't have guessed that you'd know her."

"We're not in the same social circle, no," Jane said dryly. Though he had betrayed no covenant with her, she felt hideous and ashamed; humiliation made her hostile. "Did she buy one of your masks?"

"Yes," he said.

"They are popular, then? I can't understand it."

"Yes. I take it you wouldn't want one."

"I wouldn't want to bring *more* ugliness into the world."

"I understand," he said. "Jane . . . ," and he took her hand. The familiarity of her first name on his lips infuriated her.

He had the upper hand; people like him always would. People like her had to be grateful for crumbs. She had nothing, she was no one, and she was a great big fool in her sister's dress and shoes, mooning out the window, feeling linen touch her thighs and dreaming of a different present.

"Of course you understand," she said, and jerked away. "Why wouldn't you?" The rows of masks watched her every move. "I like your daughter just fine. The house isn't even that weird." She licked dry lips as the orange rage erased all wit and tact from her tongue. "It's you. You and your horrible artwork scare people off."

Chapter 8

MOONLIGHT

"Jane," he said to that, but she was gone. His voice echoed down the stairs behind her. Her flight stopped on the landing with the mirrors, the one that flung your reflection back on you, as if you were coming to meet yourself from the other end of the staircase.

She stopped, breathing hard, watching the girl in the iron mask. Between heartbeats she listened to the stairs above.

But he did not follow.

Jane did not sleep well that night. She turned back and forth, restless. Awoke sharply just past dawn with the feeling that an unpleasant dream was slipping just out of her grasp. Some nameless terror, and she had been frozen as the terror insinuated itself into the scar on her cheek, wound itself around her, through her. . . .

She hurriedly got dressed and went down to the kitchen to see if she could find Martha. Cook was up making some wonderfully scented bread, but when Jane asked about the maid she just laughed. "Sure and you won't find that one out of bed before she has to. I'm not saying she's not a hard worker, but she won't see dawn if she can help it. But she's willing to work here at Silver Birch, and there you are. Much can be overlooked for that."

"Does she have family in town?" Jane asked suddenly, remembering the old man at the carriage house that night. "Parents?"

Cook shook her head. "Just a married sister. I tell her she should be visiting home more to find herself a man, but she just grunts." She shrugged. "Who am I to say a shiftless village fool husband's better than good honest work on your own, not I. . . ."

"True," murmured Jane.

So the attic would have to wait until Dorie's naptime, assuming they would let Jane go up at all, assuming this was not an intentional obstacle. Jane went back to her room, idly wondering what eccentricities Cook had that were being overlooked, like Martha's late hours and Jane's mask. Or perhaps Cook just had an old-fashioned sense of loyalty.

She sat on her bed and thumbed through the blue book of Ilhronian city-state politics. It seemed to be a treatise on the best ways to use treachery to hold power. Not really Jane's cup of tea. She had three books in her trunk, all read a hundred times. *A Child's Vase of Cursing Verses* was a classic nursery book: rhymes and stories about dealing with the *other*—mostly the fey, but a few of the stories were about dwarves, dragons, and other creatures. Even before the war, Jane had been fascinated by the way the book ranged from utterly real and practical advice—how to avoid the copperhead hydra—to things that were surely just tales—who, after all, had ever seen a giant?

The other two books were excellent novels, full of excitement and adventure. *Kind Hearts and Iron Crowns* was a cheap, yellow-backed, acid-tongued mystery that had been printed in Bowdler Street by the thousands. And *The Pirate Who Loved Queen Maud* was gloriously exciting, an extremely rare family heirloom from the time of Queen Maud herself, written by one of the famous dwarf authors that lived at court and were part of her infamous salons. (Queen Maud's son had been less than pleased by the lurid tale, and he later ordered all copies burned on sight.)

Still, Jane had read them all. She could not get the gloves yet, Dorie would not wake for another hour, and she needed a distraction to stop thinking of *him* and that humiliating moment in his studio when the beautiful woman sailed out of his back room. Jane picked up the blue book on politics, intending to go to the library.

But when she left the room, Dorie was out in the hall.

"You're awake!" said Jane. "Well. Good."

Blue eyes looked up and through her, mutinous and steady.

Jane's heart sank. Today was going to be just as miserable as yesterday.

Well. She'd known that, right? This was just the *hard work* part. She could do this.

Jane took Dorie's hand and led her back to the nursery. "We're going to start by eating breakfast," she said to the little girl. "With a spoon."

The tar made it so Dorie couldn't do a repeat of the applesauce incident. But it didn't make Dorie cooperative. By lunchtime she had eaten a quarter of her morning oatmeal and thrown the rest on the floor. At least she had to use her hands to throw it, Jane thought, trying to see the bright side.

Progress was progress, even when it involved oatmeal on the dressing table. Jane opened the door so Dorie could see her lunch waiting, hardened her heart—and then made Dorie wipe up every single oatmeal blob that she had thrown.

The girl fell asleep in the middle of cleaning up the last of the oatmeal from under the bed. When Martha came back to take the lunch tray, she found Dorie asleep under the bed with her legs sticking out, an exhausted Jane with her head pillowed on her knees, watching her, and a full lunch tray still sitting outside the door.

"What the—?" Martha shook her head, as if indicating this whole mess was Jane's affair. "Should I leave it?"

"We'll eat it after her nap," Jane said. Wearily she rose from the sticky, oatmealy floor, took a bun from the tray. "Can you take me to the north attic now? I have permission."

The maid nodded.

They wound through the house, a twisting maze of stairs and turns. Jane was not sure she could find the way back by herself, even if she had been allowed to go alone. All the dark and puzzling features of fey architecture were clear as they twisted higher, through steps that went nowhere, halls that curved imperceptibly, cleverly subtle mirrors that reflected extra doors.

Jane caught her breath as they went up the steep ladderlike steps to the north attic, Martha's blue-lit lantern flickering in front of her. She did not know what she expected—a row of skeletons, a murdered wife, a madwoman with a mysterious laugh? The nameless terror of her nightmares?

But Helen's lurid imaginings were not to be found. It was an ordinary attic, dim and crowded with the history of generations. The air was hot and close, as attics seem to be even in April.

Martha gestured at a grouping of wardrobes, trunks, and hatboxes, covered in dust. "Years of things," she said, in her usual succinct fashion. She tapped a chewed-on hatbox with her foot. "Got to set more mousetraps."

"A two-syllable word," Jane said absently.

Martha looked at her suspiciously. "You look while I sweep. Cook says don't snoop."

Jane ignored this and immediately opened the nearest hatbox, the one that had been chewed on. She couldn't very well find gloves without snooping, could she? But inside was the tattered folds of what might have once been pillowcases, or anything at all, and the remains of a mouse nest. Another hatbox was better equipped, with mothballs and what looked like a fancy pair of men's breeches, a hundred years out of date. A third hatbox actually held a hat, but no gloves.

"Do you think Grace's clothing is really still here?" said Jane. "Maybe her family took it." No particular reason why they would—Jane was probing.

"She just had a da," said Martha, who was attacking great swathes of cobwebs with her broom. "No need for her things."

"Poor man," Jane said, thinking of her mother's grief over Charlie. "Was he from town?"

"One town up," said Martha. "They had a shop. Don't think he has it no more." Her prods at the spiders dislodged a great pile of dust from the rafters, sending Martha into a coughing fit as it settled to the floor.

Jane had her eye on the large wardrobe against the far wall, and she used the distraction to make a beeline for it, in case

Martha would have stopped her. The wardrobe was dark walnut, old and burled. A heavy, old-fashioned piece, massive against the plaster wall. The brass key hung loosely in the lock, and Jane turned it with a click and opened the door.

Inside were rows and rows of gowns. Jane gasped softly at the sight.

They tended toward the cool colors—silvers, blues, and greens, with some gold thrown in for good measure. Jane pulled the nearest one out and found it to be a sapphire blue silk in a corseted style from a hundred years ago. The next one was a cream muslin with green flowers and an empire waist— that style was probably a hundred and fifty years old, or more. Dress after dress, myriad different periods. But the dresses appeared to all be new, or at least stored so immaculately that no fading or yellowing had occurred, and not a single moth or insect had invaded them.

She studied the beautiful dresses, puzzling over them. The obvious answer was that they really were a hundred and two hundred years old—dresses collected from generation after generation of the ladies of the household. Their condition amazed her, but perhaps some fey technology she had never heard of kept the wardrobe sealed and insect-free.

If they did all belong to the former Mrs. Rochart, then she had had odd tastes. Beautiful, but odd. Jane wished Helen were here to see the dresses and give her opinion on their age. She could probably deduce other clues that Jane could not; find the tiny details that hinted at the wearer's status, or know what kind of outing the dress was for.

Jane's fingers lingered on the dress she was studying. It was beautiful—the color of a golden flame. She pulled it all the way out. It was one of the most modern ones—pre-war styling, shapeless with layers of golden chiffon floating from the shoulders and dropped waist. Glass beading trimmed the handkerchief hem. It must have been expensive. She held it up to herself, smoothing the gauzy fabric against her plain day dress, wondering if it would fit.

The wardrobe doors had rows of drawers along the inside. Still holding the golden dress, Jane opened them one by one and found plenty of gloves, along with gilded fans, satin ribbons, paste jewels, square shoe buckles. She found a beautiful cream-colored pair of gloves in poor condition that would work perfectly for Dorie. The left glove was marred by a dark red wine stain that splashed up the forearm like blood. Jane held it up to the golden dress, imagining how it would all fit together, the gown, the gloves, the night. . . .

Martha whistled and Jane looked up, guiltily dropping the folds of the golden dress. The maid leaned on her broom, studying the ball gown with an oddly wistful expression, and Jane suddenly remembered that despite Martha's sternness and angularity, she was younger than Jane herself. "I saw her once," Martha said. "I was eight, and she came to town. I thought she was so fair. Wore deep blue silk like a queen. Saw her just once—no more."

"And then she was gone," breathed Jane, recalling the horror that Edward had described to her. Pregnant with Dorie—killed and taken over by the fey.

Martha shook her head, seeming to recall herself to her purpose. "You got your gloves," she said. "I think you're done here."

"I need some linen I can cut into child-sized gloves," said Jane.

"That box, if the rats ain't et it." Martha stared down at

Jane with folded arms till Jane and her booty were on the way out of the attic.

Dorie was still under the bed when Jane got back. Jane's heart leapt to her throat in the first instant of seeing those legs stick out from under the bed, for all the world like a rag doll, like something dead. What if the iron was poison after all?

Heart thumping, Jane kneeled down and lifted the bed skirt, looked under the bed.

The girl's eyes were open. Dorie was staring blankly at the underside of the bed, tar-smeared hands flat on the floor.

"Dorie?" said Jane. "Are you all right?" Carefully she pulled the little girl out from under the bed, out into the room. "Do you want to eat lunch?"

A hint of a shrug.

"You must be hungry," Jane said. She levered Dorie to a sitting position, surprised that the girl offered no resistance. "Let's check your arms and eat our lunch." With her rag she made sure that the flecks of iron covered every bit of Dorie's fingers and up her arms. Then she wiggled Dorie's fingers into the long cream gloves from the attic, smoothing the bloodred stain of the left one up and along the arm. Dorie sat passively and watched.

Jane brought the tray in from the hall. In accordance with her request yesterday, it was mostly simple finger foods—the first spring peas in their shells, cut in half. A bun, that Jane tore into bite-sized pieces. A small bowl of applesauce—Jane cringed.

She pushed the tray toward Dorie. "Let's eat the bread and peas," she said gently.

Dorie sighed, slumped. One gloved hand came out and

grabbed a piece of the roll, ate it. Then the next bite. Then the next. Not looking at Jane, she ate everything on her plate, then *looked* at the applesauce.

A waver—a flicker of blue. The light in Dorie's eyes flickered up in response . . . and then died away.

Sighing, Dorie held out her hand, and Jane placed the spoon in it. Spoonful after difficult spoonful Dorie went through the applesauce until it was all gone.

Jane looked down at the silent girl in astonishment.

This was victory, sure enough.

So why didn't it feel like it?

Jane felt unsettled by her odd triumph with Dorie. Uneasy from her encounter with Mr. Rochart. The nightmares came again—sometimes she was Jane, sometimes she was her brother, stiff on the battlefield. They were coming every night now, coalescing on a scene she wrenched away from, knew she didn't want to see. But when she pulled away from the vision of the battlefield, the terror came sliding in through her cheek, poured itself through her like water, until she woke up panting.

In the past there had been Helen to soothe her when she woke in terror. Now there was no one. Jane felt as though the ground were shifting under her feet, a sliding back and forth of uncertainty. Perhaps if she could just see him—she could talk to him about his daughter. Talk to him—just talk to him.

The days passed and still he did not come.

Jane looked for him in every shadow of curtain, every stroke of the clock. She lay awake in the blackest hour of the night, unable to let her failures or successes go, her mind flicking through each day's events, relentless.

Dorie on her stomach, slumped on her gloved elbows, listlessly working on her letters.

Lunch: soup with the last of the put-up vegetables, the first spring peas on the side.

Martha shutting a gossip magazine with a snap, Cook gesturing with a wooden spoon at a full mousetrap and grinning.

Mr. Rochart, where her thoughts always landed. But she hadn't seen Mr. Rochart. Hadn't seen him since he was with that redhead, Miss Ingel.

But that just recalled the incident in the studio, a week ago. Awake now, Jane writhed under her quilts, tormented by jabs of humiliation. Why had she thought she could be his equal? The entire time he let her try out her silly flirtation, he had that woman in the back room. He knew that she liked him, knew why she turned her face away. He probably thought she was standing that way in the sunlight, in that dress, to do . . . what Alistair had suggested.

She thumped her pillow angrily and rolled over. She would *not* let her thoughts turn inward. She would resist. She didn't like him, she wasn't that foolish, and she wasn't here for that. She was here to help Dorie, and that was it. She did not expect anything else.

Did not, did not. Did not . . . but why did that redhead in his studio look so familiar? Someone Jane had seen at her sister's wedding? No, it was mostly the name that was familiar. Jane's eyes flew open. Of course! The woman who had come on Jane's first day. Her name was Miss Ingel—Blanche Ingel. She even looked like this one, as near as a charcoal sketch looked like an oil painting. That Miss Ingel had had the same red hair, true, but had not been beautiful in the slightest. The two might be cousins, she supposed.

Odd, but explicable. Why did it make her so uneasy? Her damn cheek, that's why. It was unnerving her, and she couldn't trust her reactions. As if in response, it fired again. She pressed the back of her cold hand to it and thought of standing at the window in his studio, watching the woods and imagining him studying the shape of her blue dress. Shame tormented her belly like cold claws scuttling through her gut.

Nothing. She expected nothing. He wasn't even avoiding her—he simply didn't care. He hadn't even noticed that he hadn't seen her for a week. Maybe she was worth speaking to when she stood there, but when she was gone? Then, she was like the book she had taken from the library and still not returned. Because would you notice if *Ilhronian History of the 16th Century* was missing from a shelf? Not very likely. It was the sort of book you wouldn't even remember owning, seeing, or reading. And it certainly wouldn't lure you with a pretty blue spine, not when its contents were so unspeakably dull.

She was going back to sleep now.

Think of nothing.

The quilts strangled her with their heat, and the nose-tickling scent of the jar of iron-flecked tar was intolerable at this hour of night. Jane kicked the quilts off one by one, twisting her bare feet into the cooler air of the room. It was too warm for a night in April.

At last she untangled herself from the bedclothes and padded in bare feet to the window.

She thumbed on the fey-tech light and unfolded the most recent letter from Helen in its faint blue glow. She had started out hoarding its mini-bluepack, but when it winked out recently, surprise, surprise, Martha had produced another. "Aren't out yet," is all the maid would say, curtly, and so Jane thought: Fine. If they won't tell me, then I'll use as much damn light as I please.

She had been interrupted somewhere toward the end of the party description by Dorie waking up from a nap. Now she skimmed the repetitive descriptions of dresses and flirtations until she found her place.

"But enough of my popularity," Helen wrote. "What is merely good is short of perfect, you know, and Alistair reminds me that we had a setback to a proper upbringing. We are so good for one another, Jane. He has promised me that he will give up gambling at horses with that rough set, and for my part, he is finishing me off to perfection and you would be so delighted to see how I take to it. I work every day with the skin scrubs and the creams, and am performing the newfangled calisthenics to stay fit for my lovely slinky dresses. There is alas nothing I can do about the bump on my nose, but Alistair assures me he has a plan in mind, and he is quite clever."

What bump? thought Jane.

"The endless round of parties, dinners, &c I have just described for you seems less droll lately. I suppose the amount of catch-up I have to do fatigues me, for I am always treading on someone's toes, and then Alistair takes me to task, as if I were not more cognizant of it than he himself! You have little experience of masses of women friends, but I tell you it is quite shocking the way they can cut you down with a word or a lowering of the eyelids. How pleasant to be you in your solitude, I am sure!"

Jane snorted. She pressed the soles of her feet to the painted wood table legs, cooling them.

"I am trapped between two worlds, Jane, do you know what that's like? Perhaps you made the right decision to stay humbly in our place after all. And yet—no. No, I would not return to governessing for the most beautiful face in the city.

"You must come soon. Ironskin or no, I miss my strong-hearted sister more each day. Lock yourself in with me and we will face the world down together.

"Yours, Helen."

Jane dropped the letter to the desk. It was always difficult to get at her sister's real feelings; she insisted on burying them under a layer of decorative nonsense. Helen had always been fond of saying silly things passionately, like "we *must* have new ribbons," or, "you *must* eat that cake." Perhaps her willful gaiety had been good for Jane; but then, Jane's serious determination had probably been good for Helen. Certainly she had always tried to be a steadying influence. Mr. Hunting-don, however . . . Was he the reason the letter seemed sharp and sad all at once?

Jane was sorry that the only window with a screen looked onto the forest, but regardless, she needed air. She rose to crank the window open, and then, down among the black cedars and thorny locusts, she saw it.

A glimmer of blue light, streaked with orange.

Chapter 9

THE MISSES INGEL

Even as she saw it, it vanished, and then there was only pre-dawn blackness, leavened by thin moonlight. Jane stared into the forest, her eyes wide open and scanning. Had she really seen that? Surely it was just a trick of her nightmare carrying over, showing her fey where none existed.

Jane put a hand to her chest, uselessly trying to slow her heart through the touch of her fingers. She reasoned with herself. The fey had not been seen for five years. Why would one appear only when she was sleepless in the dead of the night? It was ridiculous. She had only imagined it. Wound up from her nightmares, her eyes insisted on seeing danger where there was none, lights where only blackness reigned. She turned off the fey-tech light, watching.

There.

No. Yes?

Jane grabbed her dressing gown and hurried down the side stairs by her room, out the side door. Well before she got to the back of the estate she was wondering what she hoped to accomplish by running outside without shoes or clothes or even a feyjabber. But that didn't stop her feet from flying.

She stood twenty feet from the forest, panting and searching the woods for more blue light. She didn't dare take a step closer into the darkness than that. She studied the edges of her vision as the moonlight glimmered off leaves and dew and played havoc with her sight and nerves. Had she really seen anything? And what about the last time she was out at dusk—had she really heard the sharp *bzzzt* of fey then, or was this house just getting to her?

"What are you doing out here?"

Jane spun to see Poule standing there, her sturdy form solid and black in the night. Moonlight lit her grey hair silver, spun itself along the length of the dingy red quilted dressing gown the woman wore. Picked out the glints of metal at her wrists, and a lump in an inside breast pocket such as Jane had seen the first day, and taken for a blackjack.

Jane backed up, as if she expected the odd butler to knee-cap her and haul her back. "I thought I saw a fey," she said. The grass was wet and cool on her hot feet.

Poule's grey eyebrows disappeared into her hair. She went toward the forest line, closer than Jane, leaned forward as if scenting the air. The night was quiet around them. Then she shook her head and returned to Jane. "They're not there now."

Jane's heart thumped at the turn of phrase. "But you think they were? It's not just my imagination? They're supposed to be gone."

Poule's eyes held no comfort. "The fey won't ever be completely gone, and you know that deep inside, don't you? Know it as well as we do."

We? "I guess I do," Jane said reluctantly. She felt exposed by Poule's assessment of her, and questions wrote themselves in the furrows of her brow.

"You don't have your mask on," the short woman said.

Jane realized that just as Poule said it, automatically tilted her head forward to let her hair swing over her cursed cheek.

"You're leaking, I think," Poule continued. "It's odd, feeling it from you. Usually it's just around the fey that you become bombarded by feelings not your own. Feelings you don't want. At least for dwarves—humans certainly aren't that perceptive, or you'd have been able to spot all those humans taken over by fey long before the bodies rotted and gave it away by the stink." She gestured back at the forest. "I can't swear if the blasted blue-things were there before or not, but I don't scent them now."

Jane wasn't sure how to interpret this barrage of information, but her tongue found tactless words before her brain had caught up and said: "A dwarf? You're a dwarf?" Immediately she realized how rude it was to ask, as rude as asking someone what their curse was.

It was the first wry grin Jane had seen on the old woman, and it made her seem less threatening. "Half," she said. "I'm *havlen,* which translates as a half-thing. We aren't very kind to those who stray from the mountains, you see."

Now that Jane knew the woman's lineage, she wondered how she could have missed it. It also explained the glints of metal she'd seen at Poule's wrists. "Do dwarves really wear their mail all the time?" she said. "Doesn't that get uncomfortable?"

"Well, not all our mail," said Poule. She slid up the arm of her dressing gown to show that the chain mail wristlets only covered her forearms. "You can make a concession to fashion without going whole hog. But tell me what you need for Dorie's gloves."

"What?" said Jane. The prying made her tongue rude. "How do you know about the gloves?" She turned back to the forest, watching the black branches sway in the wind.

Poule shrugged. "There are eyes in the walls. A little bird told me. Pick one."

Jane cringed against the being-watched feeling that she hated. How could she trust anybody when they refused to trust her?

Poule rubbed the back of her neck beneath the iron grey hair and stared wordlessly into the forest. Finally she said, "Have you seen him go in there?"

Jane thought she had seen—but she had no proof. Stubbornly she matched Poule question for question. "Why would he do that?"

Poule looked at Jane with a fierce black eye. Her gaze seemed to effortlessly pierce the veil of hair to the scarred flesh beneath. "If you see him go in, tell me immediately. Promise."

"I can't promise anything," said Jane stubbornly. She didn't know if Mr. Rochart really went into the forest, but she wasn't sure she trusted Poule any more than anybody else in the house. Her duty was to herself, then Dorie, then Mr. Rochart, in that order, and she wasn't about to make any promises she didn't know the meaning of.

The dwarf looked at her as if she knew what was passing through Jane's head. Snorted. Then turned and tromped back into the house, her loose grey hair swinging silver behind her, her slippers leaving darker impressions in the dewy grass. Behind her she called, "Do you want linseed oil or not? Come and get it, if you're getting it."

The night was empty when you were alone. Jane hurried after before she could be left at the boundary of the woods.

The last ray of sunlight didn't mean very much when there was no sunlight at all.

Jane followed Poule on another winding route, an echo of following Martha into the attic. Except this way led to a small white door, partway into the abandoned wing. It was all quite dark, but Poule flicked open a small electric torch that was not the blue of fey technology, but rather a warm yellow light. Jane kept thinking she should really go get her shoes, but it seemed like if she left now she would never see Poule again, and this opportunity would vanish like the master of the house.

The white door opened to a descending circular staircase. Poule's voice floated back as they picked their way down. "The iron paste for Dorie's hands is clever," she said.

"It's not that clever," demurred Jane. "A man in the city gave me the paste. I didn't think of it."

"Yes, but you tried it on her hands. Why her hands? I mean, Dorie's curse isn't exactly the same as yours, is it?"

"I don't know," Jane said, thinking about the first question. "It felt right, I guess. But her curse isn't the same at all." She shook her head, recalling what she had told Niklas. "No visible scar, no obvious drawback . . . Is it because it happened before birth? Because she was unborn when her mother was taken over by the fey?"

But the staircase stopped there, opened up on a hallway. The walls turned to living rock that oozed water into channels on the floor, and so Poule's only response was, "Mind the mushrooms."

Several steps down the quiet stone passageway was a wide, red-painted door, the bottom two inches painted with a thick off-white paint that Jane guessed to be some sort of water repellent, for when the floor flooded.

As Poule opened the door Jane heard a mechanical whirring inside, like the sounds heard around Niklas's foundry. A familiar sound, a homey sound. The large set of rooms on the other side of the door was a studio like Mr. Rochart had, except here in the cellar, down in the damp and dark. Poule pulled on a cord and switched on a glass light that burned with the same warm yellow of her torch.

"Is that fey technology?" said Jane, surprised.

"Of course not," said Poule, but she didn't look offended. "Pure electricity; runs off a generator that's the pinnacle of dwarven achievement. Or at least the pinnacle of my achievement. I do a sweat-ton to keep this old house moving, you know."

The swinging yellow light picked out odds and ends of tools and machinery that littered the room: pipes and glass jars, and in the corner a bed and dresser on a metal platform that lifted them clear of possible floods or spills.

Jane stood, not knowing where to go, but Poule motioned her to a beautiful little table made of twisting metal and wavery green glass. Jane stared at it as she sat down. Dwarf trade had been at its height two hundred years earlier, when Queen Maud favored the dwarves and kept them around her court. On her sudden death, her nephew, King Philip, declared the dwarves immoral and possibly regicidal, and they'd packed up from the court and gone home. Trade for the durable, beautiful dwarven craftsmanship had crawled to a halt.

But the dwarves had still been inventing and designing.

The table was clearly made by dwarves, and just as clearly it was no style that she had ever seen before. In human terms, it was priceless.

And it was laden with the crumby remains of teatime, a small oil can, and two screwdrivers.

Poule cleared these away, wiped down the table with the hem of her dressing gown. She sat down on the other chair, and Jane realized then how large she felt on her own seat. Poule was perhaps halfway between average human-sized and average dwarf-sized, which was why she could pass for simply a very short woman. The chairs and table were clearly made precisely for her—precisely *by* her, possibly—and it was just enough of a height difference to raise Jane's knees above her hips and put her off-balance.

"If this were full-sized you could sell it for a fortune," Jane said. "Er. Human-sized." She bit her tongue.

Poule snorted. "Haven't you humans learned to stop buying from 'the other'? That's what got you into this mess in the first place. Buying all that blasted fey technology instead of continuing to develop your own."

"Oh, you don't have to tell me," said Jane. "You should have seen the terrible state of the trolleys when I started looking for a job. It was about six months after the war, so just when the rationing of the biggest bluepacks had finally run out. Practically nothing was running." This was a good topic for an enjoyable rant, and clearly Poule agreed. "I'd grown up hearing about the incredible culture and technology in the city, you know, but by the time I got there, it had practically ground to a halt as the bluepacks all died, one by one. The factories, the trolleys, the cinemas—no one could run anything."

"You'd sat on your arses and let the fey run your lives," said

Poule. "And now you have to start from square one. That's why the dwarves never went down that road."

"We're not all as smart as the dwarves," said Jane. She felt a moment of kinship with the short woman as Poule laughed in appreciation. Here they were in the black cold basement of Silver Birch, dank and damp under the damaged wing, and yet . . . perhaps this woman could be a friend. Or at least . . . an ally?

But Poule turned the force of her attention back to Jane. "I feel your rage," she said.

"I know," said Jane shortly. She swung her hair to cover her cheek again. "It's why I wear the mask."

"I mean I feel it extra now," said Poule. "You got angrier when I talked about the fey."

"Yes," said Jane, annoyed. She had a strong urge to wriggle away from the examination.

"So you were less angry before," Poule said patiently. "Not enough that humans would notice the difference in how they feel around you. Sometimes they feel cranky— sometimes crankier. They don't know how to put it aside regardless. But like I said, dwarves are more perceptive. I feel the shifts."

"You can put it aside?" said Jane.

Poule nodded. "Not all of it. But it's a matter of thinking about what you're feeling and separating it out from what you should be feeling, if you take my meaning. Get rid of the feelings that aren't yours. Find your composure. Dwarves can do that a little—it's bloody hard, but it's something we practice, for dealing with the fey." A short, hard laugh. "Some of us have had a lot of practice. . . ." She trailed off. "Well. If sometimes you are just a little shirty and sometimes you are flying-off-the-handle, rip-roaring mad—then you do have some control over it, don't you?"

Jane thought back. "Sometimes," she said slowly, "when the fire rages up against my mask I feel it. Like a hot orange flame. And then . . . and then I try to make it go away. Imagine the fire going out. Like it's being dowsed with water or something. Or Helen used to stroke my arm and I would imagine it rubbing out the fire." She looked up at Poule. "But I didn't think it was really doing any good."

Poule nodded thoughtfully. "You might continue trying it," she said. Her calm assurance made Jane think she should take this woman seriously. Poule leaned back in her chair. "Now, tell me. What do you want for Dorie?"

"Ironskin," said Jane, unconsciously touching her bare cheek.

"What you have wouldn't work on hands."

"I know," Jane said. "I'm going to make some gloves that have the iron tar inside. I found some linen in the attic. Now I need the linseed oil to paint the linen and turn it into an oil-cloth, so I can make a sandwich of the fabric that has the tar inside it." She sighed. "Hopefully that will stop the tar from leaking out, because tar's been getting on everything and I'm sure it's frustrating Martha no end, though she only looks at us and shakes her head."

Poule drummed her fingers on the table. In the swaying yellow light she had a funny self-satisfied look, like she was bursting to tell Jane something. "What about a fabric that has iron wires woven through it? A sort of mesh."

"That might work," Jane said slowly. "I had thought of chain mail, but it would be too bulky. But can you make wires thin enough?"

"We do back home," said Poule. "We draw the wires thin enough to crochet. Some people use them to make jewelry—a different take on iron charms. Which—who knows if they work—bloody superstition if you ask me. Well. I've been experimenting with these iron threads to see what applications they might have against those blue brutes. The iron mesh cloth has potential."

"It might work," agreed Jane. "It might be even better than my idea—no tar to leak through. Do you have a sample of the cloth?"

By way of answer, Poule reached under her chair and pulled out a cotton bag. "A cloth *and* a bit of spare time on my hands," she said. From the bag she pulled a small pair of long mesh gloves and slid them across the green glass tabletop to Jane.

"Oh, how perfect . . . ," breathed Jane. She touched the metal-threaded cloth. It was supple enough to move with fingers, like a second skin. Yet it seemed like the iron was woven closely enough to keep Dorie's talents suppressed. The gloves fastened up the side with little iron clasps, so it would be possible to wriggle Dorie's hands in.

Poule pulled the gloves away from Jane's touch. Leaned back in her chair, flicking her grey hair behind her. "The question is: what do you want to pay for them?"

Jane fumbled. "I'm sure Mr. Rochart will pay you what you need, when I tell him. . . ."

Poule's eyes were friendly but firm, the creases set in a way that recalled stone. "I don't make the rules," she said. "That's the one thing about both the fey and the *dwarvven*"—and Jane clearly heard the foreign tongue as Poule pronounced the word in her own language—"there's certain rules. And one is that everything has a price. Everything between your world and ours has to be fairly bought and paid for." She flipped the screwdriver between nimble fingers like a worry stone. "And it doesn't seem to matter that I'm *havlen,* a half-thing. Some things still apply."

Jane said nothing, thinking through her history, attempting to come up with a suitable answer before she let her tongue say something foolish or insulting. The fey drove dreadful bargains, seeking your talent and life and anything that truly mattered to you that they could get; they sealed deals you didn't know existed.

Whereas no such reputation existed for the dwarves, though they were sometimes said to be cold and miserly. "Wouldn't give you a smile you hadn't paid for," was a common saying about the oft-surly folk. They traded their fine engineering and design for things of the surface: fruits and wheat and wool. Jane had none of these things.

The dwarf leaned back in her chair. Her dressing gown shifted just enough to show that whatever she always carried in her breast pocket had a hard rectangular outline, and like a flash Jane knew what it was.

The one surface culture dwarves shared with humans, that the dwarves were known to love with all their fierce, passionately intellectual hearts. Wasn't that why so many of the court poets had been dwarves, until Queen Maud's death put an end to the days of civil friendship?

Books.

The dwarves loved books. They read them in vast, devouring quantities, and they wrote them, too—in their electric-lit caves alongside their molten metal and their turning gears the *dwarvven* scribbled out great gothic tragedies, pouring out their hidden romantic souls into tales of forbidden love and secret temptation, blood-soaked mysteries and swashbuckling pirates.

A Child's Vase of Cursing Verses was unlikely to be of interest. Poule had surely read *Kind Hearts and Iron Crowns*—Jane only hung onto it for the personal inscription on the flyleaf. But the third . . .

"I will lend you a book," said Jane. "A glorious adventure novel."

Poule's eyebrows raised. Her hand went unconsciously to the book she was currently reading, tucked inside her dressing gown. "You think you have something I haven't read?"

"Maybe," said Jane. "I mean, it is a dwarf author."

"Probably read it, then," said Poule. "You'll have to think of something else."

"The Pirate Who Loved Queen Maud."

Poule dropped her screwdriver to the table with a clatter. "Not the one her son banned, and ordered all copies burned on sight?"

Jane nodded, and she mentally thanked the several-greats-grandmother who had decided she'd rather risk royal displeasure than give up a book. She leaned across the table toward those bright, eager eyes. "On page twelve he carries off a girl who looks like the queen, but he doesn't find out she's actually the court alchemist's daughter till they're halfway across the ocean, with a fleet of navy ships in hot pursuit and a nest of sea dragons just off starboard, ready to ravage the ship for its gold and tear the pirate to bits."

Poule gulped. "Done," she said hoarsely.

After the bargain was sealed, Jane slowly retraced her path back to the foyer, went up the stairs to her bedroom on the second floor. She stared out the window into the night for another hour, drifting in and out of semisleep.

But no more lights appeared.

Jane was the one with the midnight adventure, but Dorie seemed just as tired as she the next morning.

But thinking back, Dorie had been slower and slower to get out of bed each morning since they'd started the tar. It was not the stubborn revolt of the first day, but a strange passive resistance, as if she had decided she'd rather sleep than do anything that Jane wanted. Listless—slumped. It was an unusual strike for a healthy child.

A very tired Jane knelt by the bed. She was heavy on her feet and her iron mask seemed to weigh her head down. "We're not going to do the tar today," she said.

Dorie slowly lifted her head. "No?" she said.

"No. We're going to try these interesting gloves," said Jane. "See how pretty they are?" Jane produced the mesh gloves that Poule had made. As a concession to Dorie, she'd gotten up early and stitched red and silver sequins on the backs of the hands.

Dorie looked blankly at the sequins.

"Your friend Poule made them for you," said Jane, deftly wriggling Dorie's passive fingers in and fastening the catches up the side of the arm. She hoped she could get them on before the tantrum, as the reverse seemed highly unlikely. "Now the other pretty glove," said Jane, and in went the other hand before Dorie could discover that these gloves had the same effect as the tar. "Pretty, yes?"

The blank in her eyes faded, and Dorie stared at the gloves with the same intent look she used to wear when she was trying to make something move. Jane readied herself for a full-on tantrum.

But all that happened was that the intent look in the girl's eyes slowly died.

Her gloved hands fell to her lap and she stared off into nothing, through the papered wall. Jane felt suddenly alone in that white-and-silver room. The air vibrated with emptiness around that little girl who sat there, saying nothing, doing nothing, slumped like a forgotten porcelain doll.

The nightmares increased.

They grew more focused, more detailed, until Jane was seeing the same scene, night after night. A terrible, familiar scene, one she had tried to block out for five years.

She sees the blackened moor, bare rubble separating her town from the terrifying forest. She played in that forest once; they all did. Yet now she and her childhood friends take their places with jagged scraps of iron, watching the menace pour from the forest. This is how the Great War is fought, for soldiers are spread too thin when the enemy is not a human enemy, with one home base, with needs of food and water and horseshoes. This is an enemy that materializes out of every forest in the land, first here, then there, an inhuman pattern not easily deciphered.

Their misfortune, to live so close to the trees.

It is the dawn of early spring, and the moor is dense and roiling with fog. Daily there have been reports that the Great War is being won, that they are drawing ahead. This may well be propaganda, for they have not seen it. For almost four years some trick of circumstance kept them safe here in Harbrook, untouched by the ravaging, decimating war. But after the winter solstice something turned, and the enemy began appearing. Perhaps they were driven here, or perhaps it was next in their plan. They have been attacking night after night, gnawing the town's defenses one by one. Harrying the town, taking one child here, one woman there. Till at last they have been seen, blue-orange lights gathered just inside the perimeter of the barren forest, and the ragged army of Jane's friends takes their desperate stand against them.

Charlie steps in front of Mother and Helen, pushes them back with a pale, dirty hand. Helen is thirteen and useless when faced with this terror. She wrings her hands in her dirty apron and holds Mother tight. Mother is brave, brave enough to let Charlie go forth with the men, even though he is all of twelve.

I am not as brave as Mother, Jane thinks. Not brave enough to stay behind. She picks up her stave of iron and follows her baby brother onto the field where the yellow cowslips poke through the black turf.

"Jane!" Mother shouts, but she does not turn. "Jane!"

Jane thrashed herself awake. It was cold pale dawn, and Jane's buoyant hopes for Dorie were fading to despair. The days were all the same now, and Jane went through the morning rituals by rote: locking Dorie into the gloves, helping the listless girl dress and eat and play with her toys.

It felt ridiculous to complain about no tantrums . . . but Dorie wasn't doing anything at all. Jane had expected the girl's stubbornness and energy to sustain her through learning this new skill, but now?

Jane watched Dorie color on a picture of a rabbit with blue chalk. The girl lay on her stomach, her cheek on her left arm as if she were too tired to lift her head. Her right arm scribbled randomly over the rabbit, but she was using her hand, so though Jane despaired, she did not say a word. Just sat and tried to quench the impotent rage inside her that wanted to jump on Dorie for the tiniest infraction.

She tried to turn her thoughts aside from her failure, but that just turned them back to Mr. Rochart, and the frustration of not seeing someone when you wanted to change what you said, wanted to rewrite the whole scene. No, that change of subject didn't help one bit.

Jane breathed in and out on counts of three as she watched Dorie's gloved hand creep back and forth across the page in short jerks. It was a good thing Jane had the mask on, or Dorie would feel her rage no matter how hard she tried to pack it down inside her where it belonged. What was it that Poule had said? Maybe the calming thoughts really did help? Jane breathed deeply, imagining water filling the mask, the rage steaming off and dissipating.

Dorie's hand moved slower and slower and Jane reached out and gently touched her elbow. "Why don't you sit up and try a new color?" she said. "Or a new page?"

Dorie's fist opened and dropped the blue chalk. Jane placed a piece of yellow chalk on her mesh-gloved palm. Dorie did not look at the chalk, but just started scribbling on the page again.

"Do you want to color the ears yellow?" suggested Jane.

Dorie looked at the picture, moved her hand over the ears, and started her slow scribbles again. Her eyes closed as if they were too heavy to keep open.

Jane sighed, not understanding why Dorie wouldn't at least want to do a good job. She liked pretty things—surely that would be a motivator for making the page pretty. Girls this age usually didn't have to be enticed to attempt to stay in the lines, even if they didn't always make it.

Of course, Dorie wasn't like any other girls. Jane knew that.

But she watched Dorie's limp curls and slow-moving gloved hand and wondered if they were making any progress at all.

"The old servants' entrance got blown off with the north wing," Cook said. "Like as not we'll get the temporary staff wandering in at the front door today. You'll be knowing where the side door is to show them if you see them? And the passageway to the kitchen? Little matter for today, but there'll be none of this front door waltzing-in when the guests are here, I can tell you. Sure and I'm the closest thing Rochart has to a housekeeper, but I won't see him humiliated for all of that."

Jane sat huddled in the painted white chair in the kitchen, absorbing the unwanted news that there was going to be a house party in two days. "Extra staff," she repeated.

"Yes, to whip this house into something not an embarrass-ment and to be serving the guests. We'll be having to open up at least two bedrooms in the damaged wing and maybe three. As well as extra rooms belowstairs for those we're hiring and the staff of the guests. Still, better pence coming in than pence going out, though why potential clients have to be ro-manced for a week and not just an eve, I'll never know. Espe-cially when that puts them here over May Day, and won't they just be expecting a grand celebration, as if those city folk had anything to do with the ending of the war. . . ."

Dorie had just gone down for her nap, and her naps were longer these days, lasting from just after lunch to near dinner.

Jane was torn between worry for the girl and the thought that Dorie was merely tired from the extra physical and mental exertion. Still, if this strange listlessness continued, she would have to go back up to the studio and confess that she was failing. The thought was not appealing.

"Is Mr. Rochart busy this afternoon, do you know?" she said.

"Rochart?" Cook dumped a bin of fresh new potatoes into the sink and ran an inch of water to loosen their dirt. "He hasn't been here for a fortnight. He'll be meeting with a wealthy client in the city. Left for town just after he finished with Miss Ingel. Were you not knowing?"

"Oh," said Jane. "No." So he hadn't been avoiding her. Unless he'd been avoiding her by fleeing the house altogether, but that seemed unnecessarily silly for the owner of the house to do. No, he hadn't even noticed her ridiculous advances in his study, and maybe that was more humiliating. She didn't figure into his travel plans one way or another. He didn't think of her at all. Breathe, she told herself, and let it go. Think about anything else—water, tar, potatoes.

"Sure and I don't see why you would know," Cook said. "Keeps to himself, don't he, and why a young lass like you would care about the doings of a moody widower, even if he is your employer."

Jane did not want to respond to that, so she turned the conversation back to Creirwy's earlier speech and replayed her instructions, to fix on what might actually be expected of her. "The side door on the south, you said?" said Jane. "That's where I should direct them?" She wondered what the temporary staff would be like—these local wives and daughters pitching in to pick up an extra bit of money and a hamper of leftover party food. Did they normally ward themselves when they went by Edward's crumbling house? Did they rap on iron to come today, and did they come only because they were desperate, as desperate as she?

Cook nodded at the side door question, her nimble fingers rubbing the tender skin from the newest spring potatoes. Sloughed skin fell to the countertop in flaking bits of red-brown. "Some of the temporary staff were here at the last party two years ago," Cook said. "The rest said they wouldn't come back for love nor pence. Silly girls probably got themselves with babes by now. The old ones return, you'll see. Ones with heads on their shoulders, with sense enough not to let their bellies turn at the sight of Dorie's tricks. You have to be thirty before you have any sense at all."

"I'm twenty-one," said Jane.

"Sure and you don't act it. You'll be having an old heart, you will. My grandmam used to say that was the only thing that might save you."

"Save me from what?" Jane prompted. Anything to derail her thoughts. She hooked her feet on the rung of the wooden chair, watched Cook's fingers fly.

Cook stared off over the steam rising from the soup pot. The flames licked around its copper edges. "A cousin of mine was taken by the fey," she said. "Well, her parents thought she fell off a cliff, but my grandmam said Eirwen was too clever to go tumbling off cliffs. Eirwen was that pretty and clever, and she had a little wooden recorder painted all blue that she played as well as the birds. She and I would go roaming, we would, through the woods and cliffs around the sea, where we lived then. But one day we separated and she never came back. The only thing we found of her was the blue recorder, half-buried in the mud of the path. Grandmam was certain the fey took her for their own."

Jane realized she was holding her breath, that her elbows hurt from leaning on the side table. "But the fey didn't take you? Was it because you had the old heart?"

Cook came back to herself with a laugh. "No, that was because I wasn't pretty nor clever nor talented. May you be born plain, that's the way of it. Grandmam said to me: 'Creirwy, you'll be thanking your lucky stars you're ordinary, 'cause that's why your mum isn't bawling her eyes out right now.' And you know, I did." She slid the delicate potatoes into their own pot of cool water. "I suppose I'm too practical for my own good."

"Did you ever see her again?" said Jane. It seemed like the worst way to lose a child—no clean break, but the agony of waiting day after day, holding out hope against the inevitable. She imagined Cook's aunt turning the muddy blue recorder around in her hands day after day, watching it age as the years rolled by. First the dirt would flake off, then the blue paint. Then the wood would smooth under her hands until the recorder was merely a lump of wood with holes, out of tune and unusable. And still no child.

"No, that we never did," said Cook. "And they say the fey let their captives go with a gift after a certain number of years—decades—have passed. So who knows—maybe she did fall off a cliff, for aught I know. Except that was just a bit easier to believe before the war. Nowadays I reckon even Aunt and Uncle accept that the fey took her." The water roiled under the stirring of her wooden spoon. "Sure and the fey aren't just tales anymore."

* * *

Jane volunteered to steam the curtains in the foyer and direct traffic. There wasn't time to wash everything ("A party only every two years, and he can't be giving us more notice than two days?" moaned Cook), but there were plenty of ways to freshen with dusting and carpet beating and steaming.

The steamer was one of Poule's inventions: a copper and iron contraption on spoke wheels. Jane dragged the awkward machine into the foyer and poured her full kettle into it. The heavy velvet drapes were nearly wrinkle-free, but she felt oddly satisfied as she freshened the plush, uncrushed the nap of the velvet. Maybe it was because this was a simple task, she thought, not like her open-ended struggle to turn Dorie into something she was not. Steaming the curtains fixed the curtains, and that was satisfying.

She directed several men and women to the side door to apply to Creirwy for the temporary work. Most often the villagers arrived in pairs—unwilling to brave Silver Birch Hall without a friendly face in tow, she thought. They peered in cautiously or stoically, wiping damp palms on their cleanest black-and-whites, fingering iron charms fastened over their pulse points. Jane smiled at them, but she knew her unveiled face with its contoured iron wasn't likely to set them at ease.

She was nearly done with the last set of curtains when the twisted doorknocker sounded again. Jane opened the door. "Side door on the south," she said automatically, but then she looked more closely at the visitor. "I'm sorry," she said, for the woman at the door was clearly no servant. Jane wasn't embarrassed for herself, but she didn't want her employer to lose a client because she'd been too informal to her. So she bobbed an unfamiliar curtsey by way of apology. "An' ye be human—oh, just come in, please, with my apologies."

The woman laughed, her head thrown back till her throat caught the muted morning light. "I'll have you horsewhipped," she said, and she swept past Jane and into the house.

Jane looked at her sharply, uncertain as to whether the woman seriously thought that was a possibility, or if she merely had an odd sense of humor. Oddly cruel, perhaps. She wished she could take back the curtsey.

The woman was amused by Jane, judging from the expression in her snapping black eyes. She was not attractive, but Jane had to look twice to see that. The woman was tremendously distinctive, due to the fire in her face, the light in her eyes. She had clear olive skin and masses of black hair, and she knew how to dress to her advantage—she was clad in folds of black satin that slashed dramatically past her shoulders and clung to her hips, accentuated at the waist by a sunburst diamanté pin. She took the plum silk wrap from her shoulders in one fluid motion and tossed it to Jane, who fumbled for it. "You may tell Edward that Nina is here." As if there was only one Nina in the world.

"Oh, I'm not the—," said Jane, but Nina looked her up and down in a way that said she couldn't possibly be interested in what Jane was or wasn't.

Her attitude got under Jane's skin. "Is he expecting you?"

"Oh yes," Nina said, with a significant smile. "He's expecting me."

"And yet I regret to inform you," Jane said coolly, "that he's not here." Score one for the governess.

Nina's eyebrows raised, but her retort was forestalled by a movement behind the second floor railing. She elegantly inclined her head to study the small figure above.

Jane knew her words would have no effect when confronted

with one of the "pretty ladies," but still she said to the small figure: "Go finish your nap, Dorie. I'll be right there."

Dorie didn't obey. Her legs pushed through the banister railings and her head leaned against the rail as she stared down at them. Her curls were limp and matted; her iron-gloved hands hung loosely at her side in a now-familiar gesture of tired defeat. Even her eyes seemed dull.

"That child needs castor oil," said Nina. "Or a pony."

Temper rose and with it sarcasm. "I'll make a note on her charts," Jane said. "Mr. Rochart will be back the day after next. Would you like to leave him your card?"

Nina's eyebrows met along her low forehead. "I would," she said. "With a note. You wouldn't have an ink pen, would you?" Something about her tone implied that Jane would be unlikely to have anything related to literacy.

"In here," said Jane. She drew aside the freshly steamed garnet curtains and ushered Nina into the small red room.

Nina's gaze immediately snapped to the rows of masks and she studied them, touching jutting chins and hooked noses. "The Varee *chirurgiens* can't compare to him," she said in a low voice.

Jane was apparently dismissed, though she wondered if she should stay planted and wait to take Nina's message—as well as ensure that Nina did not go wandering through the house in order to find out if Jane's information was true. Of course, if she stayed for the message she'd have to make sure that Mr. Rochart got the message, and she did not wish to seem that she'd been seeking him out in his studio.

Nina's stiff posture, white-gloved fingers frozen on one misshapen mask, seemed to imply that she couldn't possibly do anything as personal as write a note without the privacy of

Jane being gone. So Jane turned, but as she did, her eye fell on a new mask hanging by the door. Her gaze caught and held, and she could not look away from the glistening skin, the bags and folds that caricatured a human.

But not just any human.

It was obscenely taken to extremes, true. But surely Jane recognized the model for those pouched eyes, that prizefighter nose, though she'd only seen them the once?

It was the leering face of the first Miss Ingel.

Chapter 10

THE EDGE OF THE FOREST

Jane's knees shook. Plain Miss Ingel. Beautiful Miss Ingel. And—"the Varee *chirurgiens* can't compare to him," Nina had said, but didn't *chirurgien* mean surgeon?

"Miss Ingel . . . ," Jane whispered. "She used to look like that sculpture."

Nina looked where Jane's eyes were fixed. "Oh, Blanche," she said derisively. "I saw her yesterday, and she tried to pretend that the hot springs were restorative. As if she could fix that face and not have it be obvious." Nina's eyes fell to Jane, still holding her plum silk wrap. "I'll take that. Now, if you wouldn't mind . . . ?"

Jane wanted to collapse to the floor right there, but she obeyed Nina, wobbled through the foyer, and sank out of sight behind the forest green curtains. She wrapped her arms around her knees, where goose bumps speckled her skirt.

It was plain as day, now that Nina had said it. Rochart-as-artist was a pretty little fiction, a cover story that certain wealthy elite knew the truth of. No artist—a surgeon. A secret surgeon, unless maybe everyone knew—everyone but Jane, who was apparently as naïve as Alistair had painted her.

No, she reminded herself, she would not beat herself up over ignorance. She had been wrapped up in her own work with Dorie; why should she see through a mystery that she didn't know existed?

Not to mention that facial surgery was so uncommon that Jane had only seen it once before, and that was to fix a boy in her town who had had his face mauled by a wild boar. She had seen the city surgeon's work, and it was obvious. It was noticeable; there were scars, and stretches. It was definitely an improvement over no work, but the boy would never look quite normal, let alone handsome.

She had heard that back when the cinemas were still running, there were actresses who went voluntarily for such surgery, that noses and chins could be tweaked. But she had never seen the result, and she had never heard that it could look like this.

But that was what it was. Edward the surgeon, Edward the artist in flesh and bone. Tweaking those like the Prime Minister's wife so they merely looked refreshed, doing major work on those like Blanche Ingel. And either way making the woman into the most dazzling version of herself. Fey beauty, the old woman at the party had called it, and that's what it would've been called before the Great War, for it was inhuman to be that perfect, that symmetrical, that flawless.

She stayed there until she heard the soft front door click of Nina leaving, and then she crossed the foyer, went to the small red room to see the faces again.

Yes, there was Miss Ingel, the stretched and exaggerated sculpture of her original face. His mockups, perhaps, his befores and afters. She thought back to something he had said about them the first time she'd seen his studio. "A reminder," he'd said. A reminder of the worst of us, extracted and displayed.

She could only guess that the sorrows in his life drove him to the extreme of making these grotesque images—perhaps he was not altogether comfortable with what he did. It was shrouded in secrecy after all, presumably because the women wanted to pretend they'd always been this beautiful—would rather pretend they'd had affairs or been on holiday than let the truth be known.

And secrecy like that had to weigh on him.

Had to cause—moodiness, as Cook had said.

Jane reached up to touch the ugly Blanche Ingel mask. The clay was smooth, the painted surface slick, almost elastic. One above and to the left caught her eye—was that the Prime Minister's wife, with the heavy jowls? The caricature was so extreme, it was hard to tell. If that Nina person had been friendlier, perhaps she could have told Jane what name went with each piece of artwork.

Slowly Jane turned, looking at the rows and rows of masks with a new eye. Each one represented a person, somewhere. Rows of people who had jumped ship on their old lives for the chance to be someone new. She might have met them, seen them in the city, and she thought of the beautiful people at Helen's wedding.

Thought of all the splendidly attired guests, whirling in their gauzy gowns of apricot and ruby in the gaslight, each holding to their faces a mask made of their worst self.

Jane did not sleep well Thursday night. There was a windstorm in the early morning that shook the house, woke Jane from her nightmare of the battlefield. She woke with the echo of her mother ringing in her ears, one heart-wrenching word: *Jane.*

She lay in bed till the last of the storm had beat itself out, dashed its brains on Silver Birch Hall. When she looked from her window, she saw the forest had been rent by winds that covered the bottom of the back lawn in dead black branches.

Jane dressed and went to Dorie's room, mesh gloves in hand. Prior to the gloves, Dorie had been awake well before Jane's arrival each morning, but no more. Jane sat down on the bed and said, "There are going to be a lot of people in the house today. And longer—a fortnight."

Dorie opened her eyes and looked at Jane, but made no move to get out of bed. Her curls looked like they hadn't been brushed in days, though Jane had helped her wash and comb them just last night. Dorie's eyelids were smeared with sticky sleep and her cheeks were pale.

"How are you feeling?" Jane said. She laid the back of her hand against Dorie's head, but the girl did not feel hot, or damp, or anything unusual. She didn't have any physical signs of sickness—it was just this listlessness, as if she was worn out by their work of eating from spoons, as if she was depressed from not being allowed to make blue lights flicker in the air.

Dorie's shoulder shrugged. She rolled over and stared out the window into the blue of an after-storm sky.

Frustrated, Jane rose and went to the window. She would have to keep Dorie well hidden from the guests if this continued—the girl looked like a lost war orphan. Jane stared into the woods, wondering what trick to try. Maybe she should admit the task was too hard for her—maybe she should bend her pride and get advice from Mr. Rochart. Mr. Rochart the *surgeon*. If she ever saw him of course, and where was he, with the party starting today?

"Father," said Dorie from the bed.

Impossible sightline for Dorie, but the instant she said that Jane saw him standing, just inside the forest, as if Jane's wishes and Dorie's words had conjured him. He was clutching a tree branch with one hand and his side with another, and she saw him take a step toward the back lawn that made it look as though he were swimming through molasses. He bent, clutching his side, as if in pain.

Concern coalesced into action. "Out of bed and wash your face," she said firmly to Dorie, and she hurried for the stairs, whirling down them as fast as her feet would go. She emerged onto the back lawn, blinking in the clear sunlight till she saw him, immobile next to a thorny locust, his hand outstretched toward the house. "Mr. Rochart," she shouted, running for the trees. "Edward!"

Slowly his head tilted up. His amber eyes took a while to focus on her, as if traveling back from a great distance. "Jane," he said wonderingly. "Jane."

She slipped in past the first tree, barely thinking that *this was the forest* in her rush to get to him. "I am here, sir," she said. "Lean on me."

He clasped her forearm. "Yes, you are flesh and blood, are you not? Not a pale mist of blue masquerading as a live girl. Say you are real, Jane."

"I am," she said. His hand still clutched her arm. "You look unsteady. Do you need assistance? Shall I find Poule?"

He shook his head, his eyes vague again. "Did you hear the windstorm last night?" he said.

"Yes," she said. A shudder rippled across her shoulders. "You must get out of the forest."

"My foot," he said faintly.

She looked and saw how his leg stretched awkwardly behind him, saw that thin scarves of blue seemed to wind around his ankle, pinioning him. His right hand held a satchel to his ribs, and blue weaved from his fingers, around it.

Sharp anger, born of fear. It rose up in Jane, and she felt the hot orange of her curse lash at the iron, so hot she thought her face might literally burn. No time for thoughts of water—she had to pull it off to find relief. She clutched at the chin of her mask, lifting it an infinitesimal bit to get air, said desperately to distract him: "Look up at the window; do you see Dorie?"

"My little one," he said, turning that way, and lurched another half-step toward the house.

Jane scrabbled at the leather straps, pulling them aside, and then the mask was suddenly off, cooling her face. The orange tongues of anger lashed out, raging at the idea that he was stolen from her, would be taken from her. He must not be caught, and she tore at his ankle with her bare hands, as if fingers alone could melt the blue shackles of air.

"No," she whispered to it, "no no no no no . . . ," and above her she felt him lurch another half-step, and another, and the blue seemed less all the time as she told it *no,* peeling off, crackling away. "You can make it," she told Edward, while simultaneously willing the blue: *no no no.*

Another step and he was past her. Another, and he was to the last tree, then out, out of the woods, onto the back lawn.

"Jane," he said, that wonder sharp in his voice. "Jane!"

"Coming, sir," she said, and there was a tremble in her voice. She shoved the mask into place, buckling it firm against her now-tangled hair. A blue flash zipped along the ground, back into the woods, and vanished out of sight.

She stumbled from the woods, shivering, and suddenly his arms were around her, holding her close.

"I should never have put you in danger, oh, Jane. . . ."

"I am fine"—gulp—"I am fine." The sharp adrenaline and rage were draining now, lessening until she was very aware of his arm around her shoulders, his hand holding her upper arm tight.

Perhaps he realized it at the same moment, for he released her.

He shook his head as if grounding himself in the present, and some of the old color returned to his face. His face closed off, became the familiar sardonic mask. He ran a hand unconsciously over his side where the blue had been and no longer was, tucked the thick satchel under his arm. From a distance he said, "I owe you a rather sizable debt, Jane, do I not?"

"Sir?"

He cast around for something to do, reached to pick up one dry branch blown free from the forest by the windstorm. He turned it to study the thorns, then tossed it into the undergrowth. "I frequently walk here to throw back the branches," he said, and there was a self-mocking note to his voice that suggested he was trying to lighten the situation. "If I let them, the trees would come right up to the house."

"Sir, how is your ankle?" said Jane.

"It is well; never mind it." He picked up more branches and hurled them into the forest. "It is the trees that must concern you. This is Birnam Wood, and as in Shakspyr's tale of madness, it is creeping toward me. But this wood is alive; it will catch me before my time is through." He was retreating again—closing himself off behind archaic, formal ways of speaking and dark thoughts.

Then he turned and saw her expression, and his mouth twisted in a sort of smile. "Forgive me," he said. "It is but a wild fancy. For aught I know this stretch of yard has the same measurements as when it was laid two centuries ago. But you did not come out here to let me lean on your arm like an old man and hear me talk of moving trees. No, there is something of far greater import on your slim shoulders. Speak, Jane, what would you have me do? Now and forever, you must see I am in your service."

She shivered at his talk of moving forests, and said, "I could almost agree with you that the trees move, sir."

"Edward," he said. "I could almost believe in your ridiculous fancies, *Edward*. If you were not so clearly a raving lunatic, *Edward*."

"You're not!" she said. "I saw the blue on your ankle!" She startled at her own outburst and stopped herself, though deep inside ran the frightened thought: five years, they had been gone five years. They were gone for good, weren't they, weren't they. . . ? She could feel her boots sinking into the mud in the silence.

"I'm not mad, eh?" He scoffed at himself. "It is gone now, Jane. Just a passing madness of a madder wood. What proof have you that I am not a lunatic, or worse?"

She was silent another moment, and then suddenly all her thoughts seemed to burst forth and off her tongue and she said, "I think you carry a dark burden, sir—Edward."

"I do?" His tone mocked her worry, but she pressed on, her brain making previously half-formed ideas into connections on the spot. It was not *just* the burden of his craft; no, there was more.

"I think you blame yourself for Dorie's manner of birth," she said. "And further . . . and further I think you go—you went—into the woods secretly, to try to find the fey, so they will undo what they've done to her."

"Isn't that rather dangerous of me? To seek out the fey? Besides, what could one little fey do to help me, even if I found them?" The dry branch broke in half under his grip. He tossed half aside and his hands closed around the remaining piece, his fingers weaving through the black thorns.

She thought back to the stories. "The Queen, then. She can make bargains. You're looking for the Queen."

"A lofty ambition," he mocked. "And when I find her?"

"You'll bargain for Dorie's soul," she said.

But this guess seemed to fall short.

Mr. Rochart tossed away the stick and clasped her shoulder, steering her back toward the house. "The guests will arrive soon," he said, as lightly as if they had been only talking about the weather. "For this tedious chore we call a 'party.' We pronounce mingling with uninspired souls 'charming,' and talking of unimportant topics 'delightful.' Oh, I despise it. Pity me, Jane, for I must smile and play the artist for all these women with their expectations."

She shuddered. "I couldn't do it."

"And yet, Jane, if I bring this fortnight off perfectly it could be a great thing for us—for all of us." Mr. Rochart shook his head and she saw the financial worries laid over him like a glove.

She remembered Miss Ingel in her aquamarines, Nina in her furs, and briefly she wondered why his situation was so dire. Surely the money was coming in—where was it going to? But merely she said, "I will do what I can to help, sir."

"Will you?" He turned his strange amber eyes upon her. "Then you must bring Dorie down to mingle with the guests."

Jane twisted away. "No," she said immediately. "She's not ready."

"*She's* not?" Edward stopped her in the middle of the mud-splashed lawn. His amber eyes shadowed and focused on hers. She felt caught, like prey. "You must. Every night, you must. Don't think I don't know what they say of my daughter. And of me—that I lock her in a garret like some madwoman, that I keep her hidden. She must come and be normal. You must come and make sure that she is."

"But—"

"Please," he said, and she was still. He studied her. "I see thoughts whirling behind your eyes," he said. "You feel like a trapped animal; you are desperate for any excuse not to sit in a dark corner of my drawing room for a couple hours each night. Am I such an ogre?"

"No," Jane said reluctantly.

"Then what are you frightened of?"

She did not answer.

Finally he said, more lightly, "I foresee one objection—you are going to tell me you and Dorie don't have any dresses suitable for evening soirees. I have brought her a new one from town, and for you I have a new pair of dancing shoes."

"You shouldn't have," she said, overwhelmed, but he held up a hand.

"No, do not thank me. I saw your sister in town and she

sent them. She said specifically to tell you that they were commissioned for you—I gather she often sends hand-me-downs?"

"Very nice ones," Jane said, but it was true, the thought of Helen having specifically made these for her was a spot of gladness in her heart. "Did she send a letter?"

"No," he said. "But she spoke of doing so soon." He hesitated. "Does she speak of being often alone?"

"No," Jane said, surprised. "Her letters are endless descriptions of parties and compliments."

"Oh." He was silent for a moment, and then he took her arm and moved on, irrevocably leading her back to the house. "I have sent Martha to the attic to fetch one of Grace's stored gowns and clean it for you. You do not have to wear them. I know how women like up-to-the-minute fashions"—with an ironic lift of his lips—"but perhaps having a choice will ease your mind."

The only choice that would ease her mind would be the choice not to attend, but she could tell that this one was to be denied her.

And . . . he needed her. "We will come," she said.

He inclined his head in thanks, and then they were at the house. He opened the back door for her and gestured her to precede him into the narrow hallway.

"I assure you, there is no one on earth who can bargain for a soul," he said softly, as if there had been no break in the earlier conversation. The sunlight cut off as she stepped into the dark hallway, birdsong and cricket buzz, all gone inside that dim swallowing house. His eyes were lost in shadow as his fingers released their hold on her elbow, leaving five spots of

cold in their place. "Bodies, however, are under earthly juris-
diction."

Jane was all the way upstairs before she realized that she had
not asked for his advice on Dorie's listlessness. And yet he
had inadvertently told her one thing that had to happen, for
Dorie could not appear before everyone in metal-cloth gloves
with sequins dangling from their backs.

Dorie was still in bed. "Father in forest," she said. "Jane in
forest."

"Yes," said Jane.

She sat down on the edge of the bed, smoothed out the
white swiss-dotted coverlet as what to do straightened itself
out in her head. Dorie stared through the wall as if she could
see the black trees.

"Here's the story," Jane said finally. "Your father wants you
to come down and meet these people tonight. You'll like that,
won't you? All the ladies in their pretty dresses?"

Small voice. "Pretty dress?"

"Yes, one for you, too," said Jane. "Your father brought you
one from the city. And." She took a deep breath before offer-
ing Dorie the bargain. "You won't be wearing your gloves the
whole time his guests are here."

Dorie rolled over and looked at her. The first spark of
interest lit her blue eyes.

"But," Jane said, forestalling. "That means you have to be
very good on your own, without the gloves." The blue eyes
flickered and she pressed harder. "Dorie. Your father is counting on you to behave. I don't know how to impress on you
how important this is to him. If we leave the gloves off during

the day, will you promise me that you won't do anything with the lights or moving things without touching them?"

"Mother stuff."

"Right. No mother stuff. Your father would get in so much trouble, I can't even tell you. Can you promise me that you won't get him in trouble?" Jane held her breath, used her tiny bit of leverage for all it was worth. Would the girl do for her beloved father what she wouldn't do on her own? She hadn't when Jane arrived, but now, maybe, maybe after their weeks of work and toil, the days of wearing the hated gloves . . . ?

Slowly Dorie nodded. "I promise," she said.

Mindful of her charge's fragile self-discipline, Jane cranked the gramophone for Dorie for most of the morning, and she did not make her do any of the hand exercises that would persuade her that "mother stuff" was a good idea after all. Even with the door shut, she heard the entrances and chatter in the foyer below, as the house party guests arrived one by one. After lunch Dorie wanted to go outside, and Jane eagerly seized on that, glad Dorie seemed to be taking an interest in life again.

When they exited Dorie's rooms, another guest was arriving. The servant's footsteps were silenced by the carpet, but the door creaked as it opened. Dorie tugged to go see, but Jane clamped down on her hand, held her fast. She recognized that plum silk wrap, that drawling, amused voice.

Jane and Dorie went out the servants' side door, wound their way past a coach and four, a shiny black steam-powered convertible, and the same reliable old Peter with his lurching motorcar who had dropped Jane here two months ago. He

pulled out onto the road, looking shell-shocked by the pas-
senger he'd just dropped off.

Jane and Dorie crossed the hard-packed road, walked out
the opposite way from the forest, walked onto the open moor.
It was the end of April, and wildflowers were beginning to
bloom in the heath: purple heather and yellow cowslip and
fringed blue-eyes like tiny daisies, no bigger than Dorie's
thumb. The fields around Jane's childhood home had been
covered in cowslip; it had been blooming early the year she
and Charlie marched into battle. So she looked away from
the butter yellow petals and envisioned the field in another
month, when it would be covered with color, the cowslip lost
in a sea of purple and blue.

The ground was damp. She leaned back on her hands,
watched bits of white and grey after-storm clouds chase each
other around the sky. The sky behind them was as blue as the
daisies, which made the clouds the white petals, blown care-
lessly across it.

Dorie ran around the field as if she'd been let off a leash.
There was already more pink in her cheeks and her curls
were bouncing back to life. Amazing what a holiday from
work could do. When Dorie tumbled on the grass in a clump
of the tiny blue daisies, Jane watched her out of the corner of
her eye.

Dorie stretched her palm over a yellow blotch of cowslip.
Jane waited, dying inside, wondering what choice Dorie would
make. Wondering what she could do if the girl refused to play
along, if she refused to keep her extra abilities under wraps. It
would look strange to have her in the mesh gloves, but there
wasn't another alternative if Dorie didn't cooperate. And if

her love of her father didn't make her try for these two weeks, what else did Jane have to bargain with?

Slowly, slowly, Dorie withdrew her palm.

No flowers jumped to her hand, no blue lights sketched patterns on the moor.

She also did not lean over and pick the cowslip with her fingers, but Jane was all right with that. Dorie didn't have to succeed in all her goals today, as long as she started to show some control.

Dorie looked over at Jane, who was careful not to show that she was studying Dorie's behavior. She put her hand over the flowers one more time.

Then she jumped to her feet and started running down the moor again, running in circles, running with her curls streaming behind her.

Jane let out a breath she didn't know she was holding, and wiped a cheek she hadn't known was wet.

Chapter 11

MASK AND SHADOW

By evening the guests were all in. All dined, already bored and ready for the amusement of repairing to the drawing room with drinks and painted chocolates. One of the younger girls sat down at the rosewood piano—to show off, but she was good, and the latest waltzes sang from the freshly tuned keys. The women laughed and flashed rings and angled their hips to display their dressmakers' concoctions of slim silk and beaded net.

And yet. Now that Jane knew Edward's true occupation, she saw the women with a different eye. Not art patrons, but women wealthy enough to buy themselves new noses and cheekbones. Not content with the normal faces she'd give anything to have. For an instant she viewed them with disdain, sad creatures focused on appearance. And in the next moment that superiority washed away in shame as she reminded herself that she was focused on her own looks, whatever justification she felt she might have.

Jane ducked out of the shadow of the doorway as one of the new hires hurried through, intent on not spilling her tray.

The woman's pinched, set mouth implied it had been a long day for her already, trying to properly navigate her new employment. Jane wondered if it would be better or worse to carry a tray rather than mind a child. More boring, certainly—but perhaps easier during times like this.

But at least she was not poor Edward, having to actually give the party. Jane was not so naïve as to think he'd rather sit and talk to his fey-scarred governess, but still. She would hate to give parties for all those frighteningly perfect people, so she sympathized with him.

Jane went slowly up the stairs and sat on the bed in Dorie's room. "Ready to wake up?"

Dorie roused, blinking sleepy eyes.

Jane gently untangled the golden curls, helped the girl from the bed. A shame, keeping her up past her bedtime. Jane lifted the rose-pink dress off the padded white hanger. "Are you awake enough to go?"

Dorie swallowed a yawn, nodded firmly, face lighting at the sight of the party frock. Jane smiled, glad a new dress could still catch Dorie's interest. She helped the girl into the frock and was attempting to tie a decent-looking bow in the silk sash when there was a knock on the door.

"Come in," said Jane, expecting Martha with their summons. And yet when she looked up it was Edward, staring down at Jane ministering to Dorie, an oddly soft look on his face.

"Father!" said Dorie, and she ran to him, leaving the sash to trail behind.

He set down the paper-wrapped parcel he held, scooped Dorie up in his arms, and swung her around till she giggled. Jane had never seen him do that, and she thought: He is happy, and look how she beams from it. How did he get that way, and can it happen more often?

Edward stopped spinning and came to a halt, still holding Dorie, and for a moment looking very boyish indeed. His hair had already gotten mussed, and one of the locks stood straight up. "You are going to be perfectly behaved tonight, I can tell," he told Dorie, and she nodded.

Jane smiled faintly at the two of them, and did not say, "We hope so."

He set Dorie down. "Your tail is trailing," he told her solemnly, and she laughed again, beaming at them both, and for one ridiculous moment the three of them were lit with happiness, because of how *normal* it all was, could be. "Be good and let Jane tie it."

Dorie let Jane catch her trailing sash, and Jane bent again to the task. Her fingers slipped on the silk, but at last she managed a creditable attempt at a bow, and she set Dorie free to spin around in front of the mirror, engrossed in the whirl of her skirt.

Edward cleared his throat.

"Yes?" said Jane, and she was surprised to see hesitancy in his face.

He picked up the lumpy brown parcel from the floor and handed it to Jane. It felt like cloth, folded and wrapped in butcher paper to keep it tidy. "The slippers from your sister, and a dress for you," he said at last. "If it would please—if you like it."

"Thank you," said Jane, but he cut in:

"It's nothing, just from the attic. Just washed and pressed is all." He spread his hands. "Perhaps I should have picked you up something in town. . . ."

"That would not be necessary," said Jane, meaning, *that would not be appropriate,* and she felt warm with embarrassment. "Thank you for this."

"So you will come," he said, and his usual assured cynicism seemed to flow back in, his mask settling back in place. "You will save me from being quite alone down there. Ah, Jane, I told you once of the tale of the beastly man, but do you know the famous tale of Tam Lin? Stolen away by the fey, and for his beloved to win him back, she had to hold him as he changed into a variety of loathsome beasts."

"I have heard it," said Jane. She wished they could return to the Edward who swung Dorie around, rather than the Edward who brooded on fey tales of misery and despair.

"I request that you not think badly of me as I change into that most loathsome of all beasts, the Gentleman," he said.

"I would hardly think badly of you for being a good host to your guests, sir."

"And yet I am certain that to once lose Jane's good opinion is to lose it forever," he said, and that bit of cowlick waved madly. "So I ply her in advance with dresses and words, hoping she will take pity on poor Tam Lin when he becomes an ogre."

Jane did not know what to say to that.

He laughed, a laugh with *dark* in it. "Jane, if you could see your face. You are certain I have quite lost all remaining sanity. Well then, never mind me, but array yourself in my finery with all speed, and bring that little terror with you. Make haste, Jane." And he was gone, even as Dorie still whirled in front of the mirror.

Jane clutched the package to her. "Wait for me," she told Dorie, and she hastened to her room.

She tore open the butcher paper and the dress spilled out on her bed.

The golden dress from the attic.

Jane held it close, warmth flooding her face. He had picked this one for her. He had thought about the gowns and said, this one. Jane will look well in this one. Their tastes had coincided on the exact same dress.

Jane recalled herself with a sigh, and with a bump came back to reality. No, Martha had seen her mooning over it; she probably picked it herself.

She quickly washed her face, sponged down her arms, and changed into the gold dress. It fit beautifully—but the flowing pre-war styling meant it would fit many girls equally well. More surprising was that the dancing shoes from Helen fit perfectly—she must have gotten Jane's measurements from the old cobbler, though the man who'd made her work boots had surely never made these beaded beauties.

Just as with the silver dress, Jane felt odd in her new attire, a different person—though in the silver dress she had felt like Jane-as-she-was-supposed-to-be, and in the gold she felt—like a fraud? Like a creature from another time, another place? This dress made her into a not-Jane, not any version of Jane. A lady in a different time, a wealthy girl in an estate like this, one of his house guests from the city. Getting ready for an exciting night of dances and meaningful looks and stillnesses of wild heartbeats. She would never have been Blanche Ingel, with her perfectly chiseled face; she could not be Nina, with her rapier wit and striking demeanor. A friend of the Misses Davenport, perhaps—those two silly girls with their wide eyes and their fits of giggles. Girls, because they had not yet had a reason to grow up. Here before the Great War, in a world where the fey were estranged and practically forgotten, and there was nothing more pressing for any of the guests than to drink too much and to meet a charming stranger. Some tall mysterious man who stepped in behind her with a sardonic quip about the party, and as soon as she dared turn around, she would look up and see his face, see who it was. . . .

Jane ruthlessly pinned back a stray lock of hair, shoving down that silly flight of fantasy.

The iron mask was cold around her eye. She readjusted the mask on the bridge of her nose, nudged the dark leather straps higher behind her head, where they blended into her hair. So almost pretty, if only she turned her ironskin away, if she only saw her cheek of normal skin, pale against her dark hair, so almost, almost, almost. . . .

"Pretty ladies," Dorie said from the stairs, breaking Jane's spell. Jane hurried after her, concentrating hard on the almost-girl in the rose-pink dress. She picked the child up and swooped her down the last few stairs, and Dorie giggled, before standing upright and saying solemnly, "No, I am grown-up tonight."

"I believe you are," said Jane, and they looked at each other and Jane thought—maybe I have done some good, after all. She curtseyed and motioned Dorie to proceed her into the drawing room, and Dorie did, pink step by pink step, looking perfectly happy, intrepid, normal.

She was surprised to see that Mr. Rochart was not in the drawing room. There was a small knot of guests by the piano where the younger Miss Davenport was still playing and smiling up at one of the men. The elder Miss Davenport had her elbow on the piano, trying to steal attention from her sister.

Dorie trotted confidently to the pretty ladies as Jane found a seat behind a table with a large plant on it. The drawing room had seemed bigger this morning before the guests, before Cook had had extra chairs brought from the attic and moved in. Now the piano was too close, the lipsticked girls in their slinky frocks too near. Edward had told her to come, bolstered her self-assurance with his confidences—but he was not here, and the girls very much were.

Dorie neared the girls, who didn't notice her immediately. Jane clutched the folds of the golden dress—Dorie wouldn't act out, would she? Wouldn't show off, to get noticed?

But then the elder Miss Davenport turned and saw the little girl, and the wheels plainly moved in her head. "Ah, what a pet!" she cried, and she began fussing over Dorie.

"What do you have there?" said one of the gentlemen, and the piano broke off as the younger Miss Davenport turned, pouting, to see.

"What's your name, sweet child?" cooed the older Miss Davenport.

"Dorie," said Dorie, and curtseyed, which sent the older girl into raptures.

Jane saw the amused look on the gentleman's face—the cooing over Dorie was likely to be of little interest except to the father, and where was he?

"Just look at these golden curls! Nearly as bright as mine."

Come to think of that, where were the other guests? Where was Nina, and hadn't she seen a redhead earlier, from above?

A gentle laugh by the door, and Jane turned to see her question answered. Mr. Rochart. And the redhead . . . of course.

That's where he had been.

Blanche Ingel slipped her arm under Mr. Rochart's, laughing. "I won't melt, will I?" she said, and she turned her perfectly chiseled face up to his. Mr. Rochart leaned closer, and Jane couldn't catch what he said, but she saw his lips move with his reply. The tall dark man swept the redhead with the unearthly beauty into the drawing room; the younger Miss Davenport struck up a waltz, and they danced.

The well-dusted curtains sagged overhead, creased and worn as if they'd not been touched for two centuries. The boarded windows were made gayer for the evening, tacked over with cloth cut from remnants of upstairs curtains. Only one of the paned windows was still whole, and it showcased the dusky moor.

Jane held her side as if it had a stitch. Her ribs were too broad for her dress, suddenly, and they labored against the golden panels. What was it to her if he danced with his clients? That was what he was supposed to do—what he had *told* her he would do. It wasn't his fault that she couldn't understand how he could say he hated parties, hated smiling, hated the dance—and now could whisk away the redhead in the slinky green silk with an air of absolute charm, smile at her as if she were the only person in the room, whirl her around as if he loved every minute of this gathering.

He wasn't supposed to dance with Jane, not in this life or any other. Even the imaginary whole-faced Jane was nothing compared to this woman's sculpted perfection (the perfection *he* had created, oh, why wouldn't he adore his living artwork), and it wasn't just her. More women were in the room now, including Nina, and the Misses Davenport's cousin, who was nearly as striking as Blanche. She was shorter, and her figure not nearly so fine, but her face was a tiny cornered thing of heartbreaking beauty, and the few men flocked around her, to the dismay of both Misses Davenport. Had the cousin, then, already been under his knife?

It mattered little if she had or not—the women's beauty was still from money, whether bred or bought. These were the people of this world, and she was a fool to believe that Mr. Rochart's seemingly unguarded moments with her could mean anything more than that she happened to be standing nearby when he spoke. A man who could swear that he despised parties and then charm a roomful of women—no, she didn't understand him, she couldn't understand him, and the familiar claws of cold humiliation tore her up inside.

The waltz rang to a bright finish, and Mr. Rochart twirled Blanche into his arms and against the piano. They stopped, breathing with the effort of the dance, and Mr. Rochart took a long time to draw away from his lovely partner in green, to let her escape his arms. Jane's shoulder blades prickled under her filmy dress, recalling how that touch felt.

The elder Miss Davenport also watched this interaction carefully, her eyes flicking from Mr. Rochart and Blanche to her younger sister and the moon-eyed boy gazing at her. Weighing options, but good luck to her, thought Jane. As if anyone in the room could surpass Blanche Ingel.

"Da!" said Dorie, and she ran to hug his knees.

Edward bent to caress the blond head. "Are you behaving yourself, my little terror?"

"Oh, you ogre!" butted in the elder Miss Davenport. "This sweet thing is an angel, a bunnykin, a darling moppet. I just adore her, and she adores me already, don't you, precious? Look at her sweet pink frock. Can you give us a curtsey, pet?"

Jane's hand crept down to the radiator to rap on iron as

Dorie smiled and curtseyed prettily at the crowd. "Oh, what a doll!" she heard Miss Davenport exclaim, and then the other girls pressed in until Jane couldn't see Dorie at all. She stood, unwilling to either leave her dark corner or risk Dorie getting out of her sight.

Too much attention might be a balm, might make Dorie sufficiently happy that she would not be tempted to destroy her father's reputation in a single flash of blue light. On the other hand, Jane had seen more than once what excessive adoration could do to a child. She did not know Dorie's measure in this situation, and she took a step in, nerving herself to fight her way into that flock.

But luckily Mrs. Davenport's broad figure moved, and Dorie came back into view. She was smiling and laughing with the pretty ladies, twirling to show her skirts. Dorie did not pick up her skirts as another girl might do, or coyly twirl one of her golden curls, but for all that she did not look strange.

Jane sank to her chair, heartbeat slowing. As long as no one asked Dorie to demonstrate perfect penmanship, perhaps they would make it through the night.

A woman in a deep turquoise silk with black net overlay claimed the next chair over. Nina. "Famished!" she said. "Dieting really takes it out of one. Enough to make you want the old fashions like you've got on." She gestured at the loose panels of Jane's dress. "You could eat a cow in that frock and no one would know."

"Don't you have other girls to bother?" said Jane.

Nina laughed and settled into her chair. "But I find you the most entertaining. There's no use sharpening my wit on those feather bolsters. Look at them, all hovering around poor Edward."

Jane hated the possessive way that Nina spoke of him. "They don't have a chance against Miss Ingel," Jane said. "Look at the way she moves."

"Like a confection of marzipan and rainbows," Nina said dryly. "She'd better enjoy the attention now, because next week this party will be mine, all mine." Jane raised her eyebrows, but Nina just laughed and dismissed her comment with a wave. Went back to assessing the chances of the women. "Well, old Ingy's a duckling imprinting on her 'savior'—you did see her *before,* yes? Men love ducklings, no matter what they might say. Then there's the bolster Davenports—two can be twice as nice—but their mother will whisk them away soon enough when she realizes he's flat broke. Makes you wonder where the money goes, doesn't it?"

"Not particularly," said Jane.

Her curt answer seemed to amuse Nina, who leaned forward. "Not even the Varee *chirurgiens* charge what he does, because they can't compare to him and they know it. And now with this jump in skill he's made, I've told him it's imperative he double his prices—after me, of course." She flapped a hand at the drawing room. "They'll all pay it, those bolsters. So where does it all go?" She tipped back her champagne. "I think he's got a secret child somewhere he's paying off."

"The Prime Minister's wife," Jane said without thinking.

"So you do have ears," said Nina. "I like a girl who listens at dumbwaiters. Not her, though. She's completely obsessed with their five drippy children and that doughy husband of hers. I think she just spent extra time with Edward trying to get those children done. At their age." Her eyebrows were expressive. "No, I think there's someone from the past. He grew up abroad, you know. Never came to Silver Birch until almost the end of the war." She clacked polished nails against jet beads. "There's something leftover from his past he's taking care of."

Jane's memory flicked back to the old man with the cane at the carriage house that one day, the old man who was not Martha's father.

Dorie ran across the drawing room floor, giggling as the elder Miss Davenport pretended to try and catch her. Miss Davenport might have had more success if she hadn't interrupted the chase to arrange her body in artful poses.

"Good to see the child acting like a child," said Nina. "That'll go a long way to making the bolsters feel secure."

"Secure?"

"Hard to entrust yourself and all your money to a man who *everyone knows* has a damaged child locked in an attic." Nina rose from her seat. "But you might not be all bad for her," she conceded.

Reflexively, Jane rose with her, watching Dorie giggle and slide.

"No, I never saw such a change in a child," said Nina. She smoothed her turquoise silk around her hips, readying to sweep back into the fray. "Very odd. It's as though she were released from chains."

Chains, thought Jane. *Iron chains,* and the image hit her like a blow.

She and Dorie, encased in iron, bound by it, enclosed by it. A sarcophagus, an iron maiden—the ironskin not armor but an airtight coffin.

She sat down hard on the chair, her legs suddenly wobbly and useless.

The iron was supposed to keep the fey curse from hurting others. From leaking out.

But what did it do to keep it in? What was it doing to Dorie?

And what had it already done to Jane?

Her fingers trembled on the folds of her dress. So she took the mask off for sleep. That was nothing compared to sixteen hours a day of steeping in the poison, year after year. She had stopped those she met from feeling transitory rage—and in return she had taken it all, until her soul was eaten away with self-loathing.

She watched the tiny blond girl smile up at the pretty ladies, her curls light and bouncing, and Jane felt sick. It had taken Nina to point out what Jane should've known immediately. It wasn't that Dorie was being stubborn and resistant, though she was. It was the iron making her ill by forcing her to bottle up her true self.

Jane rose, unsteady on her feet, fingers clutching her golden skirts to hold onto something, anything. Across the room she saw Edward's eyes go to her, saw him look worried at her distress, but she couldn't, she just couldn't, be there one more minute. She lurched from the drawing room, climbed the side stairs with nerveless feet, flung herself into the safety of her room.

The moonlight laid a square of white on the wooden floor and she stood on its edge till the light lapped her toes, glittered the hem of her dress. Breathing, breathing.

If she were right about this, then everything she had thought was wrong. The good she had attempted was bad, and not just for her.

And now it wasn't just that she would have to start working to undo years of damage.

She would have to reveal herself to the world.

Oh, say she was wrong, say it! She must be overreacting, must be mistaken. Anything so the answer was not inevitably: The mask comes off.

Jane spun to face the mirror. It was a good mirror, clear, unwavy. Unrepentant. Her iron mask looked back at her, her companion and protector, hiding the half-destruction. Skin on one side, iron on the other. Skin and iron, and her gauzy golden dress moonlit around her like fey light.

An explosion.

Through the mirror she looked until she saw, not Jane, but her past, the battlefield, plain as daylight and as immediate.

There was no sheltering past, no curtain of sleep to filter the nightmare, no, there it was, freed from its nightly confines to attack her in the day. There was her past, coming for her.

"Jane!" Mother shouts, but she does not turn. She won't embarrass Charlie by taking his hand or squeezing his shoulder, but she nods at him, and he nods back. There are no soldiers, no King's Men to come to their aid. They are all elsewhere, or dead. There is just them, clumped together on the white-grey moor, iron raised against an enemy.

Grim and white-faced they march across the moor.

That dawn Jane thought she saw no signal, no sign that the day was beginning. But she did, or perhaps she only sees it now, now in this living memory, this waking dream. An orange-blue flash like a comforting candle flame.

Then Sam—the baker's apprentice, the lighthearted boy she danced with once—explodes next to Charlie.

A cry goes up. "There! The fey! The fey!"

Bombs are costly for the fey, she knows. But fey have no body in their natural state, no way to touch humans. Their strategy is to kill the strongest humans and take over their bodies. Then in their borrowed human forms, they can fight. It is why they have been harrying the village before the battle. We knew it, Jane thinks, and yet our hearts lurch when our dead stagger out of the forest, swinging sharpened wooden picks at us.

"Stab them with the iron," she shouts to her little brother. "It's the only way to drive the fey out."

Charlie knows. And they advance, iron staves at the ready. It is gruesome work, and not all the villagers are up to the task. A man runs, retching. Jane's nerves are strung so tight that every fey she studies seems to be at the end of a long tunnel of fog. Or perhaps that is the actual fog, insistent and cruel, hiding their attackers until they are too near. A farmer she knows by sight runs at her with a sharpened wooden pole and she thinks it is all up. But Charlie trips him, and his clumsy dead feet fall over her. Jane rolls and stabs the dead farmer with the iron. Tentatively, then harder, reminding herself that war is not a time for politeness, reminding herself that this friendly farmer is now a mask worn by the fey.

As the iron goes in, the fey dies. A fey in a human body is vulnerable; the state in which they have bodies to kill is the state in which they can be killed. Blue light ripples around the stave and turns stark white, crackles, keens—is gone. For good. The farmer slumps into the dirt.

"Good work," Jane says to Charlie, who is ten feet off holding his iron bar. He smiles, that happy-boy smile she knows so well, and then a ball of orange-blue light and rock and glass falls behind him at his feet.

"Charlie!" she screams, and she runs toward him. *I think I can bat the bomb away with my iron staff, I think—I do not know what I think.* Time slows, and over his shoulder she sees the fey that threw it, a thin blue light with a carefully formed human face floating in its center. The face is exhausted, gloating.

Charlie has time to turn and see his death before it explodes.

The world is suddenly hot then, and full of rage. Her vision goes red and smeary. She loses some time then, in life, in the dream. The next thing she knows she is bent double, spearing her brother's chest with cold iron to destroy his killer. Blood drips from the left side of her face, and it seems that everything around her is very angry, though at that moment she feels nothing.

Nothing except for the weight of the cold iron in her hands. The battle has moved away, east across the moor, but she doesn't want to let the stave go. She clutches it to her chest as her other hand touches the strange whirring light that buzzes around her cheek. Her fingers come away wet and carmine and glowing. Shouts and clangs ring in the distance as blood drips down her chin, through her fingertips and onto the early yellow cowslips that dot the blackened moor.

Now in the bedroom of Silver Birch Hall, in this waking dream, the vantage point swings around until dreaming Jane is looking down at kneeling Jane. The kneeling girl raises her face, her gaze. Half of the girl's face is Jane's, clean and perfect, serene and trusting. The other half is an inky void, a *nothing,* a bottomless pit like a night without stars.

One green eye blinks in slow motion, falling like the crash of a piano lid. The girl's half-mouth moves, and words form in Jane's mind. It's a sentence, or maybe an echo of a sentence, repeated with the monotony of a ticking clock.

I am Jane, and you would be frightened to look upon me.

The room swam back into focus until Jane was merely staring at a mirror. Her fingers trembled.

She had to know.

Jane closed her eyes and unbuckled the straps of the mask as she did every night. The iron came away from her face, leaving little strips of cold where the edges had touched her around the cotton padding. The padding conformed to her face and it stayed there until Jane seized it at her chin and peeled it away, dropped it and the mask to the dresser with a cold thump. The mask rocked on the cheek plate, thrummed as it stilled.

If she was going to face the world like this, she had to know. No more hiding from the mirror.

This was the start of her new life, and from now on Jane would be strong. Would master the poison, somehow, or would learn to live with the anger she caused, or would learn to live alone. The image of herself flashed behind her closed eyes, the black nothingness splitting her face, and the girl repeating: *I am Jane, and you would be frightened to look upon me.*

I am Jane, I am Jane, I am Jane.

She opened her eyes.

Chapter 12

WITHOUT IRON

The iron mask gleamed dully in the morning sun, glinting light from where Jane had dropped it on the dresser the night before.

Jane was fully dressed for the day, her hand on the doorknob, and still she could not make herself leave the room without the mask. She could not walk out the door with that face.

That face that no one had seen in five years.

She told herself she should be bold, told herself she should not be ashamed of an accident that was not her fault. There was no reason to feel naked and exposed, as though she were walking down the street without a skirt. Her face was nothing to be ashamed of, and she needed to see what her life would be without iron.

She must go.

Jane opened the door and then heard Nina's drawling voice from the hall. "You can't possibly expect me to be up this early—oh, just give me the cup of chocolate and go. No, I don't want that leaden cow patty your cook calls a croissant."

The servant's reply was inaudible in the slamming of Jane's door.

Jane leaned against the back of the door, hand curled cold against her good cheek. Dorie she could face. Cook she could face. Maybe she could even screw up her courage to face Edward without her mask.

But she could not face all those women. She didn't really want to see any of the party guests, true, but she knew it was chiefly the women. The men were another species, out of reach, out of mind, but those horribly perfect women made her shrivel inside. Blanche Ingel with her heart-stopping beauty; Nina, who could be amusing one second and raze you with a single well-placed word the next.

Jane pressed her chest, willing her panic to slow. She would not put on the mask, but she would go veiled. Fair enough? She listened to her conscience inside, and it agreed: Yes. That will do to start.

Baby steps. Just like Dorie. Except no one would be Jane to her Dorie, so Jane would have to encourage herself, and not flay herself open over what she couldn't do. One step at a time.

Jane pinned her second-best hat to her head and wrapped the cotton veil around her bare cheek—several times, more fully than she'd hidden the first day here. At last her face was completely obscured once more. Her breath came slower as she hid herself away, protected herself.

Out into the hall.

This time it was empty. Some of the guests were on this floor, some on the third. It was just her bad luck to have Nina billeted between her and Dorie. Of course, in most regular households the governess would've been in the garret, and she would've had to brave the entire household to wend her way down to her charge.

Still, she was glad to slip inside Dorie's rooms without encountering anybody.

Dorie was in bed but not asleep. Jane saw with sinking heart that Martha had followed earlier instructions to put the gloves back on her at night. Dorie lay with her arms in iron, flat as a pancake, staring at the silver-papered ceiling.

Jane sat on the bed. Dorie did not move. "Here goes," she said, and unlocked the mesh gloves, peeled them from the child's pale skin. She rubbed Dorie's arms down with her hands as if human touch could dispel the aftereffects of iron.

Dorie finally looked interested as Jane got the blood flowing through her forearms. "Off?" she said, and there was a flicker of light in her eyes.

"Today and more," Jane said grimly. "I have a new bargain to make with you. You will work on your hands with me . . . and I will work on 'mother stuff' with you."

Dorie's blue eyes were wide.

"Only together, do you understand?" Jane seized Dorie's hands, drew them close to her, her voice falling to a fierce whisper. "This is no game. This can only be you and me in this room. Otherwise you and your father are in danger."

Dorie nodded, and there was gravity in the expression.

Jane breathed. "Now," she said. "Lift your quilt in the air. Without your hands."

Dorie spread her arms over the quilt and went silent. With a little tug and bobble, the quilt slowly rose. Then fell again, and Dorie looked surprised.

Jane nodded. "You're weak this morning. That's not surprising. Stop that for now and we'll have breakfast and do morning exercises with our hands. *If* you work hard, we'll come back to this before lunch. Understand?"

Dorie nodded. Then she smiled. "Yes, Miss Jane," she said clearly.

Jane smiled, and the action felt strange on her cheek, the skin crinkling against the cotton veil like the cracking of a porcelain mask. Or maybe the strangeness was that she almost felt like she could feel the little girl's emotions, and the strongest one was trust.

"I just don't see why you have to go without it," said Cook crossly. "Sure and if there's something that helps you withstand them, you seize it. Even if it is wearing iron across your face."

"But my worry is that it's *not* helping me," Jane said. She had offered to chop walnuts for that night's dessert, but the conciliatory gesture didn't lessen Cook's temper.

"You're still wearing a hat, aren't you then? Covered all up like a beekeeper in June. Not like *that'll* be normal."

Jane knew that the normally friendly and cheery cook couldn't help her reaction to Jane. She knew intimately how frustrating it was to react in anger when you didn't think of yourself as an angry person. She hadn't been, once. She'd been even tempered, patient with children, tolerant of others' foibles.

Cook threw chopped yellow onions in the pot with sharp splashes. "It's not right, and you not knowing how Dorie will react. Children need careful handling. You've got to be thinking of her."

"I am, truly," said Jane. She attempted a smile, though she

knew it was obscured by layers of cotton. "It's all part of the master plan."

Cook folded bay leaves and long runners of thyme into a square of cheesecloth. She didn't turn around. "There are plenty here who'd give nigh anything to stop their curses and you just let it out."

"Plenty? Who?"

"Never you mind, missy. You just sit down and give it all a good long think, that's what." Cook tied off the bag of herbs with twine and dropped it in the pot, washed her hands of the argument. "Now I've said my piece and I'm done. You'll be passing me the walnuts now."

With the back of a butcher knife, Jane scraped them from the chopping block into a green bowl. "Did Mr. Rochart need careful handling, too? When he was young?"

"And how should I be knowing that?" Cook said. "He didn't grow up here."

"Oh," said Jane, and then remembered Nina saying last night that he had grown up abroad. "But this house belonged to his family, yes?"

"It'll be the family house, sure, and we all knew the last Mr. Rochart. Cross old man, rest him—he paid his workers fair and just, but never a kind word for any soul. He died a good decade before the war, and the house sat empty till this Mr. Rochart returned. A grandson, you see. His da had run off when he was just a boy—some quarrel, and the old man never forgave him."

"Then when did Mr. Rochart come back?"

"Just after the Great War started," Cook said, "but that's enough asking into your master's business."

Jane thought it better not to point out that Cook frequently volunteered similar innocuous gossip, common knowledge that had been in the village for decades. "I liked the croissants you made this morning," she offered, like an olive branch. "With the chocolate in them."

"Sure and you got one of mine," Cook said, flicking flour into the bowl. "I'll tell you, none of these girls from the village knows how to make a decent pastry, never mind it's a skill every mother should've taught them. But no one has enough time to fold a thousand layers of pastry, let alone the cost of the butter to go between them, and it does cost, because no one has cows any more than they have the cinema, nothing is the same at all. . . ."

Detoured on the new rant, Cook briskly dumped honey and eggs into the walnuts, preparing the filling for the tart. Her treatment of Jane brought a sour feeling to her stomach. This is how it had been five years ago, hadn't it? It was as if all her time with the mask had been undone. And yet, was she wrong to try it? If one way brought frustration to Jane and one way to everyone else, what was the morally correct thing to do?

She sighed, wishing there were a third way. Poule had suggested that her water imagery was the right path, but was it really helping, or was that just wishful thinking? She would have to be pretty darn watery to counteract this curse. But it wasn't like she had anything else to try, and there was no one inside her head to see the silliness. So why not? She would be a cheerful sparkling pond, drowning the orange flames of her cheek before they could even spring up. So cool and watery that fish could swim around inside her skull, as if her head were a glass bowl. The ridiculous image cheered her.

Poule came through the kitchen door with mail in hand—circulars and a letter for Cook that the woman seemed pleased to get. She silently handed Jane a thick cream-colored envelope. Then, leaning closer, she stared at Jane's veil. Jane was surprised to realize that she did not instantly take offense at the impertinence. No, she was perfectly calm and interested, a cool still pond, wondering what Poule's reaction would be. The woman had seemed to withstand it the other night, but . . . Well. Jane didn't think she could bear it if *everyone* in the house hated her.

Poule's nostrils flared and Jane remembered how she had scented after the fey in the woods. The short woman spread her hand wide and reached high, high to Jane's face, briefly touched the crook between thumb and index finger to Jane's chin, as if she were measuring it. Jane managed not to flinch. Poule's silver hair streamed loose, iridescent in the sun, rippling like the waves on her imaginary Jane pond.

"I've felt worse," Poule said at last. She dropped her hand and turned to go, treading heavily across the grey kitchen stone.

"Wait," said Jane. "What do you mean?"

Poule stopped at the door. "I mean we have tales of a dwarf named Moum who got cursed with rage. He started three wars, and his children tore each other to bloody bits." She shrugged. "Say what you like, but I don't have any urge to rend Creirwy."

The cook laughed as she beat the filling. "I should hope not."

Jane pulled her paper knife from a drawer and slit open the heavy stationery that Helen favored. Four heavily written-on pages fell out, plus a thin blue-and-white photo of Helen in a dark gown, and a scrap of rose fabric.

She skimmed the parties and balls. Alistair had one of the last working fey-tech cameras, and here she was before opening night of a new production of *A Midsummer Night's Tragedy*. She had a new afternoon tea dress, and here was a swatch so Jane could see how it would complement her complexion. Jane laughed, imagining Helen sending a swatch of complexion as well. Then she sobered as she started on the last page.

"You asked me point-blank what I meant by 'Ironskin or no.' My ever-blunt Jane! And also you wondered if my fine friends care nothing for the war, think little of it, &c. I assure you it is true, and I am only reporting to you what I see around me. I try to be as cynical as the next woman about the malingerers who yet line our hospitals, and I try to accept it when my bosom friend Gertrude steers us clear of a begging ironskin in the street. I know she knows of you and has only pity for me, but I don't think she understands what it means, and how that iron leg she reviles is at least the common decency of that poor boy to cover up a horrible curse. And yet she thinks he should go one step farther, and shut himself up so he is not seen at all.

"They all think that, Jane, and so I wonder what would happen if you came to live with me as I previously begged you to do. I suppose we should become social pariahs after all. That is not something I thought a month ago at the wedding, but I do believe that the society here gets more and more rarefied each day, as all these fine ladies and gentlemen try to hide anything that reminds them of the war far, far away, and move on with their lives. I do not believe they can conceive of what it was like to be in the country—the women, I mean. The men who had to fight understand it well enough, though I am rather shocked at the number of men who paid a poor servant to take their place in the war. Alistair would call that naïve of me, and of course I understand that some lives are simply more important—their loss would make a greater impact, tear a bigger hole in the silk of society. And I knew full well when I married him that even my darling Alistair avoided the war, and I am glad of it.

"And yet . . . I am not certain it seems right. Sometimes I think, would Jane approve of this? I can hear your sharp tongue decrying it even as I write.

"By the time you read this I shall be past caring what others think of me. My Alistair has introduced me to a very surprising secret—a secret which you would no doubt be shocked to hear! Very soon those 'fine ladies' will be forced to treat me as one of their own, and their malicious tongues shall be well-stopped. Or rather, I shall be proof against anything said.

"Now you *must* come, for with this new capital I shall be able to champion even you. No doubt I shall hardly have time to see you between invitations, and yet I will, I must. . . . Do come.

"Your loving sister, Helen."

Worry, empathy, irritation, all snaked through Jane's core and made heavy her heart. She folded up the letter and slipped it into the bottom of her trunk.

"We'll play a game," said Jane. She was sitting across the room from Dorie, keeping a watchful eye for any uncharacteristic signs of anger. She was also still thinking of herself as a calm pool of water, because if nothing else, it reminded her not to let her temper carry her from normal-cursed Jane into orange-tongues-of-fire Jane. It seemed as though the imagery was helping with Dorie—the girl was not reacting to Jane's anger the way Cook had been. Although that could be due to Dorie's strange fey talent. It was so hard to tell.

"I like games," said Dorie. She was speaking more this week, Jane noticed, answering with short sentences rather than nods and shakes of the head. Jane wondered if it was increased confidence, or comfort, or merely practice in listening to people hold conversations—maybe the chattering party guests were good for something after all.

"I'm going to throw a ball at you," Jane said. "I want you to bat it away from you, just using your fey talent. Shall we give it a go?" In her mind this "game" was defense, but she wasn't about to explain that to Dorie.

Dorie nodded, then remembered her voice and added: "Yes, please."

Jane scrunched a cloth napkin into a ball and wrapped it with a length of string. She tossed it across the room toward Dorie's lap, where it fell on her knee, bounced, and rolled away.

Dorie examined where the ball had come to a halt, then hefted it into the air. It glowed a faint blue. She let go, and it fell to the floor again.

"Now try doing that quicker," said Jane. "When I throw the ball, grab it from the air." She retrieved the balled-up napkin, tossed it again, and again Dorie missed it.

"Again," Jane said. "Lash out at it."

Dorie tried to obey, but what she seized was her Mother doll that lay on the bed, near the arc of the napkin ball. Glowing blue with streaks of orange, the doll slipped off the bed and thumped to the floor.

It was either a problem of dexterity or a problem of being out of practice. Or both. Just as catching a ball with your hands was a learned skill, so was catching a napkin with your mind. Dorie had built towers the first week Jane was there, before she got the tar, but that was a process of raising each piece and stacking it. Jane was certain Dorie could do this—but it was different.

"Let's drop the throwing part of it for now," said Jane, after several more attempts resulted in utter failure. She paced over to the window, thinking.

Below she could see the hired servants setting up chairs and gay canopies for a tea party on the back lawn. She wondered if the fine ladies would be nervous so close to the forest. They "cared nothing for the war," but surely here in the war-torn country it would strike home. Jane scanned the trees, as she always did, but she saw no tall dark form, saw no blue flickering lights. Just yellow and white ruffled swathes of silk, casting dark rectangles on the green lawn. Near the patio, two men were setting up a maypole. April was almost through, and that meant May Day, the last day of the Great War five years ago, the day the fey vanished. Of course the guests would enjoy the dancing and drinking aspect of the war holiday—would expect some sort of celebration. They just wouldn't think about what it meant.

Jane turned and sighed. She was a lovely blue pond, who cared nothing about picnics on the lawn or thoughtless city-born guests. She picked up the Mother doll and held it in front of her. "Try pushing this away."

Dorie fidgeted, frustrated, considering. Behind the obscuring layers of veil, Jane could not see the minute changes in expression she usually relied on, usually watched like a hawk.

Yet it was odd—half-blind, she seemed to have a better sense of Dorie's mood shifts than she ever had before. Perhaps it was that she had grown close to the girl; perhaps she was picking up on body position, breaths, sighs—because she was sensing Dorie's flickering changes, pinpointing her mute emotions with a sense that seemed eerily spot-on.

"If you work hard now, you can go to the tea party later on," said Jane. The mandatory event made for good bartering.

Jane felt Dorie make the decision to try. She looked up at the doll.

Jane held the doll's waist, readying for a small wobbly pressure as Dorie tried this new trick. "Just push it away."

Dorie bit her lip, concentrating.

Blue light gathered on the doll in Jane's hands, bathing its porcelain face in fey glow.

The Mother doll exploded in Jane's hands.

Dorie's face went to utter shock, then crumpled. She ran to Jane, flung herself into Jane's arms, and Jane, as shocked by that as by anything, enfolded her in her embrace and stroked the fuzzy curls.

"There, there," Jane said. "There, there." She tugged her veil out from under Dorie's fierce hug, freeing her neck. Despite the extra warmth of the cotton swathing her face, cold shivers ran up and down her spine.

What had she unleashed?

Jane backed out of Dorie's room with an apronful of porcelain shards. Dorie had sobbed herself to sleep. In between sobs she had said once, quite clearly, "Put the gloves back on." Jane held the girl close and did not comply.

A swish of black skirts on the right—Nina's back, turning,

closing her bedroom door. Jane turned to the left, pretending not to see, hoping to move quickly on noiseless feet, but the broken porcelain clinked in her apron, and anyway, Nina was ever too aware of who might be around her.

A black satin arm snaked through Jane's bent one and Jane could not free herself without dropping the porcelain shards.

"Let me guess," said Nina, nodding at the swathing white veil. "You're a new widow with a fear of sunstroke." She eyed the apron filled with pink shards and two unbroken blue glass eyes. "And you've dropped your husband's urn. Pity about his blindness."

A blue lake, a calm blue lake where no fire could burn.

"You'll take me to Edward's studio now, won't you?" Though the words were a petitioner's, submissive, the amused drawl belied that. "He truly is expecting me this time." Nina produced a small calling card from her décolletage, one of Mr. Rochart's. In black spiky ink he had written "3:00" on the back. As if in response, the grandfather clock far below began to peal the hour.

"That could be any day, any place," Jane said, but only because Nina expected her to put up a fight. She wasn't the guardian of his studio, and it wasn't up to her to decide whom he should entertain there. She continued down the hall, leading them around the maze of stairs and turns into the abandoned wing.

"It was three a.m., and he wrote it in my rooms while lying blissfully on the chaise . . . ," parried Nina, but her words trailed off. She fell uncharacteristically silent as they went up the dark stairs.

Though Nina's face was its usual mask of arrogance—

haughty tilt of brow, sneer in the lips—somehow Jane knew, she *knew* that Nina was frightened.

They rounded the section where the stairs curved back and the hidden mirror startled them with their shadowy figures rushing in. Nina tightened her grip on Jane's arm but calmly she said, "I can't stand fey architecture."

"Personally, I'd be more worried about spiders in this wing than fey," Jane said. "And rats. Spiders and rats, everywhere you look. The rats eat hair, you know. Late at night, when you're asleep."

Nina said nothing, which made Jane all the more sure that she was right: Nina was afraid. She must be keeping an appointment—a surgical one. Because Nina wouldn't be this nervous if she were keeping an assignation with Edward, no matter what ruse she tried to imply. Nina probably ate men like him for breakfast.

They emerged at the top of the house, which was darker than Jane expected. Black wool curtains had been hung at all the windows, extinguishing the sunlight. She wondered where he'd gotten the money for those, and then Nina gripped Jane's arm closer, crushing it into her satin side. Her nails were chips of tile pinching Jane's skin. "You wait for something for so long," she said, "and when it comes, can it possibly live up to your expectations?"

"Not likely," Jane said softly.

"The bolsters think a face is as easily changed as a dress," Nina said. "You are the only one who might understand that you live in your face. As much as you long for the improvement, you know you will lose something, too. Well, you will see soon enough. I have seen your face, you know. Pretty enough if you like that sort of thing, but I would rather be me."

Jane stared at her. Nina did not notice. All her attention was in front of her, on that slab of wood, on the studio door.

"I'm going to see me now," she whispered. "The me I will soon be." Her fingers lifted away from Jane's arm, and she raised her hand to knock.

The door opened partway before her knuckles could hit the door, opened just enough for Jane to see a shadowy Mr. Rochart standing in the dark, opened just enough for Nina to slide through. His eyes fell on Jane and she backed away. The door closed and a strip of green-gold light turned on, lighting the crack under it. The top floor was dark except for that glowing strip of light.

Jane moved with nerveless feet down the steps.

Nina and Edward—no.

Well, maybe, but—something else.

Her face. Nina had seen her face.

Edward had sculpted her face.

Jane stumbled down the stairs, feet nerveless beneath her, slipping from one step to the next. The bottom dropped from her stomach as she ran through the thought of what Edward might be contemplating.

A new face. A whole face.

Normal.

The agony of desire struck her at a million points, a net constricting her skin, drawing her tight around that piercing hope.

To be normal.

She cried out, batting aside that hope, telling it to vanish, but it wouldn't, it multiplied, insinuated itself into her brain, telling of all the joys she could have if only she were whole, if she were normal, if the last five years were only a bad dream.

She stumbled to the landing with the hidden mirrors. Pictures of impossible memories blinded her sight, obscuring the Janes rushing in to meet her with a different Jane. Jane in that other timeline, that one where tall Charlie had sat beside her at Helen's wedding, that one where her family was not blindsided by war.

Jane walking through Crown Park in a yellow voile sundress, arm slung around the shoulders of a blond girl her age, laughing hysterically over an incident in her life drawing class involving a male model and his determination to pose *au naturale,* as one did in Varee. The normally dignified teacher had smacked his disrobing rear end with a broom.

Jane leaning over the opera balcony before the start of *Ma Petite Chou-Chou.* Seeing a knot of friends below waving wildly to her, trying to get her attention. "Jane," they shout, doubling over with laughter. One of the girls flips open a fan and dances with it à la Chou-Chou. Shocking, riotous, joyous. Shouting: "Jane!"

Jane in Helen's new pink sitting room, looking into the mirror before a dance. Her cheeks are flushed; her dark hair frames her face. She is solemn and fluttery, for tonight she will see him again, and tonight is the time that something important will happen, a declaration, a step into the future. She enters her sister's fancy drawing room where the rich folk flit like champagne bursting and the gaslights dot yellow against the papered walls. And there he is, tall and dark, a man gaunt with the aftereffects of war. A widower, a heavyhearted man with a bite to his tongue, a man whose eyes light when they fall on her in the borrowed silver dress. The only man she could talk freely to, the only man she could ever love . . .

Veiled Jane swam back into view.

"Edward," Jane whispered aloud to the stairwell. Her heart seemed to be breaking into a million shattered pieces, and the revelation of her face was only part of it, the crack in the frozen river that opened a hole to the raging current beneath. "I love Edward."

Porcelain shards tumbled to the carpet, spattered the floor like cracking ice.

Chapter 13

THE LAST RAY OF SUNLIGHT

Jane was still woozy when Dorie woke from her nap late in the afternoon. Desire made her nerves twitch, made every step rock with the suppressed hope that threatened to explode, to split her apart.

She sat on a bench partly concealed by the shrubbery and kept one eye on Dorie while the Misses Davenport petted her and fed her chocolate cakes under the yellow striped canopies on the slope of the lawn. She wondered if they were always so fond of children, or if it was the presence of an eligible suitor that brought out their doting. No, surely she was being catty. Jane sketched Dorie kneeling in the grass, and watched her tears from the morning vanish as the pretty ladies cosseted her. Dorie was blissful as the girls slipped her bites off of thin silver forks.

"It's perfect," marveled a deep voice over her shoulder. "Chocolate cake without using her hands for anything."

Her heart lurched as she turned.

Mr. Rochart stood behind her shoulder, half hidden in the curve of the laurels. He must have finished his appointment with Nina.

Seeing him brought back all the agony of a couple hours ago. It was the first time she'd seen him since she thought that he might be planning to help her, the first time since she truly admitted what she hoped, what she could be allowed to desire if only she weren't who she was.

"Perhaps she can get them to feed her breakfast, too," Jane found herself saying. "That is, if her father's in the room." She had not meant to say that, and the blood pounded in her damaged cheek. Flustered, she patted her cheek to make sure the veil was still in place, reminded herself to continue her thoughts of water, calm and cold.

"Wicked girl," growled Mr. Rochart. "Youngsters are not supposed to see so keenly into the faults of mortals."

"And at what age am I allowed to see what's in front of my nose? I am twenty-one, you know. I hope I shan't have to feign blindness much longer." She marveled at the steadiness of her voice.

"All of twenty-one?" He considered her for a silent moment. "I thought you were yet two years from that." His smile was mocking, ironic. "Ah, Jane. How unfortunate that you should be a third my age."

"Your numbers exaggerate, sir." Calmly, coolly, though her heart beat hard against her chest. "Two-thirds at most, I should say, for there is no grey on your temple, and you do not order stewed prunes at breakfast, like a grandfather in his dotage."

"You are too kind to me," he said, and he brushed aside her covering hand to view her sketch.

Jane willed her embarrassment at her amateur drawing to subside. He was a real artist, with a decade more experience besides. It took all her courage not to snatch the drawing away and close the sketchpad so he couldn't see it.

"The angle of the knees is off," he said.

"I know," said Jane, looking at that over-erased spot. She clamped her lips closed on a torrent of other inadequacies she could plainly see.

"And yet you have captured something of the spirit, which is far more important. It is Dorie to the life. May I?"

Jane nodded, let him take her pencil.

He studied the girl for a moment, then with firm black strokes corrected the tilt of the waist, the knees, the toes digging into the ground. "Always draw what's underneath," he said, "before you get to the folds and lace on top. You should have a life drawing class."

Jane did not say the obvious, that there were very many things that this Jane would have liked to have.

Perhaps he saw the stubborn set of her lips, for he returned to a discussion of what he did like. "Yes, something in the chin, the tilt of the head, is just right. Happy only when she is being adored. She is so like . . ."

"Her mother?"

"Though it pains me to admit it."

"Because you miss her," prompted Jane, uncertain why else the thought would pain him.

He handed the pencil back to her. It was warm from his hands. She let it lie loosely in her palm.

"And now it is expected that I should take a new bride," he said. "Dorie needs a mother, and the staff need someone else to cosset, someone who does not gruffly lock himself in an attic for weeks at a time. Miss Ingel is their frontrunner, I believe, for she is wealthy and kind and has a decade on those little chits the Misses Davenport. Yet another worry to add to my plate." His fingers rested lightly on the sketch of Dorie.

"Oh," said Jane. She did not wish to say anything, yet the syllable burst forth anyway. There were so many things she wanted to say, and did not want to say, and letting the "Oh" escape at least stopped the incoherent words of desire for him, for her, from tumbling from her lips.

There was silence in that misty air. She was transfixed by those amber eyes, caught, searching their blackening depths. Had he really sculpted her face? And why? Was he as curious as she to know what she might have been?

Silence, and him watching her veil flutter. "You're not wearing your mask," he said.

Jane's hand flew to her cotton veil. "Does it bother you? Can you feel the curse?"

He leaned close, considering.

Surely her chest did not always rise and fall this much; surely her breaths were usually even and regular, barely disturbing the profile of her dress. Water, she thought, water to suffocate the flames. I could not bear it if he raged at me.

"I don't know," he said at last. "I am certainly angry that this happened to you, but I have felt that since shortly after we met."

"Perhaps you have more practice dealing with strangeness, because of Dorie."

"Perhaps I have too much anger of my own to tell. If a man is steeped in bitter anger every day of his life, how then would he notice a small additional fire? Particularly when the fire comes in the presence of . . ."

She was silent as his eyes searched past her veil for hers. He was the source of all that she wanted, she knew that now, and the burdens of that were too much for one man to bear. She was insignificant; she could not be to him a tenth of what he represented to her.

And yet, she felt something as he leaned in. It was oddly similar to the way she had seemed to sense Dorie's feelings. Not her desire . . . but his?

His breath made his voice rumble. "Words, I fling words at you, and still you bear up under them, Jane. Yet if you knew what I had seen, accepted, nay, desired . . . it would shock you. You are too unspoiled. If *they* knew, they would all leave, all those women, and good riddance. But the hurt to me is that I would lose your good opinion forever."

The accusation of naïveté echoed Alistair's words, and she could not bear it from him. Oh, why did everyone think that because she was a scarred governess that she understood nothing, saw nothing, felt nothing?

"I cannot believe you are evil," she said. "If all the world spat on you, what care I for the world? If they all left you in a great flurry of fear, I should still be here, and stay by your side."

"I almost believe you would," he said softly.

The silence was too charged on that, and she rushed on: "Anyway, I know what you have done."

"You know . . . ?"

"Nina mentioned certain things and I uncovered the truth of the matter to my satisfaction. You are no mere artist in clay, but another sort altogether."

"Jane."

She lowered her voice. "I understand why you keep it hidden, why none of your clients talk. It would be embarrassing for them, surely."

His lips opened to speak, while that same rushing desire for *normal* welled up in her like a river that could not be contained, a waterfall that threatened to break open upon her lips.

"Jane, I—"

"Mr. Rochart, if—"

"Oh, Edward!" cooed a young voice from the lawn, and another girl giggled. "Come see what we have made for our little pet."

Silence.

"You are called," said Jane, and she bent her head away from those amber eyes.

"Of course, Miss Eliot." A sharp bow, and he straightened with a smile, stiffened his spine as if arming for the fray. "Miss Davenports One and Two! I have been too long deprived of your company."

The two girls, Dorie, and Edward formed a happy little knot on the lawn, laughing and flirting as if nothing could possibly be more important. It was very like the happy moment in the bedroom that night he brought her the golden dress, except this time she was on the outside looking in.

The waterfall of desire spilled over into her eyes and she turned away from the group into the bushes, shoulders jerking, trying to regain her composure. "Not for you," she whispered fiercely. "Not for you."

It was some minutes before she could turn back to the lawn. Edward was surrounded by Blanche and Mrs. Davenport, each clinging to an arm and holding a very spirited discussion about what Edward should do next. The younger Miss Davenport was off finding croquet mallets with a gentleman, and the elder Miss Davenport was sulking. Jane blinked, blotting her eyes with the cuff of her sleeve.

Dorie was nowhere in sight.

The sketchpad and pencil fell from nerveless fingers, thumped to the damp grass. Jane whirled, looking up and down the lawn. Any second she would see Dorie's curls bouncing around that willow, see her tumbling down the slope, showing off for the pretty ladies.

No Dorie.

Jane ran—her feet took her to the sulking girl on the divan, and though Jane had never spoken to her, she did not even notice that now she spoke firmly, commanding—"Where's Miss Rochart?"

The elder Miss Davenport sat up straight, saw for herself the girl's absence, started babbling. "It's not my fault, I'm not in charge of her, you can't blame me . . ."

There was fear in her eyes, and Jane pressed further, harder, seized the girl's silk-trussed arms and shook her. "Where did she go?"

The silly girl was unable to speak, fright at being scolded turning to tears in her eyes.

The rage rose up in Jane at the delay, broke through the calm pond. She was all hot rage and orange fire, so fierce and strong that she lost control. She could not feel her fingers pinned on the girl's arms, she did not know what she was saying, only that she was shouting something about the idiocy of city girls who spent the war sheltered and foolish, who had never learned to use their brains.

Miss Davenport was completely unable to speak now, and something snapped in Jane and pushed through her rage. It was like a shiver of lightning, a force, something hot and fierce and fine, willing the girl: *Tell me where Dorie is.*

A pale blue light flickered across the elder Miss Davenport's face, and her eyes went glassy, and she broke. "Into the woods," she said, the words forcing themselves from her lips. She seemed unable to look away from Jane's gaze. "She just wanted to look at the foxgloves. . . ."

Jane dropped the girl's arms and flung herself past the fox-gloves edging the wood, under branches, through brambles. Dimly she was aware of Mr. Rochart wresting himself away from the women to follow. The rage was white hot all through her, making it hard to think, hard to run without numb feet stumbling. This was no good; she would be as useless as the Misses Davenport if she could not bring herself back to reason.

There was a natural clearing a few yards in and Jane stopped, willing her rage to clear. The water imagery was useless in the face of that snapped bolt of rage—she could not think of anything except her anger at the girl who had done nothing more than looked the other way, not been on guard. Her rage frightened her, as well as that strange moment when it was almost as if she had bent the girl to her will.

The rage might not go, but she would not let it stop her from finding her little girl. Through the hot rage she turned around in the clearing. "Dorie?" she shouted. "Dorie?" There was no answering sound.

The already obscured view of Mr. Rochart's lawn was the only bright spot in the trees around her; on all other sides the forest was green-black and dim. Well past the last ray of sunlight. Jane's eyes flicked to rustles of leaves, small brown birds, a vole. At any moment there might be blue light slipping through the trees, back from a five-year absence to find her, to find Dorie. Blue, limning the silver birch, the parasitic mistletoe. Blue that came sharp and fast and hot, blue that whip-cracked your life like lightning striking a strong chestnut tree, tearing it in half. . . .

"Have you seen any trace of her?" His breath came fast.

Jane nearly jumped out of her boots. "No," she said. The hot orange was giving way to fear. Anger and fright could make her do foolish things. She steeled herself, trying to find her even keel. "Should we split up?"

"Not a chance," said Edward, and his hand clamped down on her wrist. "Stay with me."

He ducked under a low-hanging branch and set off carefully but purposefully, as if following a trail only he could see. Several times he lifted his head, as if scenting the air or listening—something using a sense other than sight. Though he dropped her arm so they could navigate the narrow trail, Jane stayed close on his heels, trying to keep the ends of her veil out of the grip of brambles and twigs.

A blue light flashed in the clearing.

"There, over there!" cried Jane, and she took his arm as if she could physically propel him to his daughter's side. She crashed past him, tugging, because for a moment he just stood there with stricken eyes.

"The Queen," Edward said, and his amber eyes were black and wild.

She tugged on his sleeve and slowly he moved again, running after her to where the blue light had been.

"Nothing," she said, looking at the empty clearing. "Nothing," and suddenly she whirled, thoughts flying—"What do you know about this forest? You grew up here. You were out here last week, when I found you. Where would the fey likely be?" Even before the Great War, when the fey had been half-made-up tales, still there had been signs. Rings where they gathered, clearings where they were said to bask, trees they swarmed in. All the spots that when you were five you believed might truly be fey, and not just fireflies.

But he shook his head, and that dazed expression was in his eyes. "I didn't find what I sought," he said. "I don't think. I have been losing time. There are large gaps, just like the time before that, the long time. . . ."

Jane tugged on his sleeve. "Stay with me," she said fiercely.

He willed himself back to the present with a great effort. Strain showed around the corners of his eyes. "The forest has changed," he said hoarsely. "When I knew it as a child, it wasn't evil. You could still walk there by day, at least. It wasn't a habitat." He looked around, palms spread out as if trying to determine where he was by feeling the air around him. "But . . . closer to the creek, I think. If we walk . . ." His hands groped through the air as if questing for that spot. "If we walk through here . . ."

Edward pushed through an unlikely looking pair of bushes and Jane followed on his heels. They spilled out into another clearing—the forest seemed to be nothing but round clearings linked by dense brush, which sent shivers down her spine. That was not natural growth, nor human-made—no, that was all fey.

Habitat, as Edward had said.

Edward felt forward with his hands, palms outward. "Most peculiar," he muttered to himself. "I can almost *feel* the way with my hands. . . . This way or this way. . . ."

"Is that—what is that?" She lunged for a scrap of blue just past Edward, down the first "this way." Caught her toe in the fork of a fallen branch, went flying. Her veil caught and snicked tight around her throat and she pushed breathlessly, uselessly at it, tried to extricate herself from the wild and weaving branches that framed the clearing. Spots danced in front of her sight, silver and blue.

Then strong hands were around her waist, hauling her upward, untangling her veil from the bush, and as they touched her she suddenly thought, He loves me, and in the next instant didn't know why she thought she knew it. Once standing, his hands did not linger, but took the blue scrap of cloth from her to study.

"It's hers," Jane managed, between catching her breath, trying not to look sideways at this man who had hauled her up so effortlessly. Not effortlessly in the sense of strength, though he was strong, but in the sense that he could touch her waist and recover, that it should so clearly not bother him when she could still feel the imprint of his fingers on her ribs.

How could she think that he loved her? She knew full well he did not think of her at all. How could he, when he'd never even seen her face? He had no object to fasten on—she could only ever be a cipher to him, a shadowy governess form hidden behind cotton veils, behind an iron mask.

"This way," he said, and hurried past the bush, squeezing his lanky figure past it into the next open space, hands feeling forward in that strange testing, questing motion, as if they were drawn by a magnet.

She was following him, and then she caught something out of the corner of her eye and she went that way, plowing through black branches that tore at her hands and dress and veil, pushing through leaves coated in sticky sap and spiderwebs, twigs with thorns and bark that raked her ankles and elbows. Her veil caught and pulled, but it had been unwound in the first tumble, and now it ripped free. Her hat came completely off and she felt air against her cheek, but she did not stop.

In the clearing ahead—

"Dorie!" shouted Jane, and then a blue-orange light blinded her.

Jane's cheek flamed hot and she stumbled, momentarily

sightless. As she fell, groping for purchase, she wondered wildly if perhaps there were no fey in the woods at all. Perhaps she had misjudged the limits of Dorie's abilities, perhaps— and her heart raced as she hit the ground, still waiting for the world to come back into focus—perhaps giving Dorie permission to work on her skills had changed her, developed her beyond their ability to control.

That exploded doll. Shards of porcelain.

Dorie's stricken face.

Perhaps Jane had unwittingly unleashed a monster out of this little girl.

Vision was returning slowly, like the old fey cameras did, their blue-and-white image slowly revealing itself on the page. Dorie, she only saw Dorie, raising her hands against the sky.

Jane rubbed her eyes, strained them trying to see in more detail than shades of twilight blue. Still Dorie, only Dorie . . .

The thought flashed that this was what taking chances was—you always thought in the back of your mind that doing the right thing would lead you down the right path to the right outcome. But when it came down to it, you might still fail, and everything might end in disaster. Faith in your decision did not mean that the best was going to happen.

Color leaked into Jane's sight and she froze, watching the clearing now with full vision.

In the green-lit clearing, the little girl was both there and not there, shimmering like the gold and sapphire scarves of light that whisked around her. The old instinctive fear ran sharp and hot through Jane; her fingers curled, everything tensed, and her face was on fire.

That was not just Dorie, and she was not imagining things.

That was the fey.

Chapter 14

ATTACK

The fey that hadn't been seen in five years.

The fey that would destroy you to claim your form—and you with no way to kill them in their natural shape.

There was little Jane could do without a weapon. No way to even protect herself without iron. She knew this in her bones like she knew how to breathe. And yet she staggered to her feet, stumbled into the clearing, her human instinct sure she should do something to protect her little girl. The shimmers of blue-orange fey coalesced into one form, a form with a heartbreaking female face that curled in the air around Dorie.

The fey *looked* at her. And then a wall of black fear swept over Jane, swept in through her face, and it was the nameless terror of her nightmares.

It was a fey attack, though she had never heard of one like this.

There was a strange feeling all through her—fear and attack all mixed up together—and Jane felt as though her thoughts were being scrambled away from her and into something else, some other thing.

No, she protested, *no*—and she recoiled from it, while simultaneously it seemed to be recoiling from her. Disgust—revulsion—distaste—ugly, ugly—pull back, pullbackpullback . . . The attack of fear fell away, and Jane still stood, as the fey surrounded the translucent Dorie.

Jane made her shaky legs go forward, heart galloping a mile a minute. She groped in her pockets for a nonexistent feyjabber, pushed her way into the clearing. Dorie stood in a circle of grey stones, a circle with a wall of hard air that Jane's fingers would not go through. "Are you all right, Dorie?" Her voice was remarkably steady.

Shimmering, Dorie came loose from the fey's encircling light, bounced through the hard air past the stones to Jane, sweeping through her. Jane felt the touch thrum through her body like the pattering of rain, a distinctly opposite feeling from fey invasion. "My pretty lady," Dorie said, and Jane felt those words like a smile deep in her body. Dorie bounced back to the fey, cradled herself in that light.

The fey's imaged face was calm after that first attack. Disturbingly calm, like the destroyed porcelain doll. She observed Jane. Studied the war-torn face that her people had caused. Her voice, when she spoke, was high and throbbed somewhere in Jane's skull. "You. Must leave us. It is my child."

"No," said Jane. "She is human." She remembered what Edward had said. "Just because you stole her mother's body doesn't make Dorie yours." She didn't know why, but again she tried to take a step forward, as if trying to fight a fey without shielding or feyjabbers—madness. The fey had weapons with which they could destroy her in an instant. Wasn't her cheek a reminder of that failed attempt?

The fey said, "My small part-of-me," in a voice that Jane

felt rather than heard. The fey blazed up hot and gold and shaming, and Jane despaired, felt herself being frightened from the clearing by the sheer force of fey emotion. Before she could master her own emotions, she was huddled in the brush outside the clearing, weeping at her inability to act.

Steps behind her—Edward coming up, coming past her. Her tears blurred her sight as the light dimmed, died, faded away to nothing. Jane sprang up, temper rebounding high, pushed into the clearing—but the fey was gone.

Dorie lay on the ground inside the stones, a crumpled heap of silk dress and tangled curls. One hand curled around a broken foxglove whose orange petals were lit with fey glow.

"Dorie," said Edward, and his voice broke on the word. He knelt beside her, but Jane was already there, checking, waiting, dying—finding that slow pulse fluttering in Dorie's neck.

"She's breathing," Jane said, and the tears ran down her ruined cheek. She gently wrested the poisonous foxglove away from the curled fingers, threw it. "Dorie? Can you hear me?"

Dorie mumbled something and scrunched her eyes tighter.

"Dorie, sweetheart." Pleading. "Wake up."

Dorie's breathing became stronger, more regular, and her pulse strengthened under Jane's touch. But she did not open her eyes.

Edward cradled his daughter to him and stood. The shadow was dark on his face as he raised his eyes—and looked straight at her face.

Her bare face with no veil, no mask.

Jane swallowed. She knew what he saw. She felt his shock like a whiplash against bare skin. She crushed Dorie's tiny hand in hers—could not let go of the charge she cared for, even though that meant she was standing a handsbreadth away from Edward.

How could she have thought simply—he can't love me as he's never seen my face?

Because he had. If Nina spoke true, he had made her face. Sculpted it, to see her as she should have been.

So no, what she meant was—I'm not normal. He couldn't care for her when she wasn't normal. Even the fey had rejected her. Edward and Dorie were not her family. Ugly ugly unclean . . .

"Jane . . . ," he said. Only that, holding his daughter close.

"Go," she said, hollow in her chest. "Lead the way back. You know these woods." She dropped Dorie's hand, walked toward him till he had to turn and she could follow, heart constricting in her chest. She retrieved her hat with its torn veil as they followed their path of broken branches and twigs back through the woods. Dorie's legs hung limply from her father's arms, jarred back and forth as he strode through the forest. The small limbs seemed as fragile as the porcelain doll's.

Poule was waiting for them at the edge, her lips set in a grim line. Her careful fingers touched Dorie's cheek, neck, wrists. "I'll send for a doctor," Jane heard her tell Mr. Rochart.

"Doctors won't help," said Mr. Rochart. He continued on toward the house with Dorie as though he didn't know what to do but get her *away*.

"No, but you'll feel like you're doing something," Poule said. "Let him take her pulse and tell you not to worry."

Jane searched the back lawn until she saw the elder Miss Davenport. When their eyes met, the girl squealed and turned away. Jane swallowed against the sick feeling inside. And yet . . . she could not return to hiding behind her wall of iron.

Poule was issuing instructions about the doctor to the nearest temporary servant. She turned to go, and Jane hurried after, fell in beside her. Before she could change her mind she let the words tumble out. "I need your help," she said. "Please."

Poule looked up at her, her sharp eyes seeing through Jane's hastily wrapped veil. "Better bring that book with you to satisfy your last debt. Meet me downstairs in ten minutes."

Jane slid *The Pirate Who Loved Queen Maud* across the green glass tabletop to Poule. The dwarf's eyes gleamed as she ran her fingers lovingly over the remains of the dust jacket—she could still make out the pirate's grin as he valiantly fought a busty mermaid riding a sea serpent. With a show of great restraint Poule tenderly tucked the book inside her dressing gown without even cracking it open.

"How much for this help?" said Jane. The hollow feeling was not going away. The fey had returned. The fey had harmed Dorie, had attacked Jane. Jane had attacked Miss Davenport. She cared too much for everybody, and everything was broken.

"Provided I can, then it's an even exchange for information about what you saw in the forest," said Poule. "What help do you think I can give?"

Jane rubbed her eyes behind the veil. But *everything was broken* meant start somewhere. Be the Jane who had come to Silver Birch to make things right.

Fix one thing at a time.

"You said you had tales of a dwarf cursed by rage, who started a war," Jane said. "Moum."

Poule raised her eyebrows. "Three wars. But you're not that bad."

"But what you said before that. You said 'I've *felt* worse.' Not 'I've heard of worse.' And before that, the first time we were talking about water imagery, and practicing controlling your emotions. You said you'd had a lot of practice."

Poule let out a breath. "Ah." Her short fingers touched the book at her heart, fell to the glass tabletop.

"Please," Jane said gently. "You knew someone who was cursed. Didn't you?"

Poule stared at her fingers on the table. "My father," she said. "On an ordinary trade mission."

"I thought dwarves didn't use fey technology."

Anger lit Poule's face. "We shouldn't," she said. "We mostly don't. But dwarves are bloody arse-faced mules, and we don't all agree on anything, no matter how crackbrained, how costly, how—" She breathed. "Pappa worked for the Steel Conglomerate, going back and forth between cave and sky. Things went wrong—it doesn't matter how. He came home wounded in the chest."

"Was it also rage?"

"Yes—no. Violence. Not just anger—brutality." She rubbed her silver-grey head, and Jane thought that this must have been a long time ago. "There weren't many curses back in those days, you know. I researched every rumor of a cure, pored through old books. . . . Well. During the Great War, I heard about ironskin and tried it on Pappa, though by then he was old and sick. It was just one more thing to try, I thought. But covering his curse with iron just made him sicker." Her shoulders slumped inside her old suit coat. "I know he didn't have much time left anyway, but . . ."

"I'm sorry," said Jane. But also . . . "It made him sick? The iron keeping the curse in?"

Poule shrugged. "I didn't think that might apply to humans, too. You all just kept wearing it. . . ." She looked at Jane. "But I am sorry, that I didn't think of that for you." She stood as if uncomfortable, went over to a nearby worktable, busying her hands by sorting pliers, recoiling spools of wire. "That's why I've been working on these things since then," she said. "The iron thread, like Dorie's gloves. Her mesh was closely woven, to ape the tar or your mask. But I've been working on others." She held a thin ribbon of ironcloth out for Jane to see. "Variants. More iron, less iron, farther apart, closer. Is there some level where the iron can boost the person with the curse, help them control their emotions? Help them dissipate the blight, without making them sick from the blasted fey poison?"

"That sounds very useful," said Jane. "But wouldn't it take a lot of control from the individual?"

"Yes," said Poule. "Just like the dwarves practice. Like I told you with the water imagery. So who knows if it would work with humans—at least, not without a long apprenticeship, and the will to work their arses off."

"That's the help I want," said Jane. "I . . . yelled at one of the Misses Davenport. The elder one. I couldn't help myself. It was like I was on fire. I can't keep the iron on and make myself sick—but I can't be afraid of myself, either." Her voice rose on the end of the sentence, more shrilly than she had intended. Perhaps Mr. Rochart could help her, but perhaps he wouldn't, and Jane couldn't live with herself anymore. She was the lit end of a firework, a short fuse that would burst into a thousand stars. "Do you see what I mean?"

"Calm," said Poule. "You can do this. A long apprenticeship, I said? You've been plugging away at it for five years, from what you've told me. All you need is a little more confidence that it's working. A little more focus of mind." She set down a spool of wire, rustled through the mess on the table. "Let me give you a bit of the loose-weave iron cloth." She held up a linen mesh through which only a few iron threads glinted. "Put this on like a bandage," she said. "See if the crisscross dampens the curse to where it helps you control what goes in and out."

Jane took the cloth, took several breaths to calm herself. "Actually it was rather odd," she said, holding the cloth in her hands like a life preserver. "It almost felt like I *was* doing something with the curse. When I yelled at Miss Davenport. Like I made her do what I wanted."

Poule looked at her strangely. "Well, she is easily cowed," she said. "*I* could make her do what I wanted." She bent a bit of wire back and forth. "Tell me what happened in the clearing."

Jane summarized the terrifying event, including how the fey had attacked her.

Poule nodded. "It felt like fear, you said? But you're sure it wasn't your fear."

"You know," Jane said slowly, "it felt oddly like my rage. Like Niklas's depression. Like . . . a fey curse attacking me, from the fey itself. I thought usually that came from the blue fey bombs."

"It's the Queen," Poule said grimly. "Maybe that makes a difference."

Jane shuddered, remembering. "It was almost like it was trying to get inside of me. If so, I'm not sure I stopped it—I think it stopped itself." It rejected her. *Ugly ugly unclean . . .* "And then, like it was trying to get inside Dorie. Something made Dorie all shimmery, but I don't know if that was the fey, or Dorie herself. And now . . ." What if Dorie didn't wake up? Jane refused to consider that. Dorie must wake up.

Poule looked thoughtful, but she clapped a comforting hand on Jane's shoulder. "They only invade *dead* bodies," she said. "Take heart—you're not a corpse yet."

Jane did not feel particularly comforted.

She did not want to intrude on Mr. Rochart in his worry, but she could not stand to go quietly back to her rooms and wait like "patience on a monument," as the girl in *Thirteenth Night* said.

She nudged the door to Dorie's room open a crack and saw Mr. Rochart kneeling by the bed, his forehead pressed into the white dotted coverlet and his hands wringing the sheets.

Jane turned away, unwilling to disturb them.

But as she turned he said her name.

Jane came back, stood at the foot of the bed. Dorie lay there, for all the world as if she were sleeping.

"She stirs," he said. "She rolls and mumbles, like she's talking in her sleep. But she does not wake."

Jane sat on the other side of the bed, across from Edward. He had hold of one of Dorie's hands, and Jane took the other. The small fingers lay limply on her palm. "She will," Jane said, willing it to be true.

"I should never have gone into the woods," he whispered. Jane heard in that an echo, that he did not mean today. Long ago, he meant. Regret, he meant.

"She will wake."

"I did not know there would be such a cost," he said softly. His hands closed around Dorie's.

Jane squeezed Dorie's other hand, angry now, the rage coming out. You do not deserve this, she thought fiercely at Dorie. You've had enough trouble in your five years. You deserve to be normal. Jane's head bowed, hot tears pricking the corners of her eyes as she held Dorie's hand.

Silence. Blue, gold lights, a pattern on eyelids shut too tightly. And then . . .

"Dorie," breathed Edward. "Dorie . . ."

The blue eyes were open.

A great lump of joy seized Jane. She reached down to hug Dorie just as Mr. Rochart pulled his daughter to him, cradled her tightly in his arms. Jane's arms fell away.

Dorie yawned and stretched. "I saw the pretty lady," she said. She gave her father one of her rare smiles. "She showed me pretty things."

"What kind of things?"

Dorie yawned again. "Lots of pretty ladies. I like pretty ladies." She was using full sentences now, and Jane noted it with pride even through the eerie fright the words provoked. Dorie twisted around to smile at Jane. "She said you're a pretty lady." Jane's heart thumped in her chest as Dorie turned back to her father. "Is she?"

"Well," said her father, at a loss for words, "well . . ."

Jane crumpled the bit of ironcloth around in her hands.

She wasn't. But she could be.

Her hand reached out to touch Dorie's dress, fell away. "What if," she said, and she described what he might have done, watching his reactions, wanting to know. "What if you shaped me a plain mask. Not a face of surpassing beauty, like Blanche Ingel. Or what you're doing for Nina. Not a face to attract all the men in the world." She touched her scarred cheek, then all at once pulled her veil aside until the thin sunlight poured over her entire face, over the ripples that writhed through her cheek and jaw. "Just me. Me as I was." She felt along the scar ridges that extended out, up past her eyelid, forehead. "Whole."

If Nina had told her the truth, then he did not confess to it. "You shouldn't risk it," he said. "The process is dangerous." His shadowed eyes met hers. "I do not speak lightly when I say that my past is unforgivable. You do not know what I have done, and my state of mind, my intentions, are of little excuse." His arms tightened around Dorie's body, his fingers locked. "The sins of the father are revisited on the child." Eyes on her. "Do not make me compound my sins."

"You said you were in my debt," said Jane. "All I want is to look normal. To feel normal." Fire burned hot within him. "Do you understand what I mean?"

He nodded reluctantly. "Jane . . . ," he repeated, and there was something so strained in that one word that she couldn't bear it, couldn't bear to have him pity her, or dismiss her, or say anything to contradict the way her stupid wishful thinking wanted him to feel and she burst out:

"We should tell the guests to leave. They need to get out of here, now. Before sundown." She looked at the lone button under the chest of drawers, at the silver wallpaper, at anything but Edward and his daughter. If he was going to deny her her own face she didn't want to know just yet.

"No." His knuckles were white as he gripped Dorie's form close to him, and the fire inside him billowed out, turned to smoke, vanished. The girl murmured, protesting the grip, and Edward loosened his fingers, carefully, loosening words at the same time. More softly, "No. I've worked too hard to

get them here. And they won't be ready to leave by nightfall—
you know these women—and in the dark on the road, they'd
be in just as much danger."

Dorie wriggled all the way free, and he stood and set her
back on the bed. She looked from one tense face to the other.
She squirmed off the bed, and though Jane assumed she was
going to get closer to her father, she ran to Jane and threw her
arms around Jane's skirts. Touched, Jane held Dorie's shoulders close.

"Jane?"

"Yes, sweetheart?"

Big blue eyes, confiding. "My mother's coming to get me,"
she said.

"What?" said Jane, and Edward stumbled backward, looking down at Dorie with horror in his amber eyes.

Dorie squeezed Jane's legs tighter. "Do I have to go? I
don't want to."

"Of course not," said Jane. She knelt beside Dorie, hugged
her little girl close, through the nerves, through the fear.
"What do you mean, she's coming to get you? What exactly
did she say?"

"She said she's coming to get everybody," said Dorie. Her
blue eyes unfocused, looked through the wall at the woods.
"She said it's time."

Edward grabbed Jane's arm and held it fast, but Jane hardly
noticed through the terror. "Get the guests inside, I don't
care how," he said.

"Yes, sir," she said. The silver wallpaper flickered blue as
Dorie looked at it, through it, seeing something Jane could
hardly guess. The room hummed with emptiness.

"Tell Poule to check the iron at all the doors and windows." His words swallowed themselves, dropped down his gullet like stones. "Tell her to prepare for a siege."

Poule and Jane worked as silently and secretly as possible. Poule enlisted Martha for the task, and between the three of them they slipped in and out of bedrooms and washrooms, sitting rooms and hallways, staying out of the way of the guests and the extra servants from town.

Some of the windows were solidly covered in Poule's mesh iron screens, but many had torn or been removed completely in the last five years, and had not been replaced. Too many of these screenless windows were open to the breezy spring air. Jane and Martha marked the places that needed work and watched the bedroom doors for guests as Poule slipped inside with crinkled sheets of iron mesh and a welder.

Mr. Rochart had disappeared almost immediately, leaving Jane with the admonition to keep an eye on Dorie—which she would have done in any case. She thought he must be in his studio—wondered how he could work with that threat hanging over him. But he had lived within the grasp of the woods for many years. Perhaps he was able to separate the two parts of him: the part that feared, the part that worked.

When she closed the door behind Dorie the last time, she met up with Poule and Martha on the landing.

"That's everything in the open wing but the two rooms the guests are actually in right now," Poule said. "Those will have to wait till they retire."

"All the rooms that we've *checked* are done," Jane said grimly. She pointed at the carved door between Dorie's rooms and her own room. "I haven't been able to get into Nina's room all evening. She's got herself barricaded in there."

"Then we'll have to do it in front of her," said Poule. "That or bar iron across her door and lock her in for good."

Despite the tension, Jane grinned. Mindful of her own lack of iron, she had taken the solitary tasks and continued her mantra of thinking of cool still pools of water.

"This iron will make us safe then?" said Martha. The normally unflappable maid betrayed the slightest hint of worry. From a chance word of Cook's, Jane had picked up that Martha was fifteen—therefore six at the start of the Great War. Old enough to know the danger they faced now, young enough to have only dimly grasped the point of all the scrap iron drives and melted-down ornamentation back then.

"The iron mesh is so tight they can't squeeze in," said Poule. "We're completely safe. As long as no one asks them in."

Martha's eyes widened. She rubbed one knobby elbow, nervous.

"I can't imagine why anyone would do that," said Jane, comforting. "It's hard for a fey to hold a human shape without it being obvious. They can't keep up a whole body for more than a few seconds before they turn back into light."

"Thought they could take over folk," said Martha.

"Yes, but only dead bodies," said Jane. She had the irrepressible urge to add Poule's line about them not being corpses yet, but she would not for the world scare Martha further, so she did, in fact, repress it. Gallows humor, she thought. When your nerves are wound that tight sometimes all you can do is make jokes about being as dead as King Bertram's lover.

"More precisely, it seems like they can only take over bodies they've killed," Poule was explaining to Martha. "We're not sure why, but perhaps something about the act of murder is a part of it. That's why they make those fey bombs."

Jane bit her lip and tried not to think of Charlie.

"And if the dead knock at the door, none would let them in," said Martha seriously. "All right then." She looked perfectly unflappable once more.

"So, this Nina person," Poule said, moving to the door. She lifted a fist and banged—monotonous, annoying thumps. Jane was impressed by her ability to skip politeness and jump right to the next level.

At length, Nina answered. A black satin sleep mask was pushed onto her forehead, and she held a short fat glass of amber liqueur. Her eyes met Jane's—there was a flash of the nervousness she'd seen earlier—and then it vanished as Nina glared at Poule.

"Maintenance," said Poule. She shoved the greasy bar of iron into Nina, so Nina had to either immediately back away or ruin her dress. She backed up and Poule squeezed past, headed straight for the windows.

"What is this?" said Nina. "Really, Jane, I thought you were understanding."

"No," said Jane. It felt good to stand up to Nina. She followed Poule's path into the room and shut the door. (Martha in the hallway shook a firm NO at the unspoken question of whether she wanted to join them.)

"Really, Jane," repeated Nina, and then she fell silent as Poule's tools whirred loudly on the window nearest Nina's bed. When she saw that Jane and Poule were set on staying, she huffed, downed her whiskey, and sank into a tufted sixteenth-century armchair, glaring at the room.

It was a mess. Heaps of satin and tulle straddled spindly-legged tables, arms of chairs, the canopied bed. Nina's dramatic black hat hung giddily over a vase painted with cherubs, and several glasses ringed with plum lipstick crowded the top of the vanity. The messy modernity of Nina seemed to swallow the dated, threadbare room.

This was what it was like to put your stamp on something. This was someone with presence. Whatever Nina wanted would be hers, just by virtue of being so unstoppably Nina. Blanche Ingel's charisma lay only in her face, the unearthly face that Edward had created for her. But Nina's charisma oozed from every inch of her skin. Jane thought that even now, she would place her bets on Nina to best Blanche in any social battlefield. And with the new face? Nina would be unstoppable. She'd be able to ensnare anyone, maneuver any event to her liking.

Surely Edward would be small potatoes then.

The thought was comforting—and then her eye fell on an embroidered chair holding Nina's wadded-up turquoise dress.

Under the chair were a pair of men's shoes.

The thought of glamorous Nina entertaining men visitors in her rooms made Jane feel smaller than Poule. The brief victory she and Poule had won over Nina dissipated, and she stood there feeling every inch of her plain day dress and veiled face as if it were Dorie's iron gloves enclosed around her.

The shoes were enough to rattle her, but—*whose* shoes? They could be anybody's, of course.

Nina drawled, "Edward looked very handsome today."

Jane looked up to find Nina innocently gazing at the shoes. "You weren't outside with us," Jane said.

Nina raised eyebrows until Jane blushed.

"Oh. When you saw him alone."

"He has an air so many men lack," said Nina. She looked

happier now that she was skewering Jane, wresting control of the situation. "So poised. So . . . skillful. We're going to have a fine, fine time tonight."

Jane *knew* Nina had been in Edward's studio just for a consultation . . . didn't she? Of course, Nina could know Edward in more than one way. Jane despaired, not wanting Nina's insinuations to be true. Not when Nina was capable of taking—and keeping—any man that captured her fancy.

Poule stepped past Jane to the next window, feeling it with sensitive fingers. "I suppose you'd want him to be skillful, since he's going to rip your face off," she said.

Laughter nearly bubbled out of Jane at this gruesome depiction of surgery. Gallows humor again.

Nina's expression of fury morphed instantly into calm calculation. She looked the short woman up and down, her eyes lingering on Poule's homely face. "I'd have thought you'd take advantage of his services," she said cruelly, and Jane, aghast, pressed a useless hand to the veil covering her lips, as if she could take back Nina's words.

Poule shouldered her tool bag. Outwardly she did not seem affected, but Jane, heart beating, thought surely the words wounded deep inside where the hurt did not show. "If you think I'd want to look like my enemy, you're a bigger fool than I gave you credit for."

Jane descended the spiral staircase by her room, thinking how nice it would be to be as sure of herself as Poule. She wondered if that came with growing up in the *dwarvven* culture, or from the fact that Poule could take care of herself in myriad ways. Perhaps if Jane could *do* something like

Poule—weld iron or sniff out fey or cow obnoxious women—
she could wrest control of her own life, make the Jane-that-
wasn't-supposed-to-be into a Jane she could be.

She slipped into a back hallway to retrieve her sketchpad
from the afternoon—one of the hired servants had brought
it in and placed it in her boot cubby. The fear from the forest
had dulled with the application of several hours of manual
labor on the iron screens, leaving her time to ponder other
problems.

Were those shoes really Edward's?

Jane brushed the dirt off her sketchpad, absentmindedly
eyeing the flaws in the sketch of Dorie, the parts where her
lines deviated from Edward's.

Was Nina really meeting Edward tonight?

A movement through the window next to the back door—
there, standing on the back lawn was Blanche Ingel, deep in
chat with one of the gentlemen, who seemed to be unable to
do anything but gaze into her perfect face. Exasperated, Jane
momentarily forgot her stature in the house and spoke to
them as she had spoken to the elder Miss Davenport earlier
that day. "Get in here," she said, pulling the heavy back door
all the way open.

The gentleman looked startled, but Blanche laughed kindly
and said, "I suppose we are out a little later than decency per-
mits." She came in, scraping her boot heels on the mat. "Can
you have a maid fetch me a clean white cloth?" She had a
white handkerchief balled in her left palm. "I had a little argument with one of those thorn trees. Made me quite dizzy."

"Certainly," said Jane, and did not say, "What on earth
were you doing at the edge of the forest? How foolish are
you?" Edward had not mentioned the fey, true (he had come

up with "the gardener says stay off the lawn tonight while he sprays for insects"), but anyone with half a brain stayed out of the woods after dusk. *That* had been true for centuries and centuries.

The man followed, throwing a grouchy look at Jane, but she was irritated and worried enough that she was not flustered by his glare. As with Nina on that first day, Jane did remember that for Edward's sake she should be polite and appropriately deferential to his guests, and so she thought cooling thoughts of water and said, "I apologize for my brusque request, but the other guests are gathering in the library for elderflower liqueur. Our host was worried that you had gotten lost."

Blanche flushed at that, and belatedly it occurred to Jane that perhaps that statement was no more polite, and maybe it implied that the two of them were doing something inappropriate in the shrubbery. The gentleman pushed past her into the house, grumbling, leaving tracks of mud, and inwardly Jane sighed. She had never been good at this polite and humble business, and with the mask off it was worse.

She locked the back door, and, casting around, she shoved the heavy wooden hall tree in front of it as a reminder.

As if anything would make those partygoers think.

Jane passed the evening either watching Dorie sleep or with Poule, checking iron. By midnight, the party had splintered off in ones and twos, and now when she peeked into the drawing room, only the younger Miss Davenport was there, flirting with one of the men while her mother snored on the window seat.

No sign of Nina.

She walked past Nina's room to her own. The light was off;

only moonlight shone from the crack under the door. Surely Nina was not upstairs but was in there, asleep. And if asleep, she would have her sleep mask on, and wouldn't see the door open a silent crack. . . .

Knowing full well she shouldn't, Jane edged Nina's door open. A little—and then more, searching the spill of moonlight on the unmade sheets. She unwound her veil, and both her eyes and some unknown sense confirmed it point-blank.

No one was in Nina's room.

Jane shut the door and found herself walking down the hall, away from her own room, toward the stairs that led to the studio. Knowledge of what she *should* do didn't seem to have any effect on the fact that she wanted to know.

She wanted to know if Nina was really in his studio, and if so, exactly what that meant. Was Edward really performing some secret surgery on Nina in the dead of night—or was there another, more obvious explanation for what went on behind closed doors after midnight?

What exactly had he meant by the things he had done wrong?

Was Nina one of the unforgivable things? Blanche?

It would be smarter not to know, not to torture herself with the truth. It certainly was none of her business. It was very off-limits.

And still she found herself climbing the stairs to stand at the door in the attic, an open door into a room lit with rectangles of blue moonlight.

She went softly into the room.

His worktable in the center of the room was crowded with his mask-making supplies—clay, metal tools—and a white wet towel covered his latest work. The clay bucket next to the table was nearly empty, its wooden shell containing only an inch of blue-black water.

She put her hand to the wet towel, wondering what she would see—a beautiful Nina? The grotesque version? Or more heart-wrenching still—herself, her whole self?

Her fingers trembled on the cloth, and then out of the corner of her eye, under the side door—she thought it was the moonlight, too, but no, that was light, the blue of fey-tech light.

He was there.

Jane left the cloth, slipped silently across the room to the door. Ever so quietly, before she could even think about what she was doing, she slid it open.

It took a second to resolve the scene in the small white room, and then she did. Edward, in white coat and mask like a surgeon, bending over the face of an unconscious woman wearing black satin. The scalpel in his fingers gleamed in the blue light.

On the wall hung one mask, a beautiful mask.

Nina.

Chapter 15

MAY YOU BE BORN PLAIN

Surely he could hear her heart racing. But he didn't turn, didn't look up.

Edward ran his scalpel around the woman's face, as close to the hairline as possible. Just before the ears and just under the jawline. Then he worked underneath the flap of skin with a spatulate tool until he could peel the face up and away. It hung up around the nostrils and eyelids and he had to fiddle with it until it lifted away completely.

The woman's face—Jane could hardly think *Nina* in connection with it—was horrifying underneath. All red like a war victim—Jane shut her eyes. When she forced herself to reopen them, Edward was settling Nina's skin back into place.

But no, not skin.

A mask.

A clay mask, matte white and opaque and sculpted by a master craftsman.

From Jane's angle, the clay mask did not blend with the rest of the woman at all. It was rigid, dead white. Unthinkably unlike human skin. Edward picked up a delicate brush, thick with glue, and began to attach the mask to the red scalp line, the red neck. He pulled the woman's skin, the skin of the mask, as he bound the two together. Despite his orders to the contrary, the window was open to the night, and the sheet draped across the wooden table fluttered in the breeze.

His hands—no, that wasn't just the blue-lit room—his hands were faintly blue. Jane made some sound, too tiny to be a gasp.

Slowly he turned and looked *through* her. She backed up one step. His eyes—she had never seen them like this. They were glassy, filmed over as if she were seeing them through stagnant lake water, through layers of mold and algae.

The blue in his hands died, till Jane could almost doubt that she'd seen it. A small zip, a pop. And then he was looking at her, and the glass in his gaze was gone, and he was not smiling, but he was *there*.

"How long have you been standing there?" he said.

"Long enough," Jane said in a low voice. "Long enough to see you peel a woman's face back like the skin off a rabbit. You're no artist. Nor a surgeon. Surgeons can't do what you just did." Her hands clenched, went instinctively to where she'd once kept a feyjabber at her side. "You've got fey technology."

This wasn't like Dorie, who couldn't help it.

He was in league with them.

Edward turned back to his work, running his fingers along Nina's cheek. He seemed to be searching for what to say.

Dazed, she thought: This must be what it means, his hints, his allusions. The presence of bluepacks in this household, to run our lamps and motorcars and machines, long after everyone else's have died.

He is working with the fey.

From the table he picked up a fine sandcloth, began brushing away pilled glue and blood. "You will leave me now," he said. "You will exit my life. You will denounce me to the world."

Her breath caught, hearing not command in his tone but sharp regret, an envisioned future. "Not that," she said. "Never that."

"You will make your excuses then, and leave us."

"An invented dying aunt," said Jane, and she seemed hardly to have the breath for the words. Her feet took her two steps closer, one step back—she froze there, watching as he gently teased the mask's eyelids in place with a long tool like an ice pick. One word, that she hoped would bring her closer and not farther away.

"Why?"

Why do you have this skill, why are you using it, why. Tell me, tell me why, and in that telling let there be some measure of explanation that will make it okay, will make it so I don't have to hate you, don't have to pick up my stone-still feet and run to my sister in the city.

Why.

In that silence she seemed to hear him swallow his fear. Then the words rolled out, deep and velvet, above the woman in black with the frozen white face.

"Once upon a time, a long time ago," he said, "back when the waters were low and calm and the stars were hardly hung in the sky, there was a young boy who wanted to be an artist. The fey were different in those days, back when the air was clean and the sky blue. More substantial. They had bodies, especially when they were in the forests, and they did not need to steal forms from mankind. They were as dangerous then as they are now . . . but they were reclusive. They rarely attacked unless provoked, and so they were like recluse spiders, or copperhead hydras—you hardly heard of them unless you happened to live right at the edges of the forests where they walked. And then you knew how not to provoke."

And you provoked them, thought Jane, for around the flowery description of *a long time ago* she heard this fey tale like heartbeats in her throat. *My father was cold and I was lonely. I went into the forest with my sketchpad. I sketched beauty.*

"Well, go on," said Jane when he stopped. "What sort of things provoked them? Back then." The roughness in her voice broke against the spell his words were weaving, fell away.

The ice pick coaxed eyelashes from the clay lids. "Great beauty. Great artistic talent. Passion. There used to be a saying in the towns near the fey, though it was forgotten long before the wars—"

"May you be born plain," breathed Jane along with him.

"Yes." His voice rolled on, filling the room with the long-ago world. She closed her mouth, certain her words would derail him from the only way he could get through this story. It had to be distant, it had to be a fantastical tale to spin itself out of a pile of horrid truths and a story of *me. Me, I lived this.*

"Some average men set up trade, of a sort, with the fey," he said, "and many curious things were brought over to ease human existence. Blue-lit fey technology replaced human invention, and it never occurred to the men who traded for bluepacks to run lights and cameras that everything had its own price, its own story.

"Scalpel. No, that one." She came just close enough to hand it to him, then backed away. He slid it into a nostril of the mask, cleaning up the edges.

"Now, this boy was not from the forests." *He was a small boy who rattled around a too-big house.* "He knew little of the fey, hardly any of the tales, and so he wandered into the woods, sketching birds and animals." *He was talented for a such a small boy. His birds seemed as though they would startle and take to the air.* "And when a beautiful shimmering woman appeared, he sketched her. When she invited him home for dinner, he accepted.

"Gauze." He pressed it under the woman's ear, wiped his forehead with a sleeve. Regret dripped from him like the beads of sweat.

"Go on," Jane said softly. She had heard these stories. The tales of the travelers who ate a golden apple hanging from a tree in winter, drank water from a cup held by a beautiful woman.

Ingested something belonging to the fey.

The sleeve had left a pink streak on his forehead. He bent over the woman again, his voice dropping. "But when the young boy tried to go home, the Queen held fast to the fey inside of him, and he could not depart. The Queen had chosen him for her consort. Now those whom she chooses are sometimes let go, back into the world, many years later. Decades. When their families have long since turned to dust. When her attention has finally turned to a new . . . toy." He dropped the pinkened gauze into a metal can. Studied his patient. "Again and again, the story is the same. The consort is let go, and paid, in some fashion, with a gift for serving the Queen all those years." He spread his right hand wide, as if contemplating the fey gift lurking in his fingertips.

Then he blew skin dust from the woman's forehead and turned to face Jane. For the first time he appeared to study her. Only then did Jane realize that she had never rewound the veil after peering into Nina's room. She felt shock from him at seeing her bare face when he did not expect it—how did she know his shock, when his expression did not change?

More, how did she know the myriad things she suddenly seemed to know about him, and her mind raced back through the day, hearing what he didn't say in his story just now, knowing each breath and feeling in the forest, feeling him touch her as she fell and thinking calmly—he loves me—mind racing, saying, *that was all just today, today when I was without iron, today I knew that, today*—

"Is Dorie still all right?"

"Yes," said Jane.

His shoulders moved—the tiniest bit of relief. Quietly he said, "Come, see how Nina looks."

Mind whirling, Jane forced herself to approach the table, to focus. Her first thought was that the work seemed surprisingly fake—the mask was dead white, the line where it had been glued into place clearly visible, outlined in a thin strip of red. Nina's eyes were open and staring, though she remained unconscious. They seemed to be set a long way behind the mask.

"What do you think?" He touched Nina's chin, delicately. "It will blend into her own skin very shortly. I will bandage it for now to keep it together, but in a couple days, you won't see those lines. She will look as though she was born that way."

"She will be very beautiful," admitted Jane. She could admit his talent as an artist. And yet . . . "She looks . . . fey." She remembered the face floating in the forest.

"Where do you think our notion of beauty comes from?" said Edward.

"Do you think so?" said Jane. "Somehow that's more disturbing than anything else."

The white mask glowed palest pink at the corners of the cheeks. Paint? Or life, slowly filling the clay? Jane's breath caught at the beauty Nina would have, and she thought: I could be that beautiful. But in the next instant—no. No, all I want is to be normal . . . and I still want that.

She saw him at work, she was shocked, she was repulsed. And yet it did not lessen the fierce desire.

Normal, she thought, like a hunger in her belly. He could make me normal.

Edward brushed aside another fleck of dust, picked up a roll of bandages, and started securing the woman's face. "So you see," he said, "why Dorie must not give in to that side of her nature. I fight against their gifts, and fail. Just like I once fought against the Fey Queen's hold and failed. There is great evil in that failure."

His eyes were shadowed again, even in the bright workroom light. She felt his pain, clutching deep in his chest. More—she really did feel it. She was sure of that now. She could feel his shame as if it were her own, and it was only just now, since she had removed the iron from her fey-cursed cheek. She put a hand to her bare red cheek and found it was blazing hot.

The shame of . . . letting others suffer for his mistakes? His daughter, but first . . . his wife. Fey-bombed and taken over while pregnant. A wonder Dorie had survived. "And then," she said in a low voice, "the Fey Queen returned."

A short nod confirmed that horror. "Dorie must not give in to her curse," he said. "Almost six and can't dress herself? No. She must be strong."

Jane was going to say that strength wasn't the issue—that bottling up wasn't strength, a whole host of things she was discovering this last week, this day, now. She put that aside to convince him, she must convince him that her way was right. She swallowed. "The Fey Queen told Dorie she was her mother." Something niggled at the back of her mind about that but she ignored it in favor of listening to the emotions that were suddenly rampaging through Edward, trying to sort out the cacophony she was hearing. "If I help Dorie learn how to use her fey gifts, then she'll be able to defend herself if the Fey Queen tries to take her away."

"To defend herself," he said, and hope lit his whispered words. "To be strong where I was weak. . . ." He laid the bandages on Nina's breast, and suddenly his eyes and insides were all aflame. "Tell me more about what you and Dorie have done together."

"Well, we've practiced diverting things out of the air. In case a fey bomb were thrown at her. I don't know why a fey claiming to be her mother would do that, but . . ." She trailed off, confused by his nearness, by the heat that billowed up inside him as he came toward her, nearer, nearer, one foot nudging hers now, now he stood right there, and it was not something that had ever been going to happen in this time-line, it was so *not this Jane* that she could hardly breathe.

He gently touched her chin, and when she did not jerk away, he drew his fingers down her ruined cheek. "Doesn't it hurt you when she uses that cursed side of hers?"

Her cheek flamed where his finger touched it. "Not so much as I expected." Speaking and breathing seemed impossible; she was overwhelmed by her discoveries, by him. "That's what I think is so important. That if we let the poison run out . . . it doesn't stay inside and fester and make us die a slow, lingering death." He ran his thumb along her bottom lip. "So . . . I think our work . . . is important. . . ."

Edward bent his head and kissed her. The new sense of him seemed to draw extra fire into her, fire that had been born in his body. Like drinking in the heat that he carried. She closed her eyes so she wouldn't have to see whether he closed his. With her eyes closed, she was just Jane, on any branch of time.

Then there was air around her mouth and she breathed.

"Your work is very important," said Edward. "I want you to be able to do it to the best of your ability."

"Yes."

He leaned in, kissed her again, again. "I will get you anything you need." A flicker of something dark—and frightened?—shuddered through him, and when she opened her eyes she realized his were now open. Watching her ruined face. Warmth and ice ran through him so intermingled that she could not tell what he felt, what he wanted. She stepped back, dropping his hands from her own.

The woman on the table was still and silent. Her unearthly beauty filled the room. The woman, the room, Jane, were cold, cold, but Edward's heat could drive all that away. She knew what she wanted. For that one moment she set aside all knowledge that there was something about her he feared and put a daring hand to his belt loop. "Close your eyes and kiss me again."

He obeyed. His lips touched hers and heat poured into them. She drowned, was engulfed, immolated.

But something rocked his body—tension, fear—and she realized there was noise from below, from the darkened house. Pounding on the outside studio door, short heavy footsteps bursting through—Poule. Jane stepped back from Edward, but not quickly enough for the quick-witted dwarf to miss the truth, she knew.

Poule's eyes darted around the room, taking everything in, fell on Edward within a single heartbeat. "Come quick," Poule said. "The kitchen. It's Blanche."

Edward turned for the door, pausing only long enough to say to Jane: "Stay here with Nina. I don't want her to be alone when she wakes up."

Then the two of them were pounding down the stairs and Jane was alone, trembling emotion crashing through her body, swaying her tired feet. Jane looked down at the unconscious woman. She was so stiff and silent—it was all wrong for Nina to be silent, quiet, powerless.

Despite his orders, Jane could not stay in the studio. She was propelled irresistibly after him, after Edward who both wanted and feared her. Softly down the stairs, clutching her robe around her. In the hallway to the kitchen she moved like a ghost, her bare feet quiet and cold on the scarred stone floor.

Voices. Edward, calming; a woman, sobbing and spitting words.

Jane crept closer, until she stood concealed in the shadows of the hallway.

Blanche Ingel stood in the kitchen like a crazed Shakspyr heroine, all in white with unbound hair. Her left hand, the one she had cut on a thorn earlier that evening, streamed blood onto the floor. Her right hand held a silver knife.

"Get it out, get it out," she cried, but it was her eyes that frightened Jane. They were glassy and wild.

They were like Edward's had been in the studio.

"It's all right, Blanche," Edward soothed, and he tried to reach in and grab her knife hand without getting cut himself.

Poule stayed back from the woman, nostrils flaring, scenting. She circled around them and then said, "Back away, Rochart. It's fey."

Shock pooled Edward's face. "No—she's alive."

"There's a fey inside her for all of that." The two looked at each other with grim faces, and in the shadows Jane's own face was surely white.

A fey in a live human. Such a thing was possible? It turned her world upside down.

"I don't know if it's making her go mad or what," said Poule. "Is she trying to cut it out with that knife?"

"It's not iron," said Edward.

Poule agreed. "Then we need to find some." She wrestled a steel butcher knife from the butcher block, held it up.

Jane tumbled out of the shadows, gasping. "Wait! You'll kill her!"

"The iron doesn't have to go in the heart, just a line to it," said Poule.

But Edward agreed. "No. It's too risky. And we don't even know for sure if what you suspect is true."

"You're wasting valuable time," warned Poule.

"Come here, Blanche," called Edward in a soothing voice. "Come here."

Blanche looked slightly less wild; she drifted toward Edward. Her arm raised—

"Pull him back!" shouted Poule to Jane, and Jane did, even as Poule lunged for the woman's knife arm and twisted it behind her back, causing the knife to drop from her fingers. Blanche's face smeared with pain, and Jane's breath caught, for despite her new beauty Blanche had always seemed kind, and they were hurting her.

"You didn't have to do that to her," said Edward, but Poule just grunted.

"You did her mask yourself, and you're under her spell. Blasted humans." She wrestled Miss Ingel toward the side door, and Jane and Edward hurried after. The screen at the door was sturdy, repaired just that afternoon by Poule. Poule opened it and pulled Blanche out onto the lawn. The iron door banged closed.

"Stay inside and call to her," said Poule. She released the woman and stood there, short and hefty and ready to tackle her again at the least provocation.

"Blanche," crooned Edward. "Blanche, come to me. Come to me."

The woman tottered forward, back to the door.

"Go on," whispered Poule. "Touch it."

"I forbid you entrance, Blanche," said Edward in a low voice. Through the mesh, Jane saw Blanche's eyes film over white, and she swerved away from Edward, from them, and Jane could not tell if she avoided the door on purpose or because she truly could not go through it.

Poule was many things, but nimble on her feet was not one, and Blanche easily darted past her and took off down the back lawn toward the forest. Her white nightgown disappeared into the trees and was gone.

Jane and Edward joined Poule on the lawn. Poule's face was pale. "There's definitely fey in her," she said. "Fey in a living woman. But how—and when?"

They were all frightened by the how. Fey taking over the fey-bombed dead was bad enough. If the rules had changed, no one was ever safe again.

But the when—a chill of realization coiled in Jane's chest.

"She was in the forest tonight," she said. "I know she was, because she cut her hand on the thorn trees."

"We're going after her," said Edward. "Poule, suit up. Jane, you're in charge. Keep checking on Dorie."

The two disappeared back into the house, toward Poule's basement suite to get iron, Jane supposed.

"Tell me what you suspect . . ." floated back from Edward.

Jane stayed by the door, bitter thoughts flooding her. She had invited fey in all unknowing, and the possibilities chilled her marrow. She turned and found a figure in black satin crouching behind her. She stifled a yelp.

The woman with the beautiful face wavered. "Where is Edward?"

"An emergency," said Jane. "He had to go somewhere. Are you feeling all right?"

Nina put a hand to her new face. The roll of half-finished bandages hung from her chin. "I feel so strange." A sense of *lost* drifted out from her.

"It's the new face," said Jane. "I suppose you'll feel normal soon. A couple days. Like Blanche." Blanche Ingel, who might never be normal again. . . .

Nina laughed and for a moment her eyes came through the mask, for a moment the mask seemed a real face. Then they died back and the whole of her face looked unreal yet again. "Oh, Ingy," she said. "Tried to pretend that the hot springs gave her such invigoration, revealed a beauty she always possessed. But it won't fix her marbles. She's as jumpy as a cat nowadays."

Nina had said something to that effect the first day Jane met her, she remembered. "Since she had the surgery?" said Jane. "Aren't you worried, then?"

Nina laughed again, the loose bandage swinging. "We're cut from different cloth. She's weak, born to her state—I had to fight for mine with tooth and décolletage. No silly paranoia will catch me." She leered at Jane. "Besides, we both know the real reason she keeps coming back for 'checkups.' Now, where's Edward?"

Edward and his endless supply of beautiful women. Inhuman, irresistible. Even Nina's mask was captivating—Jane had to force her eyes not to linger on the turn of brow and line of cheek. She was suddenly sure it was all true, all of Nina's insinuations, all that the gossip said. He must have been intimate with all of them, for that's what real fey glamour did to you, and each of the women had a touch of that spellbinding, unstoppable allure.

All of them. The Prime Minister's wife, whom he pretended to laugh at. Blanche. Nina. He denied any involvement behind their backs, but surely he turned around and mocked Jane behind hers. Nina probably knew all her secrets.

"Gone, I said," said Jane. Nina lifted eyebrows at Jane's sharp tone. No wrinkles appeared in that white forehead. "I'd go lie on the table upstairs if I were you. He'll be back in the morning."

"That might be what *you'd* do," said Nina. "I'm going back to my room for celebratory drinkies. If you see any of the young men, send them my way. In fact, maybe I'll go find them myself."

"I don't think so," said Jane. She took Nina's shoulder, propelled the woman back toward her room. Nina went quietly, mostly because she was still loopy, Jane thought. She jumped from topic to topic, played with her swinging bandages, and generally screwed Jane's already taut and screaming nerves to the edge. Jane put her in her room with a sense of profound relief. "Stay in there till morning," Jane said. "Or else."

"Or else, or else," mocked Nina. But she shut the door, and Jane drew a silent breath of hope that Nina would go to sleep.

Jane paced the hallway for hours. Her legs grew tired, a knot in her belly sickened with exhaustion, but she could not sleep any more than she could fly. Edward loved her, hated her—but no, put that aside yet again, and concentrate, Jane. What was the truth about her fey curse?

Something about her fey curse was also a gift—when not blocked by iron, she could sense emotions as keenly as if they were her own.

In the forest, Edward had *felt* for Dorie through his hands, as if they were showing him the path. (Don't think of Edward.) His fey gift, capable of more than he knew.

And Dorie herself. Also fey-cursed, and strongly, too . . . but possibly capable of withstanding a fey takeover.

For that's what had happened in the forest, hadn't it?

A fey had entered Dorie, just as one had entered Blanche. Had entered Jane, but had left of its own accord. Dorie had fey inside her, Blanche had fey in that mask on her face. And Jane? Jane just had her curse. The fey curse.

Her head flew up with a start, realizing what the three of them had in common.

The fey substance. Call it a gift, call it a curse—it was both. The fey could not gift without cursing—and they could not curse without gifting.

The fey substance lacing her skin gave her these fey traits—emitting anger, sensing emotions. And more—her curse was affecting people less than she feared, because she was learning to control it. Imagining herself as water was not a silly visualization, but a true manipulation of the substance on her cheek. She was doing what Dorie did, in a far less skillful way.

But the fey substance still had one great drawback, a new wrinkle that no one had ever known.

The fey-cursed were vulnerable to the fey themselves.

The fey had never taken over live bodies before—only the shrapnel-flecked bodies of the dead. Because fey bombs were meant to kill. Because humans with fey substance in them tended to be dead.

But they had never had all these live bodies with fey smeared over them, upright and walking around. And Jane wasn't thinking of the bedraggled and outcast ironskin, though it was true they were equally vulnerable.

The masks.

The masks that those women bought, that Edward put on. A hundred highly placed people, each of whom had turned herself into a host for a parasite: a silver birch waiting to be strangled by mistletoe.

Jane went to the window and looked through the mesh screen onto the back lawn. The maypole glinted in the first light of dawn, its orange and red ribbons hanging loose around it like a flame.

May Day. A time for celebration.

And all the guests who could be coaxed (the girls, mostly) would dance around it, never knowing that on several of their faces lurked a ticking time bomb.

The exact same substance that scarred Jane's own cheek.

Fear riddled her heart, and with it, determination. It didn't matter whether she was ugly or beautiful—she was just as in danger.

So she was determined to be normal. That desire had not

lessened one whit. She would have the face she was meant to have, the simple whole Jane face. Perhaps the desire for normal was tangled up in her desire for Edward. Perhaps she was no better than the women who would change their face "as easily as a dress."

If wanting to be herself was wrong, then so be it.

For once she was going to have exactly what she wanted.

Numb and taut, Jane went through the black early morning to his studio. She made her way to the workbench she had passed by earlier—her hand went to that cloth, thrown over his current project.

She stood there, fingers trembling.

Nina had called her new face pretty.

But what sort of pretty did she mean?

Jane almost fled. Almost was sick, almost ready to smash the mask without lifting the cloth.

She lifted the muslin.

Jane knew what she had feared when she saw it. Her own face stared up at her, white and pale, black eyes hollowed out.

But not her own face. Ten—a hundred times more lovely than her own face. Beauty that any girl would die to possess.

He had done a masterful job. She would be more lovely than Blanche, than Nina.

As beautiful as any fey.

Chapter 16

MAY DAY

"With a face like that, all men would be at your feet," said Edward.

She whirled, finding him there, a black hole of absent moonlight. Pale, drawn, enervated. Sagging, sad, but the fierce words still came to attack him: "I didn't ask for all men. What demon possessed you to make this?"

"You do not want to know."

"I know all too well." His warmth versus his chill—oh, she knew. She picked up the mask and shoved it on her own face.

The inside of the mask was cool on her skin. Sensuous, molding—like skin itself rather than cold clay. She peered out at him and it was like looking through binoculars the wrong way. Everything seemed distant, cut off. "How do you like me now?"

His eyes were invisible. "I like you as you are."

She could not hear in his voice whether that meant "before" or "now." Could not feel it, either. She was turned all upside down by the clay on her face. It seemed to thrum with implied power, but differently than her curse had, so that she would have to recalibrate everything she knew.

She turned past him to the mirror at the end of the room. Her eyes looked out from behind the mask. Her own visage, yet transformed. Enduring. Only her frightened eyes marred its regal beauty.

He came up behind her, slid a hand to her waist.

She could not move from the mirror.

"You think I mock you. You think I want you to be other than you are." He drew his fingers down the cheek of the mask—she felt it as a coldness that slid over her real skin, her damaged skin. "How could you not?"

"When the proof is right here."

"I used to be a fine artist," he said. "I used to find beauty in what *was*. Now I sculpt every mask and it turns fey under my fingertips." He pulled the mask from her face and she cried out as her reflection appeared again. And hated herself for the agony her own reflection stirred.

"I tried to form your face. Your face, undamaged. Yet the clay twisted under my fingers, edges where there should be none, roundness where there should be none—remaking your face into some horrid fey ideal. Turning a pretty human face to grotesque parody." He tossed the mask to the work-table, and its forehead chipped. "I had no idea what I've become."

Hardly thinking, she reached to him, ran a comforting hand on his back. "Ssh," she soothed, like she would Dorie. "It's all right." But her words didn't reach the coldness that seeped out of him again, thick and strong.

"I lose time when I work . . . ," he said, his voice trailing off. "At first it seemed no more than an artist's reverie, such as I often had in my youth. . . ." He balled one fist into the other. "Their gifts are poison, Jane! Miss Ingel . . ."

Jane formed the word on numb lips. "Dead?"

"We found her in the clearing. Poule stabbed her wrist— iron in any line to the heart works, she said. She killed the fey, but it was too late for Blanche. I fear she will be an imbecile forever."

Shock and horror. "It could wear off? Dorie woke from it."

"The only good—nay, wonderful—thing of the day." But he shook his head. "Dorie has gifts Blanche did not. I fear the worst."

"It could be. . . ." She picked up her face, held it to her chest. What was she risking?

The nearness of his body was suffocating. "The fey are drawn to beauty." Warmth, towering over her.

She could hardly breathe. She wondered if Edward had some other fey glamour besides the ability in his hands. "They are drawn to themselves," she gasped out. "I am at risk either way."

He spun at that, spread his hands as if seeing them for the first time. Was he realizing that he must also be at risk? The fey gift lurking in his hands—that too must be the same fey substance as all the rest. The masks, the curses—even the blue-packs? And what was that substance, anyway? Something they grew, gathered? Or spit out, perhaps, like a spider produces silk.

"Yes," he said, and he folded one hand in the other as if he no longer knew what to do with them. "You are at risk."

"Give me the new face," she said.

He shook his head. "I won't do that to you. The risk—"

"Is the same," she said, touching her cursed cheek. The imagined pond evaporated into anger. "I have borne the risk for five years, so tell me why the hell I shouldn't get the reward? And besides. If you use your fey skill to reverse fey damage, wouldn't that be setting something right?" Steel held her up. For once she was going to get exactly what she wanted, and damn anybody who told her she wasn't right to want it. "I resent being labeled a victim."

"I don't think of you as a victim. As a survivor."

"I resent having had something to survive. I resent the five years I spent letting fey emotions seep into me, send me down this life that is not mine. Five years their curse has grown into my soul until black rage and shame seem a vital part of me. One I cannot tear out by the roots, no matter how much calm I project. I resent that, do you understand?"

"Yes."

The fire died; the coldness was in her body, too. "No. You can't. Not you, with your . . . collusion."

"My daughter—"

"A daughter is a separate part of you. You can project your sorrow onto her. You can go out and be free of her for hours at a time."

"No."

She opened her eyes and studied the pain in his. "No, you're right. I can't understand yours anymore than you can understand mine. There. I resent that even in our war scars we are separated." She held the mask in front of her face. "I resent being alone."

He seized her hand and fire leaped inside of him. "Jane, my love. No. Do not ask this of me. If I were to lose you . . ."

Her anger threatened to crumble, her heart trembled at the caress of his words. Her words were fluttering steel. "You said you owed me. The day I pulled you back from the forest."

He leaned in as if he would kiss her again and she stopped him. She would never kiss him again with these lips.

They stood there, and then finally she said softly, "If we are both in danger, at least let me head into battle with my own face."

Deep inside a small voice said: Beautiful Jane is not you any more than scarred Jane is. Can you really pretend your motives are pure?

She could not, but she was out of the necessary will to walk away. Her hands closed around the iron-threaded cloth Poule had given her, but at that moment her focus was so hot and pure that she knew she had no need of it. She stood there and told him silently: *Give me my face.*

He started to protest, but then she saw that glassy white swell in his eyes, as her command raged forth, just as it had against Miss Davenport.

Give me my face.

Give me my face.

Silent and unseeing, Edward took the mask with the chipped forehead from her. She turned and marched to the door at the other end of the room, though her ankles shook her stride.

He made her lie down on his table.

He laid one fey-cursed hand on her forehead and one hand on her heart and then the small white room shifted into dreams.

Dream.

I am the Fey Queen, and Edward is at my command. When I tell him to go, fetch, stay, he does. I have complete power over his hands, his body, his soul.

But I would not command him to do evil, Jane thinks, I would command delightful things. Draw me a picture, I say. Paint a portrait of you, me, Dorie all together on the back lawn, with gold sunlight glinting from our clothes and hair. You swing her around till she is nothing but laughter. Show us how happy we are.

Dream further back. Go to somewhere in the middle of the Great War.

I am the Fey Queen, and I have lost Edward, I have let him go, he has won his freedom in a game of wits. (I did not pay enough attention to him; I was planning battles.) I am angry, but I do not show it. Instead I smile with blinding beauty and I grant him a gift. A special gift, the use of his hands, those sensitive artistic hands. And I tell him his hands will do grand things, and I will come to him and show him how.

No, thinks Jane. I will not be a part of this, of your plan to force Edward to give you the world. Did I coerce Edward to give me that face? Did I command? Then I was wrong. I reject this side of me, of what I could be, of what I might have been.

Are you certain? Look what you could be, with me.

Yes, says Jane. I am certain. . . .

Show me more?

Dream further back. Twenty, forty—sixty years.

I am the Fey Queen and I am listening. My people tell me that human factories are polluting our woods, destroying our homes. But another fey has an idea. We will distract the humans by solving their problems before them. Fey will run their mechanical horses, heat their habitat, power their night-time suns. They will have no need to invent, to destroy us.

Yes, it is clever and it will work for now. But it will not

work forever. The humans will go back to their factories eventually, and then . . . there may well be war in our future. Within the next century, I suspect.

Oh, it depresses me, and I need distraction. A small child wanders through the woods, red-faced from another fight with his father. I have watched him often. He cheers me with his drawings; he is the cleverest, sweetest, brightest boy. He will be gifted by my presence, for humans age more slowly in our company; three years seem as one. (A gift for us, too, or he would be over in a blink.)

Yes, here he comes, see him smile at the face I create for him, see him shyly extend his sketchbook for the pretty lady to see. . . .

Oh, he will do just fine.

Dream. One thousand years ago.

I am the Fey Queen and I am here. Through storm and change and wind and you and all that is to come I will be here forever. You may reject me, but you cannot stop me. You will be part of my always and ever, a leaf of my tree, a dress of the season, a blink of eternity falling in a slow blinding crash. . . .

No, says Jane. I won't let you, no. No no no.

I am Jane.

I am Jane I am Jane I am Jane I am . . .

When she awoke there was white sunlight on her body. She sat up and her head rang. "Edward?" she said.

But no one was in the room.

She patted her head where her hair itched—there were no bandages there. Either Edward hadn't done that part or perhaps he'd never started her face at all. She didn't know if she was ready to look in the mirror and find out.

But she would have to look sometime. Jane levered herself to the floor and wavered there until the dizziness subsided. She remembered having strange dreams, but the only fragment that was clear was a moment when someone accused her of coercing Edward. Compelling him.

Like the fey.

Deep inside she swore to herself that she would never do it again. She had not known she was doing it to Miss Davenport. But she had known she was coercing Edward. Once was enough for a lifetime.

Her feet seemed steady, so she inched along to the first door, stepped out into the workroom.

A breath. And she would turn and face that mirror, accept what she had chosen for herself.

And then a woman screamed.

Jane stumbled through the workroom, catching only glimpses of a messy workbench, a new mask hanging, things she hardly registered as she flew downstairs on stumbling feet. Dorie. Dorie.

The front door was open, but Cook stood just inside of it, blocking her way. "You won't be wanting to go out there, lass." She peered down at Jane and her kindly face went white.

"Jane," Jane said. "I'm Jane."

Cook's hand crept to her apron pocket and suddenly there was a feyjabber in her hand.

"I *am,*" said Jane. The newness of the mask was making her dizzy and she desperately wanted to lie down, but she had to find Dorie.

The feyjabber wavered. Who had screamed?

"You know me," said Jane. "You told me the story about your sister, remember? 'May you be born plain.'"

The older woman's lips trembled. "Would that you had listened."

A sudden bear hug from a small girl knocked her off balance. Dorie had flung herself through the door and knocked Jane backward. "Mother!" cried Dorie.

"I was so worried when I heard the scream," said Jane. She drew back. "What did you call me?"

"Pretty lady," said Dorie. "Mother." She hugged Jane harder and her affection billowed up bright and strong.

Jane put a shaky hand to her face. It was cold and smooth and when she ran her fingers along her cheek it was unscarred and whole. Confusion—if her cheek was unscarred, how was she still sensing Dorie's feelings without the benefit of the fey curse? Was she immediately, full-on using the mask in the same way she'd used her curse? But that confusion seemed a minor detail compared to being called "Mother."

"Where's a mirror?" Jane said to Cook, but Cook frowned.

"Don't know that you'll be wanting to find one."

The one on the landing, Jane suddenly remembered, and she led Dorie toward the garret, to the stairs where the mirror suddenly rushed out at you. Her steps faltered the closer she came.

No bandages, as she'd felt. But he *had* finished. The thin red line encircled her face where he'd finished his surgery.

But it was not the mask she'd seen last night—the beautiful version of her with the chipped forehead. "Dorie," she said. "Whom did your doll look like?"

"Mother," said Dorie, and Jane nodded, her gut cold as stone.

She had the face of the Mother doll.

Of the Fey Queen.

"Stay inside," she told Dorie, and she ran down the stairs, pushing past Cook and out the back door, rocks stinging her bare feet. Everyone from the house had hurried out and stood, openmouthed, hands to hearts or mouths.

A fey hung in the air on the back lawn by the Maypole, a swirl of blue-orange light with an imaged face like the Mother doll, the fey Jane had seen in the clearing.

The Fey Queen.

Advancing on Nina.

Jane shouted at the crowd: "Get back inside!" and they looked at her, startled, as if trying to figure out who she was. Only a few of them obeyed.

But the Fey Queen listened. Instantly dropped Nina and shot through the air to Jane. Hung there in front of Jane, reflecting her new face back to her.

"You're not taking my body," Jane croaked.

"Made for me," the fey said.

"He wouldn't . . ." But the proof was on her face.

"Was your. Purpose here." The swirls tightened; Jane felt the mental effort as the fey switched into a more human way of speaking. "He's done it before."

"Dorie's mother . . . ," said Jane. But what had been nagging her about Edward's story finally hit home. "She died almost five years ago. But Dorie is nearly six."

"*I* am Dorie's mother," hissed the fey. "That form was just the bearer. I needed a body, so I found him a town girl, someone silly enough to be pleased by the master's notice. Once I helped him seduce her, she was ours. A strong body, even in death. I kept that body a year before the villagers noticed the stink. Your live body will last me much longer. Decades, before it wrinkles and I kill it." Pitiless eyes. "Once you've been the consort of the Fey Queen, you'll do anything to regain that."

"You lie," said Jane desperately. "He has a conscience."

"A conscience, bah. A human thing, and he is practically one of us. He was with us years and years, after all. You have seen his hands, yes? How he can sculpt beauty out of earth? We did not gift him with that. This is a talent worthy of the fey if ever there was one."

"But he loves me," Jane said softly, and somehow all that was left in the words was the wishful thinking of a silly girl. "I love him."

The Queen sent a wave through her that somehow she knew was the fey equivalent of ostentatious yawning. "In one sense, you shall be with him," the Queen said. "The other form is nice enough, but yours is the one designed for me. I have seen what you are made of, you know. Your mind will accept my patterns very nicely. We will go together well, after you succumb. I will have it."

Then the blue-orange advanced on Jane, and Jane was too despairing to run, for the proof of what the Queen said was all too visible. He had given her the Queen's face, and there could be no other interpretation of that.

She had no defenses, none, and then suddenly there was a wall of iron in front of her and the Fey Queen was crashing into it.

"Run," said Poule, and she shoved her back toward the house, lifting her makeshift shield at the Queen.

Of course the Queen could go around iron, even a large piece of it, but the brief moment of surprise at hitting it dead on stunned the Queen so she only hung flickering for eight, ten seconds, before she could move again. Jane moved her nerveless feet faster and faster, flung herself over the iron threshold just as the Queen pounced on her ankles and came up with only air.

Rage in her head, from the Queen, then enticement. Lust, love, lulling, luring Jane to step back across that threshold and out into the open.

Jane slammed the door. She flung herself to the floor, on top of her hands, and though the compulsion seized her till she wept, she had just enough strength from all her work with the fey curse to keep her hands curled under her belly, her knees drawn to her chest.

From outside came Nina's voice, shouting no, no, no, and there was nothing Jane could do, for the compulsion still pulled her like a string pulls a top to its apex, plucking her with the fey call, and with her own human guilt, for despite not adoring Nina she did not want her to be consumed by the Fey Queen.

The compulsion died even as the door opened and Poule slid around it and into the foyer.

"Nina . . . ," said Jane.

"You're not to go out there, you hear?" said Poule. "For all she has Nina, she'd drop her like hot iron if she could have you."

"Just jump from one to the next?" said Jane. Who could stand against that?

"I don't know," said Poule. "I've been turning over the event with Blanche and I think perhaps the fey are stuck in a body till it dies. That's why that other fey tried to force Blanche to slash her wrists with a silver knife. It knew it was discovered and was trying to win free."

But the Queen had entered Dorie, and left, thought Jane.

She entered me, while I was asleep. Jane could not quite buy Poule's slim hope.

"It's curtains for Nina, but at least the Queen's trapped there for a while," continued Poule. "She'll either have to use the body or destroy it, and she'll have to get full control of it to destroy it. Nina's stronger than Blanche ever was."

But Jane slumped to the floor, hardly listening.

"He would've given me to her like . . . like a thing, a toy, a body for her. For her to be with him."

Poule's eyes were gentle. "You can't be trusting anything a fey says."

"He assumed no one would miss me. Like the village girl." She rounded on Poule. "*That* must have been true. Dorie had to be born out of a human form. How did it happen? Just like she said? Is that who he's been paying off all these years?" A thought flashed through her mind. "That man at the carriage house that day—the girl's father, it must have been."

"Before my time," said Poule. "Let's have you lie down in your room. You can talk to him when he returns from the forest."

Jane stumbled to her feet. "I can't see him. I can't see him ever again." Her fingers flew to the edges of the mask. "And this face, this face, get it off of me—"

Poule clasped her hands, pulled them away. Worry was in her voice as she said, "You'll hurt yourself. Don't do that."

"But I can't have it, I can't."

"I'll think of something," promised Poule. "Or Edward will fix it himself."

But that was the wrong thing for Poule to say if she wanted Jane to calm. She drew back from Poule, her eyes flooding. "I have to go," she said. "I have to go."

"Jane. Jane!"

And she ran from her, ran out the side door to where the party guests were hurriedly throwing their trunks and dresses willy-nilly into their carriages and motorcars, rousting their idle groomsmen and chauffeurs, fleeing.

Jane jumped onto the running board of the Davenports' motorcar. It was over-full, stuffed with the family and with another gentleman who had come by train and didn't want to wait for a hired hand to take him to the station. "Please," said Jane. "Are you going to the city? Please, you must take me with you."

"There's no room," said the mother, but the elder Miss Davenport, the one who had let Dorie go into the forest, looked into Jane's clay-ringed eyes and said "Squeeze in here."

Jane wasted no time stuffing herself in, could not even find it in herself to care that she was half on top of the girl, pulled the door closed on their skirts as the motorcar was peeling out down the mud road and away, away from Edward.

The Davenports' goodwill (or in the elder Miss Davenport's case, guilt) extended only so far. Jane walked the fifty-three blocks from their house to Helen's, alone with her thoughts. The afternoon sun was hot on her shoulders and the top of her head, and though she had nothing with her—not even money—she was also glad she had nothing to carry.

It felt quite strange to be on the streets without veil or mask. People stopped to look at her, and Jane was shocked over and over again to realize that they were staring because she was beautiful. She looked longingly at a roasted-chestnut stand as she passed, and a gentleman in a well-brushed suit ran after her and begged her to accept a striped bag full of them.

Jane accepted, an unfamiliar smile crossing her lips, a smile that apparently made the nice man blush and hurry off.

So she was not surprised when the butler at Helen's house dropped his respectable demeanor and said, when she told him her name, "Never Helen's sister?"

But she was shocked enough to drop the last of the chestnuts on Helen's nice clean floor when she saw Helen.

Chalk it up to another thing she should've known, she thought. Helen's hints about Alistair finding a solution, Edward mentioning that he'd seen her sister . . .

Helen was beautiful.

Fey beautiful.

Chapter 17

PRETTY LADIES

Helen was having yet another party.

Jane sat curled on a couch in the front parlor, turning over the morning in her mind as servants whisked past, dusting and setting up flower vases and carrying beaten carpets in and out. The emerald horsehair couch was slick, and her feet kept sliding off.

The mask had not fully sealed at the edges, and it itched. It was not obvious unless you looked closely—with her fingers Jane felt the ridge running from her hairline around her jaw and back—but the itching, plus the knowledge of whose face it was, made her want to hook her nails under her chin and tear it away.

Which did not seem like the best idea.

There had been tons of houseguests at Helen's wedding; today there was only one, and it was that Gertrude person who had told Jane to study art. She came in and out with Helen, who didn't seem to want to be alone with Jane— or, even, alone.

At last when they came in again, Jane swung her feet to the floor and commanded them: "Sit." She poured luke-

warm tea from the service at her side and passed a cup to
Helen.

"Ooh, aren't we high and mighty," said Gertrude, mimick-
ing a city servant's accent.

Jane was interested to realize she didn't particularly care
what Gertrude thought. That was a bit of a sea change, wasn't
it, how she had talked to the Miss Davenports, told Blanche
Ingel what to do, made decisions. . . . She turned the full
effect of her beautiful face on Gertrude and saw the other
woman redden.

She could get used to this.

"Helen," Jane said gently. "I have to talk to you about
the . . . art . . . you received from Edward."

"No art," butted in Gertrude. "She went on holiday is all,
don't you see how relaxed she looks?"

Helen did not look relaxed to Jane's informed eye; she
looked peaked and jittery, a thin and frightened version of
herself. She sneaked glances at Jane's different, fey-enhanced
face, in between looking sharply around the room as if someone were going to jump out from behind the curtains.

"I know the truth," Jane said to Gertrude. "I'm sure you've
been an asset at all Helen's balls and parties, but you don't
need to cover up with me."

"What parties?" said Gertrude in genuine confusion. "This
is the first in a fortnight, and aren't we excited? That'll show
them who was idiots to shun you."

Jane looked at Helen, confused. No parties? But the letters
had been of nothing else.

Helen dropped her head. "I need to talk to my sister," she
said to Gertrude. "I will come find you, after."

"Oh," said Gertrude. "Well, I—oh." She rustled from the

room while Helen plucked at her skirts, folded them into tiny bunches, dropped them again.

"No parties," said Jane. "You've had a much harder time fitting in than you let on."

"It was fine at first," said Helen, still looking at the voile of her skirts. "But they closed off against me. You weren't here, Jane. I did hardly anything, but this girl Annabella took a dislike to me. She had wanted Alistair, you see—even with his drink and horses and cards and all that. She started slyly putting me down at every turn, and her friends had to choose her over me—and she has a great many friends." Her hand touched her jaw in a now-familiar gesture, that moment of touching where you and the mask met. "I needed something to trump her. Your Edward was so kind."

With effort, Jane let that comment fall away like water against an oiled coat, did not let it touch her. "The masks are a problem," she said.

"You have one. Hardly fair to accuse me of—oh, I don't know, whatever you were going to accuse me of. Vanity? Self-indulgence? You try being the younger sister to someone who always has the moral high ground."

Jane burst out: "But you were there for Mother! Don't you know how I've regretted that?" Charlie and her mother, the two old guilts twined together.

Helen looked sideways at Jane, fingers opening and closing on her skirts. "Jane," she said, pleading. "You don't know how it was. . . ."

There was a sudden softness to the mask—was this a way back into understanding, after all? Jane groped for words.

But she could not find them quickly enough. Helen's face fell; she turned away and muttered to herself, "I suppose you can't expect an ironskin to understand what it's like, being thrown to the wolves with nothing but your face, nothing but your face, nothing."

Jane's blood ran cold as Helen dismissed her as ironskin. Helen had remade herself in the city, with or without the new face. Jane tabled the danger of the masks for a moment and tried a different tack. "Helen," she said. "The mask . . . it's almost like it gives me more power. Like . . . a fey."

"Fey beauty, not fey itself," said Helen. Nervous laugh. "Don't be so paranoid."

"Hear me out for once. Accept that I know things."

Helen looked around at the empty parlor, dressed up with vases of early roses for the evening's event. "If I tell you . . . don't tell, oh, she wouldn't tell, would she, but, you see. There is something different since I got this. Like the walls are pushing in, don't you remember, doesn't she remember that?" Her sentences muddled back and forth as she worked herself up, as if Jane were hearing spoken words and internal thoughts all tangled together.

"No. Tell me." Jane remembered Nina saying of Blanche Ingel "jumpy as a cat since the surgery," remembered poor Nina's lost and hollowed-out face. She felt much more tenderly about attacked Nina than she ever had about Nina alive.

"I hear things chittering," said Helen. "Like something is around me. Everywhere, just out of sight." She nodded around the room. "Behind that hideous painting of Alistair's mother, or under the piano there, or slithering under the green baize on the card table. Or that blue—oh, why would Alistair taunt me with that fey-blue pillow!" In hectic, feverish motions Helen seized the pillow and buried it underneath the sofa, out of sight. Sank back to her seat.

Silence from shocked Jane, and Helen rushed on:

"Tell me you feel it, too."

"No . . . ," said Jane. "Not except for a brief moment when I first awoke."

"You think I'm mad, I know she does think it," said Helen. "All the same, I remember you after the war sometimes. That was quite different, but sometimes . . . that's how I feel."

And suddenly Jane remembered five years ago, remembered waking up with her cursed cheek at home, in her bed. "The striped wallpaper swimming in to meet me," she said. "Everything had a voice, and it was all after me. And everything Mother did seemed amplified tenfold—her endless weeping. Her anger at me for losing Charlie." Sharp the memories came—she had known that anger though Mother had tried to hide it; she had fled from it. Yet it had twisted inside her, and taken root, and grown. . . .

"It's mad, isn't it?" said Helen, suddenly sharp and direct. "And yet that's what I think of. You, before you left us, the way you seemed then. And yet my face is not a curse—oh, Jane, tell me what I've done."

Jane took Helen's hands. "I tried to seal off my curse and that didn't work. I peeled off the iron and started to work with it. I gained power with it, and now with this mask I have even more. You can do that. You must do that. You have to learn to be strong and fight with what you wear, or . . . the fey will take you over . . . alive." The thought sparked a vivid memory of crouching inside the door that morning while the Fey Queen attacked poor Nina.

Helen jerked away, was suddenly up behind her chair. Her saucer of tea clattered to the floor and broke amber across the patterned rug. "It's them, isn't it. It's them I hear crackling through the walls. They're coming, they're coming—"

"Be calm!" said Jane. "Yes, they are a danger, but you can learn to fight it. You and all your friends, you must try. We have fey in our bodies now, and we can learn to use it to defend ourselves, or we can be victims."

Helen sneered at Jane. "Then you've made yourself in danger, too, haven't you? Bet she's sorry now, wouldn't she rather be ugly and safe—"

"But I wasn't safe," said Jane. "I had it all along." And suddenly she thought of all those ironskin who were also in danger. She would have to get to Niklas and let him know. And Dorie—she had to find out what had happened to her little girl. There was too much to do to hide in Helen's house another minute.

She stood, gathering her skirts and wits, and said with some asperity to Helen, crouching behind the chair, "Oh, buck up."

The butler swept in, then, with Gertrude behind him. Triumph from Gertrude: "There, I knew you'd upset her! You don't understand what she needs—"

The butler ignored the drama and said: "A visitor to see you, Miss Eliot. A Miss Poule."

Poule drove them through the city in Edward's old car, calmly maneuvering around the horses and holes that clogged the streets, the farther they got from Helen and Alistair's part of town.

"They can get into fey substance," said Poule. "All that is fey substance."

"Yes," said Jane, for it was what she'd figured out. "Tell me—is Dorie all right?"

Poule shook her head. "Every time I thought I saw her, she vanished. No telling whether that's Dorie. . . ." *Or something in Dorie,* she did not say.

Jane's heart twisted, thinking about it. Perhaps she should have grabbed the little girl, stolen her away. She could be here right now, safe on Jane's lap.

"You're no safer here than in the country," said Poule.

"You've said as much," said Jane.

"What I don't understand," said Poule, "is that they could've taken you, or any of the ironskin over at any time. They didn't have to wait for Edward to put on the masks."

"They could," said Jane. She had been thinking about the moment in the clearing, when the fey had seemed to invade and reject her. "But they wouldn't take over ironskin, unless that was the only option. They're drawn to beauty. I was practically unclean to them."

"Huh," said Poule. "A thousand centuries of trade with them, and yet I'll never understand the blasted things, I guess."

"But what *is* fey substance?" said Jane. "The curses, the bluepacks—are they the same? Is it like spider silk?"

"Well, that's the part the *dwarvven* did seem to have right. Speaking of trade, you see. The fey have a complicated punishment system that I don't even want to know about because the little I do know is deeply disturbing. But all the fey tech we have—the blue lights, cameras, your mask, everything—is essentially little pieces of a split-up fey. Not big enough to be a full entity that can think and act on its own. But a bit of captured and divided substance. The fey themselves."

"Heavens," Jane said faintly. Her fingers touched her new face. Edward had a bit of the actual fey in his hands. The clay must have fey worked through it. And those bombs—little torn-off bits of themselves, coiled around the fire and the shrapnel, to attach like leeches to the victim.

"When the time of the punishment is over, all those little split-up pieces are automatically released. A thousand lights— or what-have-you—die at the same moment as all the pieces of fey rush back to form one whole fey again, back in the forest."

"So all the time we were trading with the fey, they were selling us—bits of themselves?" said Jane. The thought made the hair on her arms stand on end.

"Yes," Poule agreed. "I'd take a good old-fashioned turn on the *dwarvven* rack any day over that kind of punishment. I've often wondered what kind of bizarre things Edward saw all those years he was with them. He could probably write a scientific treatise on the fey, if he'd a mind to."

Jane remembered then Edward saying "decades" in his story of long ago. The Fey Queen in her dreams, saying that time passes slowly in the forest. That three years seem as one. "He was in the forest a very long time, wasn't he?" she said slowly.

"Yes."

"That story. That he grew up abroad. But Edward said he grew up here."

"He lets people believe that his father was his grandfather," Poule said. "It's easier that way."

Jane shook her head, trying to make sense of it all.

Poule stopped the car outside the gated entrance to Niklas's forge, and Jane said: "But why did you come all this way to get me? Why really?"

The short woman twisted her grey braid away from her face, considering her words. "Because," she said finally, "because we don't have a solution to this. And we need one."

"And . . . ?"

"And it's going to come through you. You're the only one I know of who ever bested the fey at their own game. Edward used the fey in his hands for six, seven years, and I'm telling you you have to be bloody strong to do that and not go completely off your rocker. The *dwarvven* have experience blocking fey wiles in general. But you're the first to take their curse and turn it against the blasted things. I don't say you're special—"

"Thanks," Jane muttered.

"—only that you figured out how to do it, and that's got to be the key somehow to stop what they're doing. Else—"

"Else what hope do we have against them," said Jane. "Edward's probably done a hundred people by now. And naturally, all rich and well placed, or they wouldn't have had the money to do it."

Poule nodded, then looked inside Niklas's compound. "Is he trustworthy?"

"Yes," said Jane, and she pulled the handle.

This time it was Niklas himself who came to the gate, erect and striding despite the singlet of iron she knew was underneath the black leather. Suspicion grew on his face the closer he got. "If it's charms you're after, you'd better see one of the fancy shops in town." His eyes darted between them as if he could not decide who needed more puzzling out, but then finally they stayed on Poule and he said, slowly, "You're one of the *dwarvven*, ain't you now?" He pronounced it nearly as well as Poule.

"Half," said Poule.

"Don't hold with half-bloods myself," he said. "You don't know where you stand then, do you."

He seemed twice Poule's size, but the woman merely folded her arms and looked up at him, considering. "I've heard of you," she said. "You do that ironskin that doesn't work."

Jane interfered. "Please, Niklas, let us in. I'll explain everything."

"I know your voice," he said, unlocking the gate. "But that face—it seems like something I know but wish I didn't."

Jane squeezed inside before he could change his mind. "I'm Jane," she said, "and I'm wearing the Fey Queen's face."

It took a good while to calm Niklas down, and even then he was fixated on the bit of fey that he had let walk through his door. "You say the last woman went mad. I believe it's not just from the whole fey entering her, but from the piece of fey clinging to her face." He clanked a metal prybar against his hand. "We must rip it off before it destroys your soul."

"No!" She eluded him. "It's the same thing, Niklas. This mask, or my cheek. It's all the same. Either way they can come for me."

Poule stepped in front of Jane, stared up at the big blacksmith. "And they can come for you, too."

This stopped him.

"If there's fey in you, they can take you over alive," Jane said from behind Poule's shoulders. "That's what your curse is. A little bit of fey, attached to your body till you die. But you can use it against them, if you work at it. If you remove the iron and practice. You can use it as defense."

"Remove the iron," he said. "I bet this is the fey in you telling me to do that. Bet you're already all fey, and I invited you in—"

"Hush," said Poule. "Lay off Jane. This paranoia's not the blacksmith I've heard about on family retreats deep in the *dwarvven* compound."

"Heard about." He grunted, stared at Poule.

Unperturbed by his gaze, Poule helped herself to a stool at

his workbench and hoisted Dorie's gloves out of her bag. "I'm working on a mask myself," she said. "A rather special one. I hear you've got a tar suspension, and I also hear you've one of the finest minds for iron solutions outside of the *dwarvven*."

Niklas grunted. "That's as it may be." His sharp eyes flicked to the mesh cloth that formed the gloves.

"'Course, if you can't let go of your preconceptions, I can head back to the country now," said Poule. "Otherwise, we might have some skills to trade."

She held out a glove and after a pause, Niklas took it. He sat down at his bench and turned it over in his hands, examining the way the metal-threaded cloth moved and folded.

Several minutes passed in utter silence, but Jane felt the air in the room change, felt the dynamic shift as Niklas went from suspicion to grudging acceptance.

Poule winked at her. "You'd better get back to the party."

"You're all right then?" said Jane. "Niklas?"

Niklas grunted, not looking at her. But that had always been so.

Poule pressed bills into her hand for a hansom. "I'll be back by midnight," she said.

When Jane reached the house, the party was in full swing. It seemed an age since she'd seen the May Day preparations in the country—what, only yesterday morning? But where Silver Birch had been rustic, with its old-fashioned maypole and few guests, Helen's house was sharp and polished. And crammed. Everyone who was anyone was there—Jane decided Helen must have hand-delivered the invitations, to let that fey glamour wash over her invitees.

Jane saw more than one fey face, now that she was looking for them. The Prime Minister's wife. A duchess. A woman on the arm of a lord, who Gertrude whispered had been a dancing girl.

The Miss Davenports were there, too, and their eyes slid over Jane and refused to acknowledge her presence.

But they were the only ones. Jane was pulled into dance after dance, caught around the waist by eager male hands and swung in and out in gay, captivating rhythms. She was in her plain day dress of the day before, wrinkled and smudged from her journey—and yet it didn't matter, for she had that face, and the face made whatever cloth she wore look like gold.

The adulation caught her, unsettled her, swung her in a dance between laughter and tears, but the boys seemed to find even her tears beautiful, and more than one gentleman made a giddy proposal of elopement to her. Jane accepted them all, for why not? There was only this one night in the bubble, for even though Jane did not know how it would all end, she knew like a hanging in the morning, it would.

It was the blackest hour of the night before she felt it.

Like Helen had said, that chittering under the wallpaper, and more, Jane thought, a sense of a growing storm, of funnel clouds in the nice fine ballroom, of that moment when every hair on your arms stands up and is electrified by the sky.

A fey in the house, that house without iron.

She felt it and suddenly the blue-orange blur seemed to be everywhere, homing in on the pretty ladies, the women with masks. The fey swooped back and forth, and suddenly there was blue in front of her eyes, and she was under attack.

But this fey was not the Fey Queen.

This was some ordinary fey, and she was pale in comparison with the Queen's heat, and she was weak in comparison with the Queen's murderous rage.

The fey beat against Jane's face, and Jane, feeling less and less like a victim, drove it back with the satisfying beat and thump of squashing an insect. It fell away, rattled. Left for an easier target.

She looked up and into her current dance partner's eyes with fierce triumph, and then saw where the fey went next.

Helen.

The fey was drawn to her like she was a flame, a beacon. Its orange-blue light swallowed up the air around her and behind that masky blush of perfection Jane saw Helen's eyes scream.

Helen beat at the air, but that didn't matter to the fey. She screamed, which mattered to Jane. No, that wasn't just Helen screaming, it was Jane as well, shouting, "Fight back, fight back," and then thumping on Alistair's arm and saying, "Do something, damn you!"

He folded, blubbering. "I can't, you don't understand, I can't."

The last time she stepped between a fey and her brother, she sacrificed half her face. And her brother still lay dead of fey shrapnel on the black ground, and the only thing Jane could do after it was all over was stab a feyjabber into his heart and drive the fey out. And then her sister had resented her ever after, for daring to do what Helen could not. . . .

All that whirled through her head in an instant as the blue-orange light darkened with intent, whisked through Helen and into her. The other swirls of blue flicked outward and dissipated.

The light died in Helen's eyes, flickered up pale and glassy—but it was patently no longer Helen. Edward had said that by the time Poule extracted the fey from Blanche she was an imbecile.

But maybe Poule hadn't been fast enough.

Jane moved into that open space around Helen, fingers coiling around the feyjabber in her pocket.

Blanche Ingel had been occupied for five or six hours before Poule jabbed her wrist. Whereas Dorie had only had a fey inside her for less than a minute, and she'd recovered.

Jane plunged the feyjabber into her sister's forearm, driving it into the vein. Helen shuddered, her eyes rolling back in her head. Dark red blood welled up around the spike.

And then, a noise like shrieking, only inside her head—and from the looks of it, the guests heard it too. Fey death, she knew, though she had not felt it in five years.

Helen fell to her knees, slumped to the floor. Her iron-stuck arm fell limply to the side, but the crazed look in her eye died away, and her eyelids closed as if in sleep, exactly as Dorie's had in the forest.

Jane prayed Helen would also wake as Dorie had, but she couldn't stay to find out.

"Don't stand there," she shouted to the rest of the party. "Find iron, protect the others! Send for a doctor! And you," Jane commanded Alistair. "Bind her arm above the wound and don't remove the spike." He was stunned, and he looked as though he was an instant from weeping, as soon as he processed the shock. Jane stooped and, clamping her thumb onto the vein in Helen's arm, repeated her orders to one of the more capable-looking servants.

"Helen," he murmured. "My little Helen."

Jane took his hand and placed it on Helen's arm. "Hold tight until they return," she said, and he looked through her with scorched eyes, but nodded, and held.

"Don't leave us," he said, but Jane stood and looked down at him, huddled over her unconscious, fey-beautiful sister.

"Stop all the doors in your house with iron," she said. "Bar all the windows. Don't let anyone beautiful enter or leave."

Chapter 18

SHARDS

Poule drove like a maniac. Jane hung tight as the old motor-car whipped along narrow bumpy lanes and tried to reassure herself that the *dwarvven* were mechanically clever. The car was practically an extension of Poule, for all that the short woman was sitting on a tufted cushion and had put on special driving shoes with soles as thick as Jane's outstretched fingers.

The house was dark when they reached it. It was well past dawn, and yet the grey fog clung to the moor, wrapping the house in smoke.

"After Nina, the party cleared itself off," Poule said, though Jane knew that part. "I sent Cook and Martha home to their families. *He* wouldn't budge."

Jane remembered the story he had told of the damaged beast-man, lost without the girl who stayed away longer than she'd promised. Remembered, too, her own words: "If they all left you, I should still be here, and stay by your side. . . ."

And yet she had run.

When they all had left him, she, too, had run.

"I'll take the grounds," said Poule.

"Thank you," said Jane.

"It isn't much safer," corrected Poule. "Wait till you see the front door."

The front door was off its hinges, the iron screen door ripped up and torn aside. The grotesque doorknocker hung, tilting, knocking an echo against the door in the wind.

Jane stepped inside.

"Edward?" she called. "Dorie?"

Her footfalls echoed through the velvet curtained foyer. The mahogany curtain to the damaged rooms had been ripped away, and it now lay in a crumpled heap, all Jane's steam-cleaning undone. She stepped over it and through, winding her way up toward his studio. Her calls echoed back only silence.

The black and broken house felt abandoned, as if it had not been lived in for two centuries, and semihysterically she wondered if she had stepped into the clutches of the fey her first day on the moor, and all that had happened here had been a fey-drugged dream, where she had talked to imaginary pretty ladies and scavenged mushrooms and berries in place of Cook's chocolate croissants.

Through the cobwebs she went, her feet smearing dust on the stairs. Up and to the studio, where the tiniest noises of life crept around the open studio door. A small voice, talking. A giggle.

Dorie was sitting on the floor of Edward's studio, hair lit by a stray sunbeam. Her dress was smeared with dust and something that looked like jam, but she looked safe and healthy. In fact, she looked very like the picture of Dorie as Jane had first seen her, making her Mother doll dance among the motes of dust in the sunbeam.

Unlike that first day, though, she was talking to it. Full sentences narrating the morning life of a five-year-old ("I made my own breakfast, I ate all the jam,") and that gladdened Jane's heart.

Dorie broke off when she saw Jane, beamed at her and said, "You came back."

"Yes," breathed Jane. "I came back."

And then it struck her what was odd about the picture, for Dorie was playing with her old doll, the doll that had been destroyed by Dorie herself. Jane had dropped the porcelain shards in the small red room, and later picked them out of the dense carpet one by one, and carried them to the dustbin, dropped them in there with the two blue glass eyes.

Jane took a step back and said, "Dorie, what—"

—and then the doll dissolved into smoke, rose into the air and reformed, and suddenly Jane was staring at her new face, again.

Jane's hand went right for her feyjabber, but she'd left it sticking out of Helen.

"You are back," the Fey Queen said. "Your choice is made."

"The choice to destroy you." Though she had no idea how.

"The choice to be with Edward, no matter the sacrifice. I understand."

"The choice," Jane forced through dry lips, "not to be a victim. Not to be on the run, and not to let you drive me from the few people left in this world whom I care about. Who care for me."

"A battle you can never win," the Queen said, "for who can compete with the fey? Now that you creatures voluntarily attach us, you do not even have to be killed. The forms are cleaner, they live longer. A whole human lifespan, I expect, unless we are discovered. My subjects have slowly been slipping into place around the city. Ready to enact change from within. With Edward's help, we will win this war yet."

"Help," said Jane. "You really call it help when you were the one directing his hands; you were the one clouding his mind? But never mind that. The Great War is over, and you've lost. If you really thought you could win, *you'd* be taking over one of those well-positioned women. Not the governess in a tumble-down shack in the countryside."

"Edward has access to everyone. If you think a leader cannot direct her people from a sheltered seat, you are mistaken. Besides," and she sent a tendril of orange warmth to flicker through Dorie's hair, "this is where my child is. My small-part-of-me."

"Your child who can't live in either world—"

"Who can live in both."

"You would use her, as you used Edward—"

"If she and Edward are useful to me, do I love them the less?" She glimmered at Jane. "But I weary of maintaining this human form when the real one is present, and more comfortable to wear in your polluted world. I weary of talking like a human without a human mouth and brain to do the heavy lifting. I weary."

She dissipated into blue-orange light and then a rage like fire swept across Jane.

It was the attack, finally the true attack, and no Poule there to fling iron in front of her. The Fey Queen was trying to slip in her body through the front door of her face.

But it wasn't as strong as she had expected. Jane pushed back, blazing hot herself, pushed back and beat the Fey Queen from her body.

The Fey Queen hung in the air in front of her, paler than before, the imaged face only a sketch over colored light. "You. What?"

But Jane knew. "I have had fey substance in me for the last five years. I am not as helpless as you think."

Deep down inside she knew that the Queen had not used all her force the first time. Jane's proud words were only that—the last-ditch words of a victim.

No, not a victim.

A defeated warrior is not a victim.

Jane bent her knees, steadying herself, readying herself.

The orange light deepened, blotting out the blue, and there was sneering in that vibrating voice. "Only means I could have taken you anytime, you with fey on your cheek. Except you were hideous."

"You caused it."

"The original purpose of the fey bombs was to hook our substance into you so we had an entrance to slip into your dead forms and use them. By accident we discovered that the living maimed made more suitable, if more disgusting, bodies. Once we figured out how to attach small bits of our substance to you without killing you, we understood we could take you over alive." She swirled. "Of course, there was still the problem of taste. My people wouldn't wish to live a deformed life like you had. Hideous, disgusting . . . a half-life."

"It was still a better life than you'll ever have," said Jane softly, for here at the last she knew it. "Mine was real." It was real and I fought for every piece of it, she thought, and those other Janes that didn't happen wavered in her sight.

"Do you think we like taking over your forms?" said the Queen. "All we want is our fair share of the land again. We lived in peace until you started to ruin the world. We gave you pieces of ourselves to get you to stop—but you humans never stay satisfied for long. Soon enough the factories were blazing once more, as if we had done wrong by granting you all your wishes. We were forced to fight." The orange light was red now, and a thrumming crackled through the air which made it hard to think.

"Not forced," said Jane. "You and I, we chose to fight." She had chosen to make a stand for her village. She had chosen to stand with Charlie. And that Jane who had not been touched by war, that Jane who had never understood what it was to stand up and fight for herself, thinned out, turned insubstantial.

There was roaring in her ears, and the Fey Queen's words seemed to enter by the base of her skull.

"The first step was infiltration, which Edward solved for us. The second, to get rid of all of you. Oh, you ridiculous thing, see how you stand, so frail, against me. If you think your tiny bit of fey can stop me, you're a fool."

And then the Fey Queen reared back and attacked again, and this time it was like a wave crashing over Jane, thick and hot and thrumming with power, and her slim defenses crumbled as the Fey Queen rushed into her body.

From a far-off distance the door opened. She was dimly aware of her own voice crying "Edward!"—but whether it was her or the Fey Queen calling through her lips she did not know.

"Edward, my love, my thanks," said her voice again, and now she knew that was the Fey Queen, crackling through Jane, erasing her like a sponge crossing a chalkboard, rewriting the slate with the Queen's thoughts, words, ideas.

From a long way off she saw terror on Edward's face, despair. He was losing someone he loved, but Jane couldn't bear to hope that person was her. If he had to make a choice between Jane and the Fey Queen, Jane shouldn't give a fig for her own chances. That was what the Fey Queen, laughing, was telling her now, deep inside and all through her marrow.

It was up to her. The warrior.

The Jane who had chosen to be here.

Jane sent all her will into her fingers, still her own fingers, and dug her fingernails into the red line that surrounded her face. The Queen recoiled in surprise, and Jane used that tiny moment to summon all her internal strength, to compress the crackling, questing tendrils of the Queen back into the fey substance that Jane wore. With the lesser fey, Jane had been strong enough to shut it out completely. The Queen was far too powerful; but if Jane could just push her past a certain point, just into the mask only . . .

Push and shove, till her will met the Queen's at the razor-thin line where the fey-infused mask met her blood and bone. Jane was all Jane; the mask was all fey.

And then Jane tore.

The mask wanted to adhere, but she pulled on all its edges, ripping the attack away. Surely it must hurt, but her adrenaline and fear were too high to notice. The new face peeled off, popping away from her eyelids, nostrils, lips. Slowly the fey was torn from her body.

And as she tore she lost all her strange fey sense. All knowledge of Edward's feelings died away. Jane threw the fey-ridden mask from her and as it hit the floor it shattered into a million pieces.

"Jane!" Edward cried. He fell on his knees before her,

cupped her face with his blue-lit hands, healing her. "Jane, stay with me, Jane, Jane . . ."

But using his gift was his undoing, because the disoriented Fey Queen went rushing from the mask into Edward, Edward who had fey thrumming in his fingertips, and Edward stiffened and lurched, his eyes rolling back in his head.

"Edward!" cried Jane. Time slowed for her then, and she saw everything through a blue-and-white haze of fey light.

He was putting up a fight, she realized. For the first time.

His decades spent with the Queen had not left him as unprepared as Nina, as Blanche. The Queen's blue light went through the studio garret like waves as she poured herself into Edward in pulses of force.

Edward staggered toward the window and with a great effort lifted it up, tore it from its nailed roots into the sash. The iron nails stuck through the wood, long and spiked.

Yet there was enough space around the nails that an agile man could climb out and through, could squeeze past the iron to dash his brains on the flagstones below.

Then the Queen would be free to try again. To enter someone weaker, more docile. Was this the Queen trying to sacrifice Edward? Or Edward trying to sacrifice himself, preferring to die rather than be the Fey Queen's pawn ever again?

Jane saw both possibilities flickering before her and she ran to Edward, even as his shoulder hefted the pane high and he placed his hands on the windowsill. His eyes as he turned— oh, those beloved amber eyes were thick and glassy as he fought the Queen for dominion over his own body. Her own face stung, but no more, her trauma held at bay by Edward's momentary touch.

"I'm sorry," he whispered to Jane, and then he drew his

shoulder back from the window. Drew back the support, and the window, free and heavy with iron, fell. It slammed into his fey-cursed hands, and blood welled thick and fast from the cut veins and broken bones of his pierced palms.

His neck corded in pain, he slumped to his knees beneath the sill, hands caught above him, iron in his blood.

There was a noise—or maybe it was only a feeling, a feeling of shrieking. All the air in the room crackled and Edward's cowlick jumped on end. The air seemed to rush into Edward and implode with a sharp bang, so that Jane's ears popped and her vision blinked blue and white.

And then—nothing. The air cleared out and the room colorized.

The Fey Queen was dead.

Dorie ran to her father, threw herself onto his chest, and he gasped with pain. But he was alive, alive, and the glass in his eyes slowly receded. He levered himself to his feet, and his face was wet and streaked, and he was quite caught by the window, speared through his broken, mangled hands.

But alive.

Jane sunk to the floor, spitting clay dust that tasted like iron. The last of Edward's fey touch on her face receded. Everything was red—but of course, that was just blood. Just blood. And then the pain rushed in at last, and she groped for one of Edward's work cloths, put it to her face, where it instantly soaked itself. She was dizzy, and this was no good. "Dorie," said Jane. "Run for Poule. Quickly."

But the short woman appeared at the door, panting, taking in the situation. In her hand she held something white and metal, ovoid, and she beat a path to Jane, holding it up to Jane as she ran.

It was the beautiful Jane mask with the chipped forehead. But different.

It was criss-crossed with a web of threaded iron, iron that went above the clay, through the clay, behind the clay. The fey substance in the mask was both exposed and trapped— iron ringed the mask's edges, outlining its eyes and lips in metal.

"Dorie," Poule said, from a distance. "I'm hoping you can do something your father could." She nodded at Jane: Yes?

"Yes," said Jane, and Poule pressed the mask to her face. Iron and clay? No, iron and *skin*, it would be soon enough. This was true ironskin at last. It was cold and stiff and yet felt like an old friend, warming to her touch. She could feel the power of the fey substance inside, already sensing the emotions in the room, feeling waves from Dorie, sadness, confusion, determination. This time she would not spurn the blessings of that curse.

Dorie reached up to Jane's face, and her tiny hands molded the mask as if they knew instinctively what to do. Jane's face throbbed, stung, but the blood running down her neck slowed to a trickle as Dorie fitted the mask in place. Even the pain lessened. Dorie was saving her.

"Help me to my feet," said Jane. Dorie stood still while Jane put weighty hands on her shoulder, standing. Together they moved to the window where Edward still hung, pinned, and then Jane and Poule freed him. He sunk to the floor, defeat written all over him despite their victory over the Queen. His nimble, beautiful hands hung limp.

If Edward could mend faces with that clay, surely she had enough fey substance in her to do that now herself.

She pressed the fey-infused clay to his wounds and saw it

start to mend, saw the broken bone wiggle under its touch, straightening. It thrummed under her fingers, and she felt suddenly what power that was, to mold something into the shape of life and have it walk and breathe.

"No," he said, and jerked his arms away, rubbing the blood and clay from his limp hands on his shirt with a gasp at the pain. The thrum died. "I am not strong enough to hold their gifts, Jane. I am not as good as you."

"But your hands . . ."

And they fell to his lap, trembling, even as Poule ran to his worktable for cloth and gauze and scalpel, and he said, "You were always too good for me, Jane. The Queen never really let me go—just sneaked into me after she returned me, manipulating me—and I refused to believe it. She ruined that poor village girl. And now I have not even a home to offer you, for not only do I have no talent, I no longer have any skill at all. For who knows when these shall mend, if ever." The amber eyes were delirious with pain; he stared past her, half-blinded by it. "Now I am quite dependent on your goodwill and stubborn nature, you see?"

Quite helplessly, she laughed, a short distraught cry. "Of course, sir. You always were, you know."

"No, no." Heavy sigh. "I will not take your pity, Jane. You are too kind to leave if I do not make you. But you must."

But the cold words didn't fool her any longer.

Because she could feel his emotions behind the words, and now it was warmth alone—the chill gone. The fear of what his past could do to her was over, for it had done it, and there was no other way he could hurt her. All that was left was his own fear that she would leave him again, and he would be quite alone in that house, helpless and dependent on Poule and Cook to feed him and dress him and never leave him alone with his crippling despair.

She knew all this and he knew none of it, and she did not know how to convince him that she truly loved him.

But she knew how to provoke.

So she said, cruelly, "You are glad of an excuse to be rid of me, then."

Poule straightened one of his bones at that moment, and that might have been what caused the cry.

She pressed on: "You are glad of such a convenient excuse to be rid of me. It's more believable than an invented dying aunt."

"Wicked Jane!" he said. "And wicked Poule, you are both murdering me together."

"The splinters better come out sooner than later," said Poule.

"I know the future, you see," said Jane, pressing her advantage. "A return to public life, a long affair with each of your pretty ladies, starting with the clever and charming Prime Minister's wife—"

"So help me, if I had to spend any more time with those silly women, I'd jump from that blasted window this instant," he said, glaring at her.

She laughed joyfully at his reaction. Then gasped, suddenly dizzy, and he reached out to her, worry sharp on his features.

"Jane, my Jane, you're bleeding—"

Her fingers touched her temple and came away wet.

"You're crooked," Poule said critically. "And you're still leaking around the temple, because you're more concerned about provoking this poor man you're besotted with than your own face. Lie down and let Dorie finish. And you,

Edward, stop grinning so foolishly, because this next bit is going to hurt."

Jane obeyed, though crooked scarcely mattered now. She would always be this Jane and it would always be plain on her face. This Jane who had fought the fey and survived, this Jane who was taking their power for herself.

And the first thing she would do was restore human faces to all those pretty ladies, make them safe against the fey.

For on the wall above, those rows of masks still leered. A hundred faces, and each one a human, somewhere. A race between Jane and the dead Queen's followers.

It was a mission. It was her purpose.

This Jane was meant to fight.

The red blood splattered the floor like drops of paint. Dorie's fingers crept around, smoothing the ironskin mask of her face. Jane closed her eyes and let the girl adjust her eyelids, felt the cold iron, hard and comforting against the bone.

Her hand crept to her left just as Edward's foot found hers. Her fingers touched his elbow, his ankle her ankle, as Poule and Dorie worked above them, deft and sure.

Soon, soon, she would be whole again.

Acknowledgments

Where to begin with this enormous pile of thanks? I feel very fortunate to have received so much help and advice and (constructive) criticism over the years, and I hope to continue to pay that forward.

A big thank-you to my treasured and overworked second readers, K. Bird Lincoln and Caroline M. Yoachim, who have each read nearly everything ever, including novels that will continue to live in a drawer.

Another thanks to the rest of my novel reader/critiquers, including Josh English and Mischa DeNola, who read this particular novel, and Tinatsu Wallace, Meghan Sinoff, Julie McGalliard, Gord Sellar, Ian McHugh, David A. Simons, Nicole Gresham, and Shawn Scarber, who read others. A thanks to K. D. Wentworth, who loved the original novelette, which sparked the idea of turning it into a novel, and thanks to someone who pointed out that the original story was trying to be *Jane Eyre*. I have no idea who that was. Hey, thanks to Charlotte Brontë while I'm at it. I loved *Villette*.

I am also grateful for the support of the Clarion West class of 2006 as a whole with its awesome group of students, teachers, and administrators (including Tristan, who graciously let me use his last name for the bolsters), and the local PDX writers crew (including Camille Alexa, at whose Vermont writing retreat I wrote a large chunk of *Ironskin* [2K every morning before heading out to eat cheese.])

Enormous thanks to my rock star agent, Ginger Clark, for her hard work and keen eye, to everyone at Tor and Curtis Brown for their support, and especially to Melissa Frain for loving this novel in the first place and then giving me a billion brilliant insights on how to make it into what it was meant to be all along.

And of course to my wonderful family, who told me I was going to grow up to be a writer long before I knew it—Mom, Dad, Mike, Amy, Andy, Rick, and Grandmere & Papa, who would have loved to see it happen. My husband, Eric, who kept me focused and talked me off of ledges and read me poetry. And the new baby, who hasn't really helped my writing at all, but is awfully cute.

All that and I'm still going to miss someone. Sorry. I blame the new baby for eating my brain.